Rave reviews for Elliott Roosevelt's novels,
featuring
ELEANOR ROOSEVELT—SUPER SLEUTH!

"Perfectly wonderful!"
The New York Daily News

"Light, bright, and delightful!"
UPI

"Charming!"   *AP*

"Eleanor is even more brilliant in fiction
than she was in real life."
Seattle Post-Intelligencer

"A series that's fun!"
Library Journal

"Move over Sam Spade, Lew Archer, and
Mike Hammer . . . Eleanor the detective
is back."
Houston Chronicle

"A delightful romp
and a dazzling
mystery"
Mystery News

MURDER AND THE FIRST LADY and
THE HYDE PARK MURDER
are available from Avon Books

ELLIOTT ROOSEVELT

MURDER AT HOBCAW BARONY

AVON BOOKS ▲ NEW YORK

AVON BOOKS
A division of
The Hearst Corporation
105 Madison Avenue
New York, New York 10016

The St. Martin's Press edition contains the following Library of Congress
Cataloging in Publication Data:

Roosevelt, Elliott, 1910–
    Murder at Hobcaw Barony.

    1. Title
PS3535.0549M83   1986   813'.54   86-3807

First Avon Printing: June 1987

**As always and forever,
To Patty**

I would like to express my thanks to my friend the novelist William Harrington who has been my mentor in the craft of mystery writing and has given me invaluable assistance with the First Lady mysteries.

Elliott Roosevelt

1

"Bernie," said Mrs. Roosevelt, "is a most generous man."

"Ingratiating," the President murmured.

The First Lady ignored the negative implication she knew the President had fully intended. "Generous with his fortune," she went on. "With his advice. With his hospitality."

"Oh, I think we should accept his invitation, Babs," said the President. "Exactly as it was given. You pop on down to Hobcaw Barony and enjoy yourself. I'll get away and join you for the weekend."

"You should come for the whole week. You could use the rest."

"Can't take it right now. The President of the United States can't take a holiday every time he feels a little weary. Anyway, a weekend of Bernie Baruch is quite enough for me. In a week he'd talk me into going back on the gold standard."

Mrs. Roosevelt shrugged. They were sitting in the Oval Office. The President's lunch tray was on his desk and he was munching on an apple while they talked. Mrs. Roosevelt was dressed to go out, to a luncheon of the Business and Professional Women's Club, where she would be the guest of honor and give a short speech. She wore a brim-

1

less blue satin hat, a loose-flowing blue silk dress, and her black coat. A fur was draped around her shoulders.

"I understand the other guests will be chiefly from Hollywood," she said. "Movie people."

"Yes," he said. "It will give you a chance to hobnob with the aristocracy of the silver screen. And, uh, discreetly."

"No reporters," said Mrs. Roosevelt. "No interviews. No cameras. Isolation."

"Seventeen thousand acres," said the President.

"But, Franklin . . . are you sure? You do seem tired, and if I'm here—"

"You always try to carry part of the load," said the President affectionately. "But there are some parts you can't carry. No, I'd much rather you went on down to Hobcaw. Take your riding togs. I understand his daughter Belle is much given to riding, and I suppose Bernie keeps a superb stable. For me, I'll want to get in a day's fishing. Tell Bernie to round up the fish and herd 'em in toward shore."

So it was that on Monday afternoon the First Lady alighted from a train of the Seaboard Air Line at the tiny station in the village of Andrews, South Carolina. A spur ran on to Georgetown, but Bernard Baruch was waiting on the platform at Andrews, as his telegram had promised. They would drive to Georgetown, a matter of some twenty miles, and from there take his launch three miles across Winyah Bay to Waccamaw Neck and Hobcaw Barony.

"Mrs. Roosevelt!" boomed Baruch, to be heard by the small crowd that had assembled on the platform; but when he took her hand and spoke quietly to her, what he said was, "Eleanor! Oh, it's damn good of you to come. Marvelous to see you!"

Bernard Baruch was easily the tallest man on the platform, but even if he had not been the tallest he was certainly the handsomest, the most impressive. His white hair and lined face told his age—he was past sixty-five—but his erect carriage, firm and confident step, the alert, darting eyes behind his pince-nez, and his ebullience suggested a man at least twenty years younger. He wore a tweed cap, tweed jacket, riding breeches, and polished leather boots. With discreet but authoritative gestures, he dispatched people to pick up Mrs. Roosevelt's luggage, clear a way through the crowd to the car, and form a small motorcade of three cars led by a police motorcycle.

Everything directed by Baruch moved efficiently. Only one small element of his arrangements was changed—when Robert Wilkes, the Secret Service man who would remain with the First Lady during her visit, firmly insisted he would ride in the car with Baruch and Mrs. Roosevelt, not in the second car. Mrs. Roosevelt noticed how Baruch's eyes hardened for an instant when his gesture to Wilkes was met with a shake of the head.

Ordinarily, Mrs. Roosevelt refused to allow a Secret Service agent to accompany her on her travels. She had been adamant on the subject. The presence of Wilkes was an exception, which she had agreed to at the President's urging, because she would be visiting a rural area where law-enforcement services were apt to be informal—and, besides that, Hobcaw Barony was across the bay from the sheriff's office in Georgetown. Besides, she knew Wilkes as an affable young man with a sense of the proprieties. She could count on him not to dog her every footstep. She had secured his agreement on the way down to sleep in his own room, which Baruch would provide, and not to insist on spending the night on a chair outside her room.

In the car, Baruch's affability was complete. "Is there no way we can encourage Frank to come on down and not wait for the weekend?" he asked. "Autumn weather like this is to be savored, treasured; it is not to be missed. The fishing is exceptional right now. How about you, Wilkes? Do you fish?"

The Secret Service man, who sat by the chauffeur in the front seat of the long, dark blue Packard, turned. "Only if Mrs. Roosevelt does," he said.

"Oh, yes. Of course. But, as I recall, you don't care for it, do you, Eleanor?"

"I wouldn't mind going for the boat ride if Mr. Wilkes

wants to fish," she said. "I shall take the sun. I could use it. It's been miserable in Washington."

"It's invariably miserable in Washington," said Baruch. "Those politicians in the First Congress did us an evil turn when they stuck the nation's capital in a malarial swamp."

"Personally, I should have preferred New York City," said Mrs. Roosevelt. "Washington is . . . well, provincial."

"At least you have the right address."

"Yes, 1600 Pennsylvania Avenue *is* a nice house." She laughed.

Baruch's launch waited at the dock in Georgetown. He escorted Mrs. Roosevelt to a comfortable seat inside the small, glass-enclosed cabin. While they waited for men to bring aboard her luggage, some boxes of groceries, and a leather bag of mail, she took the moment to study her surroundings: the handsome southern town, romantic of façade though possibly squalid behind; the green, white-capped waters of Winyah Bay; the low-lying wooded neck on the other side of a mile of water. The house, Baruch told her, was hidden from sight from here by an island. As she watched, a flock of hundreds of white birds rose from the water near the shore of the neck, visible at this distance because of their numbers.

The bay, she had been warned, could become dangerously choppy; but today the swells were gentle, and the launch rolled easily as it headed out. Half a dozen hopeful pelicans took a station just over their wake and followed their southward course. The salt air was refreshing, and Mrs. Roosevelt drew deep breaths and savored it. She peered into the sunlight and tried to make out the house in a break in the woods on the still-distant Waccamaw Neck.

The name Hobcaw Barony was not a Baruch fancy, she knew; the plantation on Waccamaw Neck had been so called since the eighteenth century. Besides that, she knew the house she was about to visit was not the old plantation house, which had burned in 1929. Baruch had built the new Hobcaw House since then.

"It means 'between the waters,'" said Baruch.

"Hobcaw?"

"Yes. It's an Indian word. The first Spanish settlement on the North American continent was made on Waccamaw Neck. In 1526. Six hundred colonists. Three quarters of them died the first winter, so they gave it up. George II granted Hobcaw to Lord Carteret in 1718. He thought he was giving him twelve thousand acres, but his survey was inaccurate, and actually the original grant was of almost fourteen thousand. During the American Revolution, the British built a fort on the Barony. You can see the graves of British soldiers down at the edge of the woods. For a long time, the Barony was a rice plantation. Old abandoned rice fields are ideal for ducks. There must be millions of them. And wild turkeys. And bald eagles, Eleanor! Woe betide the man who takes a shot at one of those."

"It's fascinating, Bernie. It really is," she said. "But tell me about my fellow guests. Hollywood people, you said."

Baruch grinned. "Looking for money," he said. "They hope I'll put up some, or direct them to someone who will. You ever hear of Darryl Zanuck?"

"Indeed."

"Well, he just engineered the merger of Twentieth Century with Fox. His new outfit, which they're calling Twentieth Century-Fox, has just one surefire money maker: Shirley Temple. Zanuck needs more stars, and he needs money. Interesting fellow. He's only thirty-five years old."

"He's made some fine pictures, I believe."

"Well, he made *Little Caesar* with Edward G. Robinson. *I Am a Fugitive from a Chain Gang* with Paul Muni. But those were with Warner Brothers. He left the Warner studio."

"Who else?"

"Benjamin Partridge," said Baruch. "Same idea. When he left Goldwyn two years ago, he formed Par-Croft International with William Bancroft. The problem seems to be they've run through Bancroft's money. From what I hear, Partridge believed he was going to pick up Jean Harlow's contract, and . . ." He shrugged.

"And Jean Harlow died," said Mrs. Roosevelt.

Baruch nodded. "He has other problems. Anyway . . .

Joan Crawford is here. And Humphrey Bogart. And Colleen Bingham."

"Stars."

"Yes. Partridge has Colleen Bingham under contract, but both he and Zanuck would like to pick up contracts with Joan Crawford and Humphrey Bogart."

"I'm not quite sure I understand why *they* are here, though."

"Neither do I, entirely. Maybe Zanuck and Partridge want to impress me with the kind of talent they hope to employ for the pictures they want me to finance."

Mrs. Roosevelt smiled. "Would it be too much of a cliché to refer to the group as a galaxy?"

"No. And I will add one more. I'm expecting a friend of mine this evening. Speaker Bankhead's daughter, Tallulah."

"I've seen her on the stage twice," said Mrs. Roosevelt. "Once in London, once in New York. I'm afraid I don't recall the titles of the plays, but I remember her well. She is a striking young woman. She was something of a scandal in the London play, for taking off most of her clothes onstage."

"She's a talented actress," said Baruch. "She's had great difficulty finding a suitable vehicle in America. Her American plays, since she returned from London, have not been financially successful, though her work's been highly praised by Brooks Atkinson, among others. I'd like to see her find something good. She deserves it."

The launch passed the wooded island that had hidden the house. It turned toward the shore of the neck then, and Hobcaw House lay before them, at the crest of a long lawn that sloped down to the water. Although built of red brick, it was reminiscent of Mount Vernon, long and low in the Georgian colonial style, with six tall white pillars across the front. It was framed by huge oaks hung with Spanish moss.

"Welcome to Hobcaw," said Baruch as they stepped onto the small dock.

They walked up the sloping lawn, onto the wide front

porch, then through the tall, broad white doors into the house. A smiling black butler welcomed them in soft tones, allowing his eyes to linger admiringly on the First Lady. Dispatching a maid and underbutler to pick up Mrs. Roosevelt's luggage, he led her and Baruch along the hall and to the left, toward the first-floor bedroom suite.

"There are two bedrooms and two baths here," Baruch explained. "They can be shut off from the rest of the house very conveniently. I thought you might enjoy this one"—nodding toward the bedroom and bath to the right, at the rear of the house—"and the other one will accommodate the President when he arrives."

Although the day was not cold, a cozy little fire was burning in the fireplace in her bedroom, and Mrs. Roosevelt surveyed the room with delight. "You are a marvelous host, Bernie," she said.

Baruch bent down and kissed her gently on the cheek. "You honor me by coming, Eleanor," he said. "I hope you enjoy every minute."

"I am sure I shall."

"May I suggest riding clothes? We will dress for dinner; but for the balance of the afternoon, when I suspect you will want to relax, jodhpurs and boots will be comfortable and much in order. Of course, we *will* ride, but perhaps we should save that for tomorrow."

"Yes," she said. "I look forward to that."

A few minutes later, dressed in riding boots, khaki twill jodhpurs, a white blouse, and a tweed jacket—with her hair tied back by a broad band of yellow silk—Mrs. Roosevelt emerged from the first-floor suite. A black housemaid told her that Mr. Baruch was in the gun room and pointed her toward the door.

"Ah, Mrs. Roosevelt," said Baruch when she walked into the room, where he seemed to be showing a short, not-very-attractive man the collection of shotguns and rifles in glass-fronted cases. (He would address her as "Mrs. Roosevelt" in the hearing of others, as "Eleanor" only when they were alone.) "I don't believe you have met Humphrey Bogart."

She was amazed at how small the man was. She had seen him on the New York stage in *The Petrified Forest,* as the menacing gangster Duke Mantee—a role he had also had in the film. He had played the snarling villain of a dozen other crime films, and it was surprising to see that he was not just short but slight. Otherwise, he was the Humphrey Bogart of stage and screen: heavy brows, intent, insinuating eyes, scarred lip distorting his mouth slightly, suggesting a permanent sneer. He was wearing loose, broad-bottom corduroy slacks, a knit golf shirt, and a gray cardigan sweater. He pulled the cigarette from his mouth and shoved it between two fingers of the hand that held a glass.

"It's a very great honor, Mrs. Roosevelt," he said, coming toward her with his hand outstretched. (He pronounced the name "Rose-vult.") "I'm an admirer of yours and of course of the President's."

"Mr. Bogart," she said, taking his hand. "I've seen you on the screen, of course; but I saw you on the stage, too, in New York, some years ago."

"In something good, I hope. Please. Call me Bogie. Everyone does. It's what I answer to."

"Bogie and I were thinking of walking down near the water to see the ruins of the old English fort, and the graves of the English soldiers," said Baruch. "Would you like to join us?"

"Of course."

"Would you like a drink?"

"What's that you are having, Mr. Bogart?"

"What I call loudmouth," said Bogart. "This happens to be Scotch. You know—a loudmouth is what I become if I drink too much of it."

"As would I," said Mrs. Roosevelt with an amused broad smile. "So I believe I will forego for now, in the anticipation of having some later."

Baruch chuckled. "Twelve-year-old Scotch. 'Loudmouth.'"

"Twelve!" Bogart laughed. "I thought this was some you'd made yesterday, right here on the place."

Baruch adjusted his pince-nez. "I had the still dismantled," he said, "shortly after the repeal of Prohibition. We made good bourbon, but our Scotch was rotten. I think the boys put too much iodine in it."

"Iodine?"

"Of course, Mr. Bogart," said Mrs. Roosevelt sweetly. "Didn't you know? Scots whiskey is just bourbon with iodine added. That's why my husband favors gin."

"Well, it's a pleasure to have a President who knows the difference between them," said Bogart. "The last one who did was Harding."

The three of them were grinning amiably when they left the gun room. They walked into the central hallway in time to meet Benjamin Partridge, who had just reached the bottom of the stairs.

"Ben!" exclaimed Baruch. "Come over here and meet Mrs. Roosevelt."

"An honor," said Partridge, turning toward them and extending his hand. "You promised her, Barney; and you've delivered." (Although the Roosevelts called Bernard Baruch "Bernie," he was more commonly called "Barney," by friends and in the newspapers.) "It is *marvelous* to meet you, Mrs. Roosevelt."

The First Lady smiled and nodded and allowed Partridge to take her hand. "A pleasure," she said.

Partridge was a squat, solid, heavy-faced man, with a formidable bald dome. His mouth was broad, his chin strong, his brows black and bushy. He smiled as he greeted her, but somehow Mrs. Roosevelt felt something important was withheld behind that smile, that Benjamin Partridge was not a man ever wholly revealed. He was dressed in a dark blue, double-breasted business suit that obviously had been carefully cut to fit his thick frame precisely and lend it a dignity it would not have had in ill-tailored clothing. A white silk shirt and a wide red silk necktie completed his wardrobe.

"We are on our way out for a walk," said Baruch. "You're welcome to join us, Ben. We can wait while you get on some boots. If you haven't any, I can supply."

"I think I'll be an indoorsman today," said Partridge. "It was a long trip, you know."

"Miss Bingham is . . . ?"

"Asleep, I think," said Partridge. "Went to bed as soon as she got here. She had an exhausting trip. Got some bad news en route that was a personal shock to her."

"Does she need any kind of help?" asked Mrs. Roosevelt. "Was it something personal?"

Partridge shook his head. "No, just a business matter. I received a wire, delivered to the train in St. Louis. Merle Oberon will do the role of Sissy in *Ironweed* for me, which means Colleen doesn't get the part after all. She was hysterical about it at first. I mean, she was so upset that she walked out of the station in Evansville, Indiana, where we had to change trains, and I began to wonder if she was coming back. It turned out all right, though. She was back in time to catch the train—a little the worse for a few drinks she'd had somewhere in town, which seemed to make her feel better. She'll be okay."

"She's a sweet kid, Ben," said Bogart.

Partridge smiled faintly. "Of course she is." Then his smile broadened. Bogart was trying to light a fresh cigarette, snapping on a balky lighter and getting no fire. "Light?" asked Partridge, snapping flame out of a handsome gold lighter. Bogart scowled as he accepted the light.

"Anyway," said Baruch, "where are Miss Crawford and Mr. Zanuck?"

"Oh, fishing," said Partridge. "While you went to meet Mrs. Roosevelt, DFZ and La Crawford took rod and reel and a boat and went out to catch our dinner."

"Well, I wish them luck," said Baruch. "Unless they catch mud turtles, that is. I don't think I could stomach a meal of those."

"Knowing La Crawford's prowess, we may expect she'll come back with an alligator," said Partridge. "Or whatever's the biggest catch around."

A blond young man stood on the stairway. He had followed Partridge down from the second floor and had stood a bit apart from the conversation, listening apparently but reluctant to inject himself. Now, as there was a break in the talk, he spoke diffidently to Baruch. "May I? It would be such an honor to meet Mrs. Roosevelt."

Baruch looked up, faintly surprised. "Of course, Johnny," he said. "Mrs. Roosevelt, this is John Crown, Ben's . . . uh, assistant."

The young man, smiling happily, descended the last two steps and put out his hand to take Mrs. Roosevelt's. "What an honor!"

"I'm pleased to meet you," said she.

"You forget yourself," said Partridge coldly to the young man.

"I'm sorry, Mr. Partridge," murmured John Crown, blushing and backing away.

"Oh, it's quite all right," said Mrs. Roosevelt quickly. "I am happy to make your acquaintance, Mr. Crown."

"John is a servant," said Partridge. "He knows better than to intrude himself into—"

"Partridge," said Bogart. "God made you a complete ass. Be satisfied with that and don't be forever at an effort to be a bigger one than He made you."

"Well, God didn't make you Duke Mantee, Bogart," said Partridge. "So don't suppose you are, and don't try to play the tough guy with me. If I have to settle you, I won't pull any punches."

"Any time, fat boy," growled Bogart. Then he turned to Mrs. Roosevelt. "I'm sorry, ma'am," he said quietly. "Sorry, Barney." He looked again at Partridge. "And lay off the kid, Ben. He's a bigger man than you were on the best day of your life."

Partridge shrugged. "Actors," he said to Baruch and Mrs. Roosevelt.

2

Bernard Baruch's guests were invited to join him for cocktails at seven, in the great living room at the southeast corner of the house, and he was there promptly at seven, as was Joan Crawford. The sun had set. The house was brightly lighted. A cheering fire crackled in the big fireplace. Mrs. Roosevelt, too, was punctual and walked in from the hall only a minute or two after the hour.

Baruch stood just to the side of the fireplace, wearing a dinner jacket, which lent emphasis to his height and strong figure. Immediately he invited Mrs. Roosevelt to stand at his side, as though she were hostess. She was wearing a tea-colored gown of silk and lace, and she accepted a glass of sherry from the tray the underbutler had hurried up to present to her.

"I don't believe you've met Joan Crawford," said Baruch, nodding toward the actress, who had been chatting with him when Mrs. Roosevelt entered the room.

"No, but I've been looking forward to it."

Once more, Mrs. Roosevelt was surprised by how small these people were. She had seen Joan Crawford on the screen and would not have guessed she was only about five feet four. "Ah'm pleased as Ah kin be t' meet ya, Mrs.

Roosevelt," she said—another surprise: a deep southern accent she never used on the screen.

"It's a pleasure to meet you, Miss Crawford. I admire your gown."

Joan Crawford was wearing a sleek white silk dress that hung loosely around her shoulders and small bust but clung tightly to her slender hips and thighs. "A Bill Haines original," she said. "D'you really like it?" The famous wide blue eyes seemed to appeal for approval.

"I shouldn't call it flattering, should I?" said Baruch. "You require no flattery, Miss Crawford."

The eyes fluttered. "Oh, Mr. Baruch, Ah'll take flattery whenever Ah can get it."

"As will I, Miss Crawford." Mrs. Roosevelt laughed. "As would any woman."

At seven, John Crown came to Benjamin Partridge's bedroom, to finish the unpacking of suitcases and the arranging of the clothes in closet and bureau drawers, precisely to his employer's detailed requirements. Partridge had brought a trunk and three suitcases. Most of his clothes were out now, some of them scattered over the bed and on the bathroom floor, in the anticipation that Johnny Crown would arrive dutifully at seven, as ordered, to tidy up.

Shirts. Partridge had ordered two dozen packed for him. He would not, he had said, find anyone in South Carolina who could do shirts to his specifications, so he had to bring along enough to last his stay. Socks. Two dozen pairs. Eight pairs of shoes. Fourteen neckties. John knew exactly what was in the trunk and suitcases. He had packed them all. He worried now that he had forgotten something. Anything. He would be made to regret it if he had forgotten anything.

Four corsets. Those had to be washed by John, in the bathroom basin, and dried in the bathroom, out of sight. John would have to make the bed, replace the towels, and keep the room orderly. Partridge would not allow Baruch's household staff to attend to *his* room. He never allowed hotel staff in his room during a stay. They might see his corsets hanging to dry. No one was to be permitted to discover that Benjamin Partridge, the famous Hollywood producer, flattened his belly with strong lace-up corsets.

John Crown was twenty-four. He was a good-looking young man, blond, apple-cheeked, broad-shouldered, tall. He had learned to be careful of his duties as a valet, but every moment of it was painful to him. He thanked God his father did not suspect he had become a household servant.

After dinner, Partridge would return to this room and inspect the closet and drawers, and if he did not find the shirts lying parallel, each one overlapping the other precisely four inches, he would throw everything from the drawers on the floor and summon John from his room in the servants' wing to arrange it all again—no matter what time of night. Socks had to be ironed and stacked in neat vertical piles, a pair one way, the next pair the other. Underwear, similarly. Handkerchiefs, tie clasps, cuff links— everything had to be precisely as Partridge specified, exactly as they were always arranged in his closets and drawers at home.

In a briefcase that John had carried personally on the train from California was the can of sixteen-millimeter film—the ominous can, the one that was so damned valuable. The briefcase was in the closet, and he used his foot to shove it to the right, out of sight in a corner of the closet.

He was making a final circuit of the bedroom and bathroom, hoping everything was where it had to be, when he heard the light tap on the door.

"Who . . . ?"

"Baby! It's me!"

He opened the door.

Colleen Bingham stepped quickly inside and closed the door. She threw herself into his arms and kissed him.

"He—he's not coming back? You're sure?"

"He's downstairs, where you're supposed to be. Don't worry. We have a minute. I've looked."

She stood for a moment just inside the door, looking all around the room. "You've looked?"

John Crown sighed. "Everywhere."

Colleen looked around. "He has it. He showed it to me."

"Well . . . oh, Colleen!"

"John!"

Entangled in each other's arms, they staggered across the room and fell on the bed. "Oh, God! God!" each whispered in turn as they clung to each other and kissed.

"John . . ." she said after a minute.

"Colleen . . ."

"It's gone too far. I'm going to break it off, one way or another."

"We don't dare. Not yet."

She stroked his cheek. "We have friends," she said. "In heaven, if not here on earth."

"Don't do anything precipitous," he said.

"No," she agreed. "Nothing stupid. But soon."

"Time . . ." breathed John. "Always just a little more time."

She sighed. "I'm late. Look, I've gotta use the bathroom, repair my makeup. You go on, get your dinner. The room's okay. You go on and get something to eat."

"Oh, yes," he said. "In the kitchen. With the other servants."

"Not for much longer, honey. I promise. Not for much longer. Go on now, get your dinner. I've gotta fix my lipstick."

"Don't leave anything out of place," said John. "Blot with toilet paper. For God's sake, don't leave a dirty towel."

As she passed his room, Bogart opened his door.

"Colly! Y' look great."

"Will you escort me down to dinner, Bogie?"

"Damn right. And glad of the honor."

Colleen Bingham had not yet enjoyed the success that had come to Joan Crawford, but she was an established star, not what Hollywood coyly called a "starlet." She was a more beautiful young woman than Joan Crawford, her features more regular, more youthful, though they were probably the same age. She was taller, and her figure was fuller. She wore her golden-blonde hair coiffed smoothly, curled under her ears. Her light blue organdy dress followed the curves of her stomach, hips, and legs. Frills over the bodice saved her modesty. She wore long white kid evening gloves and carried a pouch-shaped velvet bag by its drawstring.

Baruch was still standing chatting with Mrs. Roosevelt and Joan Crawford when Bogart and Colleen entered the living room.

"Mrs. Roosevelt," said Humphrey Bogart. "Let me present Colleen Bingham."

Mrs. Roosevelt smiled at the young woman and said she was pleased to meet her. "I saw you in a film called *Glory Valley,* did I not?"

"I'm afraid you did," said Colleen with a wide smile and a little chuckle. "I wish you had seen me in some better effort."

"Well, I don't get to as many movies as I might wish."

"We must all join and persuade Colleen not to give up making movies altogether," said Bogart. "She's thinking of announcing her retirement."

"I'd hope you wouldn't do that," said Baruch. "I saw you in *Young Flame* and admired your work very much."

Colleen sighed. "Well, I . . . you see, I—"

"She had her heart set on doing Sissy in *Ironweed,*" said Bogart. "But . . ." He shrugged. "Ben Partridge is giving that to Merle Oberon."

"Why is that role so important, Miss Bingham?" asked Mrs. Roosevelt.

"It's a matter of art," said Joan Crawford. "Colleen and I would like to think we're actresses, not just faces or bodies. We're always looking for good roles—and finding precious few of them."

"Amen," said Bogart.

"It would have been..." Shaking her head, Colleen wiped her eyes with the back of her hand.

"Well, there will be other good parts for you," said Baruch. "Maybe before your visit here is over, something even better will come up. I believe we *are* here to talk about making movies, are we not?"

Colleen forced herself to smile.

Bogart slipped his hand around her waist and gave her an encouraging pat on the hip. "Join me in a smash of loudmouth, Colly," he said. "We'll both feel better."

"Do that," said Baruch. "We poured an extra tot of iodine into the bourbon, just for Bogie."

"You *what...?*" Colleen laughed. "Mr. Ba-*ruch!*"

Baruch lifted a gently summoning finger toward the butler, who came instantly to his side. "Some loudmouth for Mr. Bogart, George," he said. "And something cheering for Miss Bingham."

Bogart and Colleen stepped away from the others, Bogart putting an arm around her and speaking softly in her ear.

Benjamin Partridge and Darryl Zanuck arrived together a minute or so later. They had been in Zanuck's room for the past half-hour. The conversation that had begun there concluded just outside the living room, where no one else heard.

"You're a dirty, lying son of a bitch, Ben."

"You're a *little* man, Darryl. You've always been a little man, and you always will be."

It was true, in a sense. Zanuck was a little man, hardly as tall as Humphrey Bogart; and, though he was thirty-five years of age he had the appearance of an eighteen-year-old. His curly hair had begun to recede; his thin little moustache resembled one a teenager might try to grow, with mixed success; and his smile revealed a pronounced gap in his protruding front teeth. Otherwise, he was trim and looked as if his muscles were exercised and hard. His dinner jacket fit him well. He was, in Mrs. Roosevelt's judgment, a man possessed of himself and full of confidence.

He bowed and lightly kissed her hand. "An honor," he said.

"I have seen films with your name on them, Mr. Zanuck," she said. Her smile broadened. "I believe, however, you are an outspoken Republican, are you not?"

"I am a dedicated Republican, Mrs. Roosevelt," said Zanuck. "But I am, nevertheless, a great admirer of your husband—and, of course, of you."

"I could not ask for a better kind of Republican," she said.

"Do you mind my cigar?" Zanuck asked. "If you do—"

"Not at all, Mr. Zanuck," she said. "Provided only that you keep it at least six feet from my nose."

Zanuck laughed. "Six feet," he said. "I believe I can meet that requirement by stepping back two paces. Rather than do that, I will..." He glanced around, and the maid was at hand, to take the butt of his cigar in an ashtray.

"Ben," said Baruch to Partridge. "We've heard a little more about the problem with Colleen Bingham and the *Ironweed* role. Is there any solution to that? The poor girl is deeply distressed."

Partridge chuckled. "Barney," he said. "If *you* could get Merle Oberon to take a dramatic part, would you give it to her or to Colly? Look—" He stopped and nodded to Mrs. Roosevelt. "Forgive me, but Colly's got legs. What would you do, Darryl? You'd put Colly in pictures where you can show her legs, right? Sissy, in *Ironweed*...it's not for Colly."

"Apparently she thought she was going to get the part," said Crawford.

"You're an actress, kiddo," said Partridge. "You get big ideas about what parts you're going to get, sometimes. Don't you? Well, so does Colly. Hey, look. You folks. The players. You're kids, most of you. Colly needs to grow up. Same as Bogart over there. He seems to think he's really a tough guy."

"Ah had understood," said Crawford with cold hostility, "that Colleen Bingham had given you ample evidence of her *maturity* as a woman."

"As have you, my dear," said Partridge.

"Only inadvertently," said Crawford angrily.

"I am afraid I've been left behind in this conversation," said Baruch.

"My apologies," said Partridge. "Labor problems. I imagine you know how it can be. We will never have a strike, though. They all understand. There's not a film player in the world that can't be replaced in five minutes by somebody as good or better—out of a pool of tens of thousands of bright-eyed hopefuls that hang around the gates of every studio, just dreaming of the chance to get inside."

"And Ah suppose the same is true of producers," said Crawford icily. "Forgive me, Darryl—Ah happen to think you have talent—but producers like you, Partridge, and the Warners and the Mayers of this world could be replaced in less than five minutes, with men with a modicum of talent and intelligence." She looked up at Baruch. "I hope you'll decide to become a producer, Mr. Baruch. Others bring money. You'd bring money and taste—a combination that's been entirely absent from Hollywood throughout its history."

Partridge grinned and clapped his hands. "Speech!" he said. "That's one thing they can do: make speeches. Good going, Billie."

Crawford smiled at Mrs. Roosevelt. "My real name is Billie Cassin."

"Is it really?" asked Partridge. "I've heard several versions of that."

"I've heard several versions of yours, too," said Crawford.

Partridge's rotund face darkened and his bushy black brows tipped inward. "Did she catch any mud turtles?" he asked Baruch.

"No, but a fine sea bass," said Baruch quickly, obviously anxious to change the tenor of the conversation. "I think the President is going to find good fishing when he gets here."

"Let us hope so," said Mrs. Roosevelt. "He is looking forward to it."

"Darryl's the fisherman," said Crawford. "I never saw salt water until I went to California."

"I hope I'll have the honor of fishing with the President," said Zanuck. "Meanwhile, Joan, uh . . . Please excuse us." He offered Crawford his arm and led her away, toward Bogart and Colleen Bingham.

"I am sorry about the exchange," said Partridge to Mrs. Roosevelt and Baruch. "Film players, you know. They're . . . Well, Billie there—Joan—has no education whatever. I mean, she never finished elementary school, even."

"She seems to have married well," said Baruch.

"Doug Fairbanks, you mean?" asked Partridge.

"Franchot Tone," said Baruch.

"He's not as big a star as Doug Fairbanks," said Partridge.

"But his father is the president of Carborundum," said Baruch.

"Oh, yes. I understand Franchot is having a hell of a time trying to polish her up enough to be presented to people in his circle."

Mrs. Roosevelt shook her head. "I am surprised," she said simply.

"Well, we talk rough to each other, Mrs. Roosevelt," said Partridge, "but don't take it too seriously. It's the business."

She settled a cool eye on him. "I shan't," she said.

Even so, when Partridge separated himself from Mrs. Roosevelt and Baruch a moment or two later, she looked up at Baruch and asked, "Why does the man go so far out of his way to make himself unpleasant?"

"I suspect he doesn't know he is," said Baruch.

"I'm not sure I can name any of his pictures."

"Well . . ." mused Baruch. "Do you recall *Fire and Dance,* with Colleen Bingham and Dick Powell? The poor girl is not much of a dancer, I must say, even though Partridge did find her in a Busby Berkeley chorus line; but the dance numbers gave him a chance to show her off in some pretty skimpy costumes."

"Yes, he likes to show her legs."

"He showed more than that in *Flaming Dance*. Then, of course, Partridge produced *The Shame of Mrs. Tierney*, with Helen Twelvetrees and Gary Cooper. Last spring he released *Judge Knot*, another one with Colleen Bingham. You understand, of course, that there's another relationship between them."

"I suspected that," said Mrs. Roosevelt.

Humphrey Bogart returned to them, having been out of the room for a few minutes, apparently to the bathroom. "Having a little smash of loudmouth, Mr. Baruch?" he said.

Baruch nodded. "I am indeed," he said. "And you can call me Barney."

"Why, thank you, sir," said Bogart. He spoke with a cigarette hanging from the corner of his mouth. The satin lapels of his dinner jacket were streaked with ash.

Again at dinner, Mrs. Roosevelt was treated as hostess. Baruch presided at the head of the table, she at the opposite end. Joan Crawford sat opposite Darryl Zanuck, Colleen Bingham opposite Benjamin Partridge, and Humphrey Bogart opposite the empty chair that was to have been occupied by Tallulah Bankhead.

The table was set with heavy silver and fine English bone china, on heavy white linen, warmly lighted with a dozen candles standing in gleaming silver. Baruch's butler, underbutler, and two maids served. Wines sat on the sideboard, four bottles in ice, four bottles of Bordeaux, breathing. Dinner began with a clear turtle soup.

"Not mud turtle, I trust," said Bogart.

"To be honest-to-God truthful, Bogie, I think it's alligator, really," said Baruch.

"Strange," said Mrs. Roosevelt. "It has the distinct flavor of boiled typewriter keys."

"Oh, God!" Bogart laughed. "Jesus, dear lady! I was going to eat it."

"*I* fully intend to," said Zanuck. "Without comment on what it tastes like, which I've tasted many times over many years."

"We've heard that of you, DFZ," said Joan Crawford.

"*Turtle!*" Baruch laughed. "Turtle. I'm sure George can show you the shell," he added, looking up at the black butler standing behind him.

"Yes, sir. I definitely can," said the butler.

"Well, there. So," said Partridge.

"The wine . . ." suggested Mrs. Roosevelt.

"We are fortunate to be guests of a host who knows wine," said Bogart. "Even if he does put iodine in his Scotch."

"You said that before, Bogie," said Colleen. "What's the joke?"

"It . . . What—?"

An automobile horn honked loudly to the rear of the house, followed shortly by the peremptory shocks of the knocker on the back door. The butler nearly ran from the room.

"Ah! Ah! Barney, you will *never* forgive me! And you shouldn't. Late! My *God!* Dinner is on the *table*. Never mind, I shall take a tray in my room. Oh, *Jesus!*"

"That is your chair, Tallulah," said Baruch quietly, pointing to the chair opposite Bogart. "You've only missed the soup. Sit down. Do you know everyone?"

"Only Mrs. Roosevelt," said Tallulah Bankhead in her characteristic low, dramatic voice. "My father would *kill* me if he knew I was late to dinner with *you*, Eleanor!"

Tallulah swept around the table, extending her hand to Mrs. Roosevelt. She was dressed in deep red slacks, loose around the ankles but body-tight above, with an even tighter black sweater that covered her figure like nothing more than a coat of paint. Her bronze hair swept around her shoulders as she strode and gesticulated. She was, oddly, barefoot.

Mrs. Roosevelt, accustomed to more than this apparition, smiled and gave her hand to the actress. "How very nice to see you," she murmured.

"Oh, God! See me is what you do! Barney—"

"Sit down, Tallulah," said Baruch.

Tallulah glanced around the table, at the women in gowns, the men in dinner jackets. "Well." She shrugged. "Except for you, Barney, and the First Lady, the company is all Hollywood. As you warned me. H'lo, Bogie. God, I'm supposed to be your dinner companion, aren't I? Well, so." She took the chair opposite Bogart. "George. Some Bourbon, please. It's been a hard day."

"Miss Bankhead," ventured Partridge. "Allow me to—"

"Oh, *you*, Ben!" she cut him off. "You look *fat!* Fatter than you used to. What—"

"Miss—"

"Benjamin Weinvogel, Leipzig's gift to the art of cinema." She laughed. "Haven't seen you since—"

"London, 1925," said Partridge darkly.

"Yes, possibly," said Tallulah. "I think that's probably right. Have you missed me as much as I've missed you, *dah*-ling?"

"No, not as much, I should think," snapped Partridge.

"I would gladly have murdered you in 1925," said Tallulah. "Except that they *hang* people in England. They only use the chair here. If I'd known you here, I'd have risked it."

"Oh, dear!" protested Mrs. Roosevelt with an amused smile, taking what she heard for banter only.

"Ben is surrounded constantly by people who'd like to kill him," said Bogart. "He's quite comfortable with it."

"I am for sure," said Partridge. "I have complete confidence in the cowardice of those who talk about murdering people."

"Well, I for one," said Zanuck, "would like to talk about something more pleasant. Our little fishing expedition this afternoon was wonderful, wasn't it, Joan?"

Crawford nodded. "Tomorrow he's going to teach me to bait my own hooks. I can't tell you how much I'm looking forward to that."

"The President is also looking forward to the fishing,"

said Mrs. Roosevelt, though she wondered what he would make of this collection of egos.

Baruch led the company back to the living room after dinner, and shortly afterward Mrs. Roosevelt excused herself. "It has been a long day for me," she said. "A long journey on the train, a delightful evening—"

"Allow me," Baruch interrupted quietly, "to have coffee brought to your room. And . . . brandy? A liqueur?"

"A pot of tea, actually," said Mrs. Roosevelt. "And thank you, Bernie. The dinner was marvelous."

Baruch bowed. "We shall do better as the week goes on," he said. "Would you like to ride in the morning?"

"Oh, indeed."

"Then, breakfast at eight," said Baruch. "And if the weather permits, we will be on horseback by nine."

Baruch sat down for bridge, playing with Tallulah against Zanuck and Crawford. Partridge stood behind the table and watched first one player's cards and then another's. Bogart, still sipping Scotch, though sparingly now, sat before the fireplace and talked with Colleen Bingham.

"Partridge tried to cheat me out of the role of Duke Mantee," said Bogart quietly. He crushed a cigarette in the ashtray on the table. "He wanted Eddie Robinson to play it."

"I don't see what Ben had to do with it," said Colleen.

"Well, that was when he was with Warner Brothers," said Bogart. "Assistant producer. He didn't want some aging juvenile from Broadway, was the way he put it. He wanted a *star*. I'd been given the part, you know, and came to California to do it. I got there, and the first word I heard was, Yer out, kid. Ben Partridge has given the role to Edward G. Robinson. Leslie Howard saved my ass. I got him to send 'em a wire, telling 'em he wouldn't do the picture without me."

"Ben *promised* me the part of Sissy in *Ironweed*. There wasn't any 'maybe' about it."

"His promises are worthless."

"*He* is worthless," she said. "He's a monster."

Bogart sucked a tooth. "You want to make him mad? Come sleep with *me*. I'm a better man anyway."

"So's Jackie Coogan," she said. "I'm going to sleep in my own room tonight, with the door locked."

Bogart shrugged. "Well, that's gonna *half* make him mad."

Colleen smiled. "You're a dear, Bogie. But your wife would kill me."

"No. She'd kill me. Which is nothing new."

At the bridge table, Darryl Zanuck was discovering that Joan Crawford was a poor bridge player. Baruch concentrated on the game, and Tallulah Bankhead played offhandedly as if her mind were somewhere far away; but the Baruch-Tallulah team piled up points as Crawford misplayed her cards time and again.

Partridge drank coffee and sipped brandy. He was silent. From time to time he stole a glance at Bogart and Bingham, but he was subdued, as if making a conscious effort to avoid any further confrontations. He moved away from Zanuck's cigar smoke, without comment. When the butler came to his side with a fresh snifter of Courvoisier, he accepted it with thanks.

"Oh my God, Bogie! Look!"

Tallulah, dummy for the hand that was being played, had pulled her sweater over her head and tossed it on the floor by her chair. As Bogart turned to look, she unhooked her brassiere and tossed it away, baring her breasts. In another moment she had struggled out of her slacks and panties and was nude.

Baruch frowned. "It's a bit chilly for that, Tallulah," he said quietly.

She shrugged. "I'm comfortable," she said.

"*My God!*" Colleen whispered to Bogart.

"You didn't know?" he asked casually. "That's one of Tallulah's favorite acts. Relieves her boredom, I guess. I'm glad she waited until Mrs. Roosevelt went to bed."

"She does that often?"

"Often enough," said Bogart, glancing at Tallulah. "Truth is, she's crazier'n a bedbug."

Zanuck and Crawford pretended not to notice they were now playing bridge with a naked woman. Tallulah studied her cards and sipped from her brandy in complete insouciance. Baruch raised an eyebrow at Partridge, who shrugged and continued his determined effort to be the bland, appreciative guest. He did, though, move around the table, for a better view.

"What happened between them in England, do you know?" Colleen asked Bogart.

Bogart shook his head. "I don't know, but she called him 'Weinvogel.' What's that mean?"

"I don't know," said Colleen. "I know he's from Germany, but he never talks about it. 'Weinvogel.' What do you suppose . . . ?"

Bogart frowned. "'Vogel.' It means 'bird' in German, as I recall from school days. Let's see. 'Weinvogel.' Some kind of bird. Not 'wine bird.' Maybe—"

"German for 'Partridge?' " she guessed.

"Could be. Anyway, he didn't like it. I bet you got it. He was Weinvogel in Germany and calls himself Partridge here."

Colleen smiled at the naked Tallulah. "She said she'd have liked to kill him. I wonder why."

"I'm afraid Barney Baruch regrets the combination of guests he's put together for this party."

Colleen turned to look at Baruch. He sat with his cards in hand, studying them intently through his pince-nez and just as intently ignoring Tallulah. Her nakedness had made no visible impact at all on his imperturbable calm and dignity. The only ones visibly embarrassed were Crawford and Zanuck, who, all things considered, Colleen would have supposed would be the last people to be affected.

Partridge put his snifter aside, though there was still a sip of brandy in the bottom. "Well," he said. "If all of you will excuse me, I think I will go to my room."

"Before too long, all of us will probably be doing the same," said Baruch. "So, good-night, Ben."

"Good-night, Barney. And all."

Partridge turned to Colleen and summoned her with a lift of his chin.

She smiled. "Good-night, Ben. See you tomorrow."

Partridge hesitated for a moment, then turned and strode from the room.

3

Bogart yawned. He raised his glass and emptied it of the last of his Scotch. "Even Partridge has a good idea once in a while," he said. "I think I'm going to say good-night, too. The . . . uh . . . invite stands."

Colleen smiled at him. "You're a sweet man, Bogie. I appreciate you. I really do." She reached forward and stroked his cheek with the gloved fingers of her right hand. "I really do," she whispered. "You're a wonderful friend."

Bogart smiled wryly. "The words every man wants to hear from a lovely dame he's just asked to bed."

"Anyway," she said nervously, shaking her head. "You don't want to—"

The house shuddered under the impact of a quick, powerful shock, followed by the crash of breaking glass and the mutter of falling debris. Crystals in the chandelier were set tinkling crazily. A glass fell from the mantel and shattered on the hearth.

Baruch stood. "What—?" Zanuck pushed back his chair and rose. Crawford clapped her hand over her mouth and suppressed a scream. Tallulah shook her head, frowned, and took a heavy gulp from her glass.

"That was in the house," said Bogart grimly. He was on

his feet and striding toward the door. "Something . . . Gas?"

Colleen ran after him. "Gas! Escaping gas!" she shrieked.

Baruch hurried after Bogart, into the hall. Wilkes, the Secret Service man, ran headlong across the hall toward the entrance to the first-floor suite. He pushed back the door and entered the suite, calling, "Mrs. Roosevelt! Mrs. Roosevelt!" George, the butler, had run out from the kitchen and was standing hesitantly at the foot of the stairs; now abruptly he bolted up the stairs, yelling, "It was up here!"

He was right. The explosion had happened somewhere above. Bogart and Zanuck ran up after him. The long second-floor hall was filled with dust and smoke. George began to choke. Bogart and Zanuck stopped. George ran back toward them.

"It was in that room!" he yelled, pointing to the third door on the north side. "Door's busted! Git a breath . . ."

The butler, coughing, descended the stairs a few steps, into unfouled air. Baruch was halfway up.

"George?"

"It was . . . it was in one of the bedrooms, Mr. Baruch. Big 'splosion, look like. Fireplace . . . ? I—"

"Whose bedroom, George? Whose?"

George glanced up at Bogart and Zanuck, now hovering at the top of the stairs, then at the hall below. "It's the . . . the one we put Mr. Partridge in," he choked.

"He's up there!" yelled Baruch.

Bogart pulled his handkerchief from his breast pocket and covered his mouth and nose. He trotted down the hall to the door the butler said was broken. That was easy enough to see; the panels of the door were in fact shattered. He tried the knob. The door was locked. He pushed in one of the broken panels just as Zanuck, his face buried in a handkerchief, reached the door.

"Oh, Jesus!" groaned Zanuck.

Bogart turned away from the door and staggered back to the stairs and cleaner air. Zanuck followed, and they came down a few steps. George was about to go up again, but Zanuck grabbed his arm and shook his head.

"There's nothing we can do," he said. "Just open the windows, get some air into the house." He paused. "And George," he added, "don't even look."

"Partridge?" asked Baruch quietly.

"Dead," said Bogart. "There's no question about that."

"There's nothing we can do for him," said Zanuck as he sat down on the stair.

Baruch gripped the banister to steady himself. *"How? Can you tell?"*

"Hell of an explosion," said Bogart. "Lucky it didn't bring the house down."

"The place was built to be fireproof," said Baruch, frowning distractedly. "It's strong. It—"

Mrs. Roosevelt emerged now from the first-floor suite. She was dressed in a quilted robe and slippers. Wilkes followed only a pace behind her.

"Whatever, Bernie?" she asked.

Baruch drew a deep breath, then blew it out. "There's been an explosion in the house," he said weakly. "Ben Partridge's room. He's dead."

"Ohh," murmured Mrs. Roosevelt. "How? Why? What happened?"

"We haven't the remotest notion," said Baruch.

"Well—"

Mrs. Roosevelt stopped. Tallulah Bankhead stood outside the living room, at the corner of the library, still stark naked, glass of bourbon in hand, regarding with unexcited curiosity the irrational scene in the main hall.

"The ceiling is cracked," said Mrs. Roosevelt dully, pointing at the damaged plaster above the door to the gun room.

Wilkes strode forward. "An explosion," he said. "An accident. Are you sure?"

Bogart cast out his hands in frustration. "Come up and breathe the fumes, copper," he said.

John Crown, wearing a blue wool bathrobe, came around the corner at the end of the hallway to the kitchen.

He had come down the back stairs, from the servants' wing, and he stopped when he came on the naked Tallulah. He stood there, mouth agape, for a moment before he turned to Colleen Bingham.

Tallulah was calm, detached, but Colleen and Joan Crawford stared, stunned, at the men on the stairs. The underbutler and the maid who had helped serve dinner had come around the corner from the gun room. The blue smoke from the second floor had begun now to flow down, fogging the light on the first floor.

Wilkes remained by the side of Mrs. Roosevelt. He spoke to her quietly. "Let's go back to the room. Whatever, it's nothing you need to see."

"No, Mr. Wilkes," she said. "A man is dead. I—"

"Why and how?" asked Wilkes. "We can't be sure it wasn't—"

"Am I supposed to retreat down a hole?" she asked indignantly. "No. What has happened here?"

She walked into the center of the hall, to the bottom of the stairs. "Bernie."

Baruch came down. "I don't know," he said, stricken. "Eleanor, I—oh, forgive me for having you here when—"

"Forgive?" she cried. "No. What has happened? We must know."

"It's simple enough, Mrs. Rose-vult," said Bogart, coming down from the upper stairs. "Somebody has killed Ben Partridge. And, excepting Mr. Baruch and you yourself—plus the servants—I'd guess there's not a man or woman in the house that's not glad he's dead. I'll admit I am. The rest of us have reason enough to pour a smash of loudmouth and raise a toast. In fact, I'm going in and tip the decanter. Glorious! Weinvogel is dead! The gods are with us!"

"No, they're not, Bogie," said Baruch. "The First Lady is in the house. And all of you. A murder." He shook his head. "The gods are somewhere else."

Almost two hours passed before the sheriff of Georgetown County arrived. The guests sat in the living room, drinking the coffee Baruch's household staff brewed and brought in successive pots.

Tallulah Bankhead had pulled on her clothes and sat drinking bourbon until she was only occasionally and momentarily rational. John Crown, still in his blue wool robe, sat at the table where bridge had been played, staring vacantly into a cup of coffee. Joan Crawford and Colleen Bingham slumped on the couch, drinking coffee, smoking, talking softly to each other. Their gowns seemed inappropriate now, but neither of them wanted to go upstairs.

Baruch was in command. He had sent a man to bring the sheriff. Now he insisted that no one enter the room where Partridge lay dead, until the sheriff had been inside the room first.

Bogart and Zanuck climbed the stairs to the second floor once more, to peer through the broken panel of the door. They returned hard-faced, and Bogart filled his glass with Scotch.

Wilkes hovered over Mrs. Roosevelt, never allowing himself to be separated from her by two paces; and she sat, still in her robe and slippers, in a chair by the fireplace: filled with thought, glumly considering the implications of what had happened, wondering if she had any alternative but to sit here and wait for the sheriff, followed by newspaper reporters, to arrive.

The household staff—the butler, George, the underbutler, and the maid, plus several other black men and women who had not before been seen by the guests—hurried on orderly tasks. The ceiling in the hall was in fact cracked, and bits of plaster had fallen to the carpet. They removed those chips and the dust. They opened doors to let the house clear of the sickening odor of the explosive and of plaster dust and corrupted air. All the while, they watched the coffee pots and the cups, keeping them filled.

"It is, I suppose," said Mrs. Roosevelt to Bogart, "a distressing sight."

"Yes, ma'am," said Bogart. "He died quick, I suppose. Didn't suffer. I don't know—a time bomb under his bed, I'd guess."

"Horrible." She shuddered.

Bogart sighed. "I'm sorry I was so callous. Any man's death . . . You know, the poem."

"'Any man's death diminishes me, because I am involved in mankind,'" she said.

He nodded. "Right. *Any* man's death. It's easy to forget that when the man is so . . . Well, you saw a little of it."

"But someone," she said, glancing around the room, "*did it*."

Bogart nodded again. "We are in the presence of a murderer," he said.

Wilkes bent over Mrs. Roosevelt. "It would be well if we got out of here," he said. "And we could, before the sheriff arrives."

"But when it becomes known we were here, Mr. Wilkes," she said, "the speculations that would arise from our having fled would be worse than those that will arise from our having been here."

"I'm thinking of the newspapers, ma'am," he said.

"They are among the things I am thinking of."

Virgil Thompson, Sheriff of Georgetown County, was a bulky, fleshy, red-faced, puffing man: a wearer of little round gold-rimmed eyeglasses, a shiny black suit, a white shirt loosely bloused out around his middle, a gray fedora. He came alone, arriving at the back of the house in a Model A Ford.

"Ho, Mistah Baruch," he puffed. "Ah come soon's Ah could. Y'all got—"

"An explosion, Virgil," said Baruch. "A death. A murder, I'm afraid."

Sheriff Thompson stopped at the door of the living room. "Why . . . *Missus! Mrs. Roosevelt!* An'—"

"I hardly need introduce them, do I, Virgil?" said Baruch. "Ladies and gentlemen, Sheriff Virgil Thompson. Mrs. Roosevelt. Miss Joan Crawford. Miss Colleen Bingham. Miss Tallulah Bankhead. Mr. Humphrey Bogart. Mr. Darryl Zanuck."

"Well, Ah, well. Ah'm *honored*," said the sheriff.

"And this is Mr. John Crown, who worked for Mr. Partridge, the man who is dead. And—there with Mrs. Roosevelt—Mr. Robert Wilkes of the Secret Service."

"Well, I'm happy to have a Secret Service man here," said the sheriff. "You can prob'ly he'p with the investigation."

Wilkes glanced at Mrs. Roosevelt, then favored the sheriff with a measured smile and a curt nod.

Sheriff Thompson looked around the room, alternately frowning and smiling as if he still could not believe the identities of these people. "The, uh, man who is dead. He was also, uh, famous?"

"A Hollywood producer, like Mr. Zanuck," said Baruch. "Not quite as well known, I should think, but still well known."

"Y'all don't know *exactly* what causes this man to be dead, I s'pose."

Baruch shook his head. "Unfortunately, no," he said.

"Well, then," said the sheriff. "Maybe the other folks will forgive us if you and me and Mrs. Roosevelt goes off in another room to talk a minute."

Wilkes accompanied Mrs. Roosevelt, and the four went across the entrance hall and into the library. Mrs. Roosevelt sat in one of the leather chairs, as did Baruch. The sheriff and Wilkes stood.

"I haven't looked at the body yet, of course," said the sheriff. "What makes y'all sure he was in fact murdered?"

"We haven't looked ourselves," said Baruch. "Only Mr. Bogart and Mr. Zanuck and my man George have been upstairs. They say Mr. Partridge is dead. There was an explosion. They believe that was what killed him."

"Let's suppose that's true," said the sheriff. "How do we know he didn't kill *himself*—maybe messin' around with somethin' that would explode. What was it, anyway? Do we know *that*?"

"I'd guess nitroglycerine," said Wilkes. "From the smell. Besides, the ones who were upstairs are complaining of headaches; and the fumes of nitro, or of a nitro explosion, cause severe headaches."

"Touchy stuff, nitroglycerine," said the sheriff. "The man *could* have killed himself, accidental-like."

"Why would anyone in this house *have* nitroglycerine?" asked Wilkes. "How could they have brought it here? I understand all the guests except Mrs. Roosevelt and me arrived here by car, over those rough roads that come down through the estate. I wouldn't want to carry nitro in here that way."

"No, neither would I," said the sheriff.

"I am afraid," said Baruch, "that investigation will disclose that every one of my guests—with the sole and emphatic exception of Mrs. Roosevelt and Mr. Wilkes here—had motive to wish Mr. Partridge dead. Indeed, some of them have expressed as much, quite openly."

"What? *All* those people?" the sheriff exclaimed, pointing in the direction of the living room. "All hated him?"

"I am afraid," said Mrs. Roosevelt sadly, "that Mr. Partridge was not a very nice man."

"I'm afraid that's so," said Baruch. "Any one of them could have killed him."

"Then—"

"Then we have a mystery on our hands," said Mrs. Roosevelt.

"I do wish we could settle the question quickly," said Baruch. "It is distressing to think of the publicity—"

"Way I see it," the sheriff interrupted, "I've got two obligations as the Sheriff of Georgetown County, South Carolina. One is to find out who killed this fellow Partridge. The other'n, just as important, is to protect the names of the famous people in this house. You in particular, Mrs. Roosevelt, and you, too, Mr. Baruch. I don't want you bein' embarrassed while you're a guest in my county. What's more, I don't see any reason why you should be."

"Well, we do have a murder here," said Mrs. Roosevelt.

Sheriff Virgil Thompson lowered his head and looked at Mrs. Roosevelt over the tops of his little eyeglasses. "Who, besides us, knows it?" he asked.

"Actually, no one," said Baruch. "As you know, Virgil,

I've made a point for many years of not having a telephone here. The man I sent to wake you is completely trustworthy. I'm sure he did exactly what he was told: to notify you only and speak to no one else."

"This man Partridge. He have a family? Wife?"

"I don't think so," said Baruch. "John Crown has been his manservant for some years. He can tell us."

"If there's no wife, no children, no close family that has to be notified right off," said the sheriff, "then we can take a day to figure out what happened, before we let out any word."

"Keep a murder secret?" asked Mrs. Roosevelt. "What will happen when the word *does* get out?"

"S' far's I'm concerned," said the sheriff, "what I'm lookin' at right now is an accident—man some way blew himself up. 'Course we may find out it was a murder. When we do—*if* we do—then we put the word out. I'll tell the newspaper fellows it was only tomorrow, or maybe even the next day, when we found out the man didn't die accidental. Why, who knows? Maybe you'll be back in Washin'ton before we figure it out."

"What about the body?" asked Wilkes. "We can't leave it upstairs in the bedroom."

"You let *me* worry 'bout that," said the sheriff. "My cousin Douglas Forsythe, he's the funeral director in Georgetown. He'll take it into town, embalm it, patch it up, and make it look nice. If anybody has to see it later on, it'll look right natural."

"But—"

"Douglas is the coroner, too, of course. He'll make out a death certificate. 'Died of accidental means—explosion.' We find out later it wasn't accidental, he'll change it."

Mrs. Roosevelt looked up into the calm, grave face of Bernard Baruch. She touched her lips with an index finger. "Oh, I don't know..." she said.

"Y'understand," said the sheriff, "I'm just offerin' a suggestion. I mean to be helpful. We're *honored*, here in Georgetown County, to have visits from people like come to Hobcaw, and we want to be neighborly and do whatever we can to make folks' stay real nice and pleasant. Of course, I do have my duty. But I don't have to do it in such a way that—"

"We are grateful, Virgil," said Baruch. "And I suggest to Mrs. Roosevelt that we confront this matter in the way you have suggested. After all, we should do what we can to avoid embarrassing the First Lady."

"That's how I see it," said the sheriff.

"It will be understood," said Mrs. Roosevelt, "that the investigation must go forward and that we will have to accept the results it produces, no matter how much we may dislike them."

"Why, sure," said the sheriff.

"Let's not forget there are others who have to accept our decision," said Baruch. "Any one of them may want to leave."

"I'll hold 'em all as suspects," said the sheriff darkly.

"No," said Mrs. Roosevelt. "Please."

"I feel sure they will cooperate," said Baruch. "Let's talk to them."

The household staff was assembled with the guests in the living room, and Baruch spoke first.

"Sheriff Thompson will investigate the death of Mr. Partridge. He feels we may have been hasty in concluding it was murder and that it may have been an accident. In any event, all of you had planned to remain here as my guests for the balance of the week, and the sheriff asks that you do as planned. We—"

"We're all suspects," said Joan Crawford.

"*Except I!*" cried Tallulah Bankhead. "I arrived while you were at dinner and was with you all until the explosion."

"You made your big entrance when we were at dinner," said Bogart, his cigarette flopping up and down in the corner of his mouth as he spoke. "You could have been in the house for an hour. And don't forget, dear, you're the one who told Ben Partridge you wished you could have murdered him."

"Anyway, I don't choose to stay," said Tallulah airily. "I have obligations: places to be, things to do . . ."

"Where were you the hour before you came into dinner with these folks?" asked the sheriff.

"En route!" she cried. "I drove up to the house and came directly in."

"So you say," said the sheriff. "No. You're a suspect, too, Miss Bankhead. If you don't want to stay till we get this thing figured out, I guess I'll have to hold you as a suspect."

"I suppose," she said to Baruch, "a room in your house is more comfortable than a cell in the sheriff's jail."

Baruch smiled wryly. "Most people describe my hospitality as offering more comfort than a jail cell."

"Very well, dah-ling. Very well, then. You won't run out of bourbon?"

4

Baruch suggested that Mrs. Roosevelt go back to bed whenever she wished. She excused herself and returned to the first-floor suite. Baruch suggested, too, that he and the other guests would have to make themselves comfortable as best they could in the living room, until the household staff could close the windows and restore some heat in their bedrooms—perhaps, in fact, until the body of Benjamin Partridge was removed by the undertaker. The man who had gone to Georgetown to waken Sheriff Virgil Thompson was dispatched to Georgetown again, this time to wake the undertaker-coroner.

Robert Wilkes accompanied the sheriff to the second floor, for an examination of the room and the body. Wilkes was a young man: of greater-than-average height, sandy-haired, with a thin, pointed chin and nose. He was still wearing the light gray double-breasted suit he had worn on the train—with his revolver in a holster under the jacket.

The bedroom windows—glass and frame—had been blown out by the force of the explosion, and by now so much air had blown through the room that it was free of acrid fumes and smoke. The explosion appeared to have been centered in the bed, which had been blown to bits. The springs lay twisted but intact in the wreckage of the frame, and shreds of the mattress were scattered over the room, some of them charred.

The body of Benjamin Partridge had been blown apart. His head, shoulders, arms, and upper trunk lay face up in the doorway between the bedroom and bathroom. His legs were apart, one in a corner of the room, the other in the fireplace in the tangle of the firescreen, andirons, poker, and firewood. His blood was everywhere.

"I'd like to jus' turn around and walk out of here, is what I'd like to do," said the sheriff. "But..." He shrugged. "Duty... I seen a nigrah once, hit in the belly with the blast from both barrels of a twelve-gauge shotgun loaded with buckshot. Near to cut him in two. But this here. Brother!"

"I'm trained to protect people," said Wilkes. "I'm not a detective. But I'd guess it was one of two ways—either he was sitting on the bed with the bomb in his hands or it was under the bed."

"What set it off, you figure?"

"If somebody wanted to kill him," said Wilkes, "it was easy enough to set the bomb under the bed and rig up some kind of detonator."

"How much nitro you figure it'd take to do this much damage?"

"I don't know. A pint maybe. Maybe a quart."

"In a bottle? Can? S'pose we can find pieces?"

"It could have been dynamite, too," said Wilkes. "Dynamite is made of nitroglycerine, smells the same, gives off the same headachy fumes."

The sheriff nodded. "I've heard so. Easier to carry, too."

Wilkes knelt by the baseboard on the north side of the room. "Look here," he said. He picked up a fragment of the neck of a heavy bottle. "He didn't bring whiskey in that."

The bottle had been made of heavy clear glass, faintly tinted a blue-green color. Air bubbles trapped in the glass when it hardened in the cast glinted like tiny jewels.

The sheriff squinted at the piece of bottle glass. "Bet

there's more of that," he said. "Bet Douglas finds some in the carcass."

"Doesn't prove anything," said Wilkes. "But I'll guess the bomb was a small bottle of nitro."

The sheriff took the piece of glass in his handkerchief—Wilkes had picked it up the same way—and wrapped it and stuck it in his pocket. "No point in lookin' for fingerprints, I bet," he said. "But I suppose I should."

"Well, if you find *his* prints on it, that would prove something," said Wilkes, nodding toward the upper part of Partridge's body.

"I won't kid you," said the sheriff. "I hope they're on there. That'd settle the whole business."

"Not really," said Wilkes.

"Why not?"

"We still wouldn't know what Partridge was doing with a bottle of nitro. Who'd *he* intend to kill?" Wilkes shrugged. He was looking around the room again. "Look here," he said.

"Now, *I* know what that is," said the sheriff. "That there's from a *battery.*" He took from Wilkes's hand the scrap of torn zinc, still clearly recognizable as the bottom and a bit of the body of a large dry cell. "And that's how the nitro was set off. Blasting cap wired to this battery, some kind of a switch. Easy enough."

"Well, not easy, I'd say," Wilkes disagreed. "I wouldn't want to handle nitroglycerine. Somebody had to carry it—"

They were interrupted by a cautious tap on the door and turned to see John Crown standing just outside. He was still dressed in his blue wool bathrobe, tied with a braided cord.

"Uh . . . gentlemen."

Crown clapped his hand over his mouth as if to hold down something coming up from his stomach. He had caught sight of the head and upper body of Benjamin Partridge, and he shuddered violently.

"We told everybody to stay downstairs," said the sheriff.

Crown swallowed violently. "There's something you should know," he said. "Something in this room that—"

"What?"

Crown looked past them, into the shambles of the bedroom. "In the closet," he said. "A can of sixteen-millimeter film. It should be destroyed."

"Why? What is it?"

Crown sighed. "I—" He stopped, stiffened his shoulders. "The only thing to do is for you to look at it, Sheriff. You'll have to see for yourself what it is. Don't take my word for it. I wouldn't want you to take my word for it."

"Be more specific, son," said the sheriff firmly.

"Blackmail," said Crown. "Run the film, look at it. See for yourself. It's in the briefcase in the closet."

Wilkes pulled the briefcase from the closet and opened it. "There's no can of film in here," he said.

Crown rushed past the sheriff and peered into the open briefcase in Wilkes's hand. He fell on his knees at the closet door. Partridge's suits still hung in order, even though the door was scarred and broken. Crown felt all around the closet floor.

"Gone!"

"*What's* gone, fellow?" Wilkes demanded.

Crown peered frantically around the room. He rushed to the bureau. It had been broken off its legs and tumbled over, but the drawers were intact, and he began to jerk them open.

"All right, son," said the sheriff firmly. "Enough clownin' around. You jus' stand still and start makin' sense."

"Will you come with me and look just one place?" Crown asked. "Please! It's important. It has a lot to do with—"

"Where we goin', to look for what?" the sheriff demanded.

"Down the hall, just two doors! While it's still there. Before she—"

They did not obstruct him but followed him out of the room and to the right, along the upstairs hallway. All the doors were open, since the butler had opened all the windows to let the house air. Crown led the sheriff and Wilkes through the second door, into another bedroom. This one was a little smaller than the shattered room they had just left, and it was furnished very differently from the way that one had been. It too had a fireplace and bathroom, and the clothes spread about were a woman's. Crown began to pull drawers open.

"Here!" he cried triumphantly. He pulled a film can from beneath some clothes. "See! *She* got it! She somehow got it!"

"Okay, so she got it," said the sheriff sternly. "But what the hell is it?"

"It's a film," said Crown. He pried open the can, revealing a four-hundred-foot reel of motion-picture film. "See?"

"A film of what?"

Crown handed it over to the sheriff. "Don't take my word for this. Run it and see. It's what they call a stag film. Of her."

"Of who?"

"Her. This is her room. Joan Crawford."

The sheriff and Wilkes exchanged glances. The sheriff jerked his thumb over his shoulder, and they left the bedroom. They led Crown downstairs and into the library. Wilkes remained with him, and Sheriff Thompson went to the living room to invite Baruch to come to the library.

Baruch, still wearing his double-breasted dinner jacket, sat down. Wilkes closed the door, and the sheriff took a moment to explain to Baruch what Crown had told them and how they had found the can of film in Joan Crawford's room. As he spoke, the sheriff pulled a yard or so of the film off the reel and peered at it against the light, trying vainly to see what was pictured on the successive tiny frames. Crown sat watching.

"Let's hear an explanation," he said to Crown as he rolled the film back onto the reel and replaced the reel in the can.

Crown sighed. He slumped in a leather chair. "Some

years ago," he said. "I don't know how long ago. In the twenties. Anyway, Joan Crawford—I suppose she was then called Lucille Lesueur—did this film. It's a stag film, the kind of thing that's run at fraternity smokers or the Legion hall. It's awful raw, gentlemen. Everybody in Hollywood has heard of it. Almost nobody, though, has seen it. Not for a long time anyway. The story is that after she became a big star, Louis B. Mayer offered a lot of money for the prints and bought up all of them and destroyed them. Well, maybe he did and maybe he didn't; but if he did, he didn't get this one. Mr. Partridge had it."

"So why did he bring it to Hobcaw Barony?" asked the sheriff.

"Mr. Partridge brought it here to sell to Miss Crawford. Not just for money. He wanted her contract. He told MGM he'd have a hundred prints run off and distribute the film everywhere—which would of course make her worthless as a star property—if they didn't let her switch from MGM to Par-Croft. He told her to come here this week. He was going to announce to you, Mr. Baruch, that he'd bought Miss Crawford's contract and ask you to invest in her next film, and he wanted her here to confirm what he said and join him in proposing you back a film. Of course he had a couple of other ideas in mind, too. I don't need to tell you what those were."

"I suppose you've seen this film," said Baruch dryly.

"Yes," said Crown. "I was Mr. Partridge's valet. I took care of everything of his—everything personal, that is. I ran the film one day when he was away from home. I wanted to see if it was what he said it was. I thought of destroying it myself, but . . . I was in no position to do that."

"And when you learned that Partridge was dead," said Wilkes, "almost your first thought was to see to it that the sheriff took possession of the film. To protect Joan Crawford's reputation, I suppose."

Crown shook his head. "No, I'm afraid I can't claim so unselfish a reason," he said. "Actually, I . . . well, I suppose I'm a suspect in Mr. Partridge's death. I wanted you to see that someone else in the house had a powerful motive to kill him."

"Why do you suppose you're a suspect?" the sheriff asked.

Crown raised his chin high and drew his body erect. "You'll find out, if in fact you don't already know, that I was probably the last person to be in his room before the explosion. In fact, while all of you were at dinner downstairs, and while the household servants were busy in the kitchen and carrying food and drinks, I was alone upstairs." He shrugged. "I didn't kill him, but—"

"You hated him," said Baruch.

"Didn't everybody?" replied Crown defiantly.

"Apparently," said Baruch. "But why you?"

"He made me a servant. He treated me like dirt."

"Why'd y' work for him, then?" asked the sheriff.

"I owed him money," said Crown. "I've been working it off."

"You have ambitions to be an actor yourself, haven't you?" asked Baruch.

"Yes, and he promised to help me, once I repaid what I'd borrowed from him."

"How did you come to borrow money from him?"

"I lost a lot of money at the racetrack. I owed almost two thousand dollars to bookies. You know what they'd have done if I hadn't paid."

"How much do you still owe?" Baruch asked.

"More than half of it," said Crown. "He paid me twenty dollars a week to work as his valet, and he withheld half of it as my payment on the debt. In two years—"

"You still owe more than half of it," said Baruch. "But I want to change the subject, Mr. Crown. Who must be notified of Benjamin Partridge's death? What family did he have?"

Crown shook his head. "He never mentioned anyone. He was an immigrant, you know. He came here from Europe in the twenties. I suppose he has family somewhere. Doesn't everyone? But he never mentioned a wife or a child. I sorted his mail at home. He never received a letter from Europe. I don't know who you notify. His partner, Bancroft, I suppose."

"All right," said the sheriff. "You can prob'ly go on and go to bed now, Mr. Crown. And I b'lieve I'd keep right quiet about what you've told us. Above all, don't you say nothin' to Miss Crawford. Y' hear?"

"Yes, of course," said Crown. "I understand."

"Do you have a projectah in the house, Mr. Baruch?" asked the sheriff.

Baruch smiled faintly. "Yes. I do."

"Well, I think we gotta know if this here film is what that young man says it is."

"My own thought exactly," said Baruch.

"Do we let Joan Crawford know we have the film? That we've seen it?" asked Wilkes. "Do we confront her?"

"Unless Crown's a big liar and was settin' her up, she was in Partridge's room sometime," said the sheriff. "If she went in and got the film, she could have planted the bomb."

"Once she got the film, why would she kill Partridge?" asked Baruch.

"First thing, we've gotta see the film," said the sheriff.

Baruch returned to the living room, ostensibly to inquire about the comfort of his guests, actually to be sure they were all there while the butler, George, brought the sixteen-millimeter Bell & Howell projector down from a storage room on the third floor and carried it to the library. Before he left them to return to the library, Baruch told his guests they could use their bedrooms now and were welcome to sleep there if they would not be disturbed by the commotion the undertaker would make as he carried away the corpse.

In the library again, Baruch fumbled with the controls of the projector. "I never tried to run it myself," he said. "It shouldn't be—"

"'When all else fails, read th' instructions,'" suggested Sheriff Thompson. "Ain' that what they say?"

Wilkes set up the screen that George had also brought.

After some more fumbling and two false starts when the machine was grossly out of focus, Baruch managed to get it running, pulling film off the top reel, hauling it through the complexities of the projection mechanism, and reeling it onto the takeup reel at the bottom. Wilkes switched off the lights.

The film was grainy, ill exposed, and jerky; but it was a stag film, just as Crown had said—silent and almost ghost-like as whitish figures moved over the surface of the screen.

"It's her," said Baruch grimly. "Joan Crawford."

She had been fleshier eight or ten years ago, but the face was hers, unmistakably—the eyes, especially, could not be mistaken. What was more, the moves, the expressions were hers. Not for a moment on the screen was she covered by a thread of clothing. She was naked, and the film was without a story line. She displayed herself for a minute or two, then welcomed a partner and began a performance that was purely physical, without the slightest suggestion of emotional reaction to the use of her body. She performed in obedience to an offscreen director, to whom her eyes occasionally turned for instruction; and, on receiving instruction, she would nod and proceed to do whatever she had been told. Toward the end of the twelve-minute film, the second of her two male partners walked off camera, and a young woman came on. The two young women performed then, the same way. Almost everything that two human beings could do, physically, was pictured—yet without an instant of shared emotional involvement. At the end, the camera panned up and down the chief young woman's body, as she lay feigning—perhaps actually having experienced—exhaustion.

"Kee-rist!" exclaimed the sheriff.

"There can be no doubt," said Wilkes, pretending at least to be calm and analytical. "I've seen a dozen of her movies. That's her, beyond any question."

"It is of course true," said Baruch, "that the public would crucify her if it knew about this reel of film. Her career—"

"She could start a new one." The sheriff laughed.

"The Legion of Decency—"

"The Hays Office—"

"The morals clause in all their contracts," said Baruch. "MGM could cancel her contract in a minute. No other studio would dare touch her."

"Ah think—"

"I think we should destroy it," said Baruch. "Even if it is evidence—"

"Them's my thoughts," said Sheriff Virgil Thompson. "But right now it's evidence, so I s'pose we have to keep it. I can put it in a safe in my office."

"Would you mind if I put it in a safe *here?*" asked Baruch.

"Why, not a-*tawl,* sir," said the sheriff.

"Then I shall do so," said Baruch. "And may I suggest that perhaps now the night is too old for us to achieve much more? I assume Douglas Forsythe will be here soon and will know his business. A short drink, Virgil? Mr. Wilkes? And then to bed?"

They sat in the living room a few minutes later. The sheriff slumped wearily on the couch and stared into the fireplace—over a generous splash of bourbon poured over two ice cubes. Wilkes sipped brandy. Baruch had gone to his vault and locked away the film. He had returned and was just pouring himself a sip of brandy when Joan Crawford entered the living room.

She wore a sheer pink peignoir over a sleek pink silk nightgown. Her shapely legs were exposed through the peignoir, but otherwise the ensemble was modest enough. She entered without a word, poured herself a sip of brandy without being invited, and sat down at the table where much earlier four people had sat so casually at bridge.

"Did you run it?" she asked dully.

"I beg your pardon?"

"I noticed the projector set up in the library. I suppose you ran the film."

"I'm afraid we did," said Baruch. "Unhappily, it has

become evidence in the matter of the murder of Benjamin Partridge."

She looked at Sheriff Thompson. "Do I have to go to jail? I mean, do I have to go tonight?" she asked.

The sheriff drank from his glass. "I don't have no reason to take you to jail, Miss Crawford," he said. "That is, I don't 'less you got somethin' you want to confess."

"I didn't kill him," she said. She tipped the snifter and sipped brandy. "Honest to God, I didn't."

"When'd you go in and get the film?" the sheriff asked.

She sighed heavily. "You can imagine the demands he made on me," she said. "Do I have to tell you? He summoned me to his room, to be there about a quarter to seven. He said he would be meeting with Zanuck in Zanuck's room, and I was to go in his room and wait for him. When I got there, his door was unlocked. I went in. He wasn't there."

"So you looked for the film," said Baruch.

"Yes, of course. Wouldn't you have? Wouldn't anyone? I couldn't believe my luck—to have a chance to look for it, then actually to find it and to get out of there with it! I took it back to my room. I meant to burn it in the fireplace before the night was over, but for the time being I hid it under some clothes in a drawer and locked my room. After that—I mean, with the film in my possession—I figured to hell with Ben Partridge. I didn't go back to his room. I came downstairs. You were here, Mr. Baruch, and we began to talk, and shortly Mrs. Roosevelt came in."

"You didn't tell anyone you had the film?"

"No. I was going to burn it. When I went up, a little while ago, I lighted a fire in the fireplace, and then I opened the drawer, and the film—"

"Was gone," said the sheriff. "How'd you figure out that *we* had it?"

"I supposed you'd searched all our rooms. If you had found the film, you would know I had been in Partridge's room, so I supposed I had better come down and find out how much trouble I was in. Also, when I came downstairs I noticed the projector. Why else would you have a sixteen-millimeter projector set up in the library?" she asked.

Baruch sighed. "I regret we felt we had to run the film, Miss Crawford. It is evidence. You say you didn't kill Benjamin Partridge, and I'm inclined to believe you didn't. But you had motive."

"He paid ten thousand dollars for that reel of film," she said. "I can't be sure it's the last copy. I can only hope it is."

"Motive enough to do the man in," said the sheriff.

"Others had motive," she said. "Bogart . . . Zanuck . . ."

"Them, too?" asked Sheriff Virgil Thompson. "We cain't seem to simplify this case no way." He sighed wearily.

5

Bernard Baruch sat his horse with ease and confidence. He was so big a man that the big black stallion did not in the least overwhelm him; and it was plain, merely from seeing him sitting comfortably in his sadle, reins casually held in one hand, that he was the absolute master. He wore tweed riding clothes, complete to tweed cap, and his pince-nez was firmly seated on his nose.

Mrs. Roosevelt governed her chestnut mare with practiced skill, not quite so confident as Baruch but clearly in control. She was dressed as she had been the afternoon before, in khaki twill jodhpurs and a brown tweed jacket over a white blouse, with her hair tied back by a band of yellow silk.

Robert Wilkes had been chosen to accompany her on this trip because, of all the Secret Service agents who might have come, he seemed most likely to be able to ride without difficulty; but his bay had taken his measure, and he was at constant pains to manage it, to discourage its sidestepping and calm it. He had brought breeches and boots but only a dark blue sweater and no jacket, and he had tried unsuccessfully to conceal the revolver under his belt by pulling his sweater down over it. Baruch and Mrs. Roosevelt had invited him to ride with them, not to keep a distance, and he sat with them as they paused atop a small wooded rise and looked out over the waters of Winyah Bay.

"That's Pumpkinseed Island," said Baruch, pointing at the smallest island in the bay. "It's part of the Barony. The white birds are white ibis and snowy egrets. We don't go on the island. We leave it to the birds."

Somewhere to their left a grunt sounded above the general chatter of the woodland. They searched but did not see the creature that had made it. It had left its track on the mud bank down which it had slid—a full-grown alligator that had chosen the moment to launch himself into the water of an inlet.

"Certain animals and fish would prosper more if those big fellows weren't here," said Baruch. "But we don't interfere with the way nature has arranged things. We impose some restraints on man, but don't try to control anything else."

He turned his horse and led the way along the bank of an inlet. Birds rose as the three horses approached. Turtles slid into the water. Another alligator rose on its stubby forelegs, regarded them coldly, then slipped into the water and made its slow way to a depth where it had the option of submerging.

Only the three of them—Baruch, Mrs. Roosevelt, and Wilkes—had appeared for breakfast. They had taken coffee and pastries—Baruch also a cut of melon—before they had gone to the stable.

It had been difficult, in the peaceful early-morning house, to believe that what had happened the night before was anything but a bad dream; though when they went out they could glance up and see the blown-out windows of the bedroom where Benjamin Partridge had died. On the wall of the east wing, the house had been scarred by glass flying like sharp bullets. More glass glinted on the lawn. Shortly before daylight, the undertaker had come and removed the body. The room was being cleaned and repaired. As they rode away, Mrs. Roosevelt had noticed a workman pushing a wheelbarrow load of debris away from the house. Before the day was over, the plaster would be repaired, the floor would be restored and refinished, and reglazing and repainting would have begun.

Bernard Baruch did not mean to dwell on the misfortune of a man having been murdered in his house. He felt an obligation, nevertheless, to report to Mrs. Roosevelt on what had happened after she went to bed. He told her all they had learned so far, in some detail. He told her about the film.

"Oh, that *poor,* poor young woman!" was Mrs. Roosevelt's reaction. "Imagine what she must have suffered."

"Well, I—"

"To have to do something like that to win her chance for success in Hollywood. And then, having achieved success, to have that horrid film come back to threaten her career! You *will* destroy it, Bernie. Won't you?"

"Of course."

"Even if it is evidence," said Mrs. Roosevelt firmly. "Destroy it anyway."

Baruch glanced around at Wilkes. "I'm sure the sheriff will agree," he said.

"Whether he does or doesn't," said Mrs. Roosevelt.

They rode north, through the pinewoods and out into the abandoned rice fields that had once made ten plantations. Every kind of bird native to America—so it seemed—rose from the watery land.

"We find shells," said Baruch. "Great accumulations of broken shells. The Indians must have gathered shellfish and carried them to campsites, where they cooked them and tossed the shells in trash heaps that accumulated for centuries. We find bits of pottery, too."

"We must decide, Bernie," said Mrs. Roosevelt, "whether to send a message up to Washington and advise Franklin not to come."

"This is Tuesday," said Baruch. "If we don't know by Thursday who killed Benjamin Partridge, then we'll probably never find out."

"Oh, but we *must* find out. Otherwise, everyone in the house is a suspect."

"Except you," said Baruch. "Even I might have killed him."

"But you had no reason," she said. "Everyone else—"

"Well, Mr. Wilkes had no reason, we may assume," said Baruch. "And none of the members of my household staff. Otherwise, I'm afraid everyone in the house had motive."

"If—"

"Haloo! Haloo!"

They turned in their saddles. Tallulah Bankhead was calling, urging her horse into a gallop as she crossed a hundred yards of open grassland toward them. Her horse splashed through water, repeatedly lunging to regain its balance as it stepped into soft mud.

"She'll be thrown!" cried Mrs. Roosevelt.

Baruch shook his head. "There's a saying, Eleanor. 'God looks out for little children, drunk men, and the United States of America.' Anyway, I've seen her ride to hounds, down in Alabama, going over fences like a maniac. I'm more afraid for the horse than I am for Tallulah."

"Oh, *dah*-lings!" yelled Tallulah as she reined up her horse and covered the final few yards to their side at a slow trot. *"What* a morning!"

She was wearing a ragged sweater and a long gray skirt that rode high around her bare legs. Her feet were barefoot in the stirrups. She was without makeup, and her uncombed hair hung around her face; but she grinned broadly.

"Good morning, Tallulah," said Baruch sternly. "Don't you think there's some hazard in riding barefoot?"

"Not so hazardous as going to bed with a bottle of nitroglycerine, hey, Eleanor?" Tallulah laughed.

"I'm afraid I don't find that very funny," said Mrs. Roosevelt.

"Ah," said Tallulah. "Well, forgive me. Crude of me. But I knew him, don't forget."

"Did you kill him, Tallulah?" asked Baruch.

She shook her head. "As God is my witness, I did not have the pleasure."

"You knew him in England, I believe you said."

"Yes, I did. Herr Weinvogel."

"A German?" asked Mrs. Roosevelt.

Tallulah nodded.

Baruch frowned. "A Jew?" he asked.

"Partridge?" Tallulah laughed. "Weinvogel? No, Barney. A Nazi."

"Seriously?"

Tallulah shook her head. "Actually, I don't know about that," she said soberly. "But he was no Jew. He knew every ugly anti-Semitic word and phrase ever invented and used them more than Adolf himself."

"What did he do that made you hate him, Tallulah?" Baruch asked.

She shrugged. "Something that doesn't have to be dredged up."

"Maybe it will have to be," said Baruch. "You are a suspect in his murder. Not one of the chief suspects, I suppose, but all of us who were in the house last night are suspects, with Mrs. Roosevelt almost the only exception."

"Well, if I have to tell, I suppose I will. The sheriff has already threatened me with durance vile. But until I have to, I will keep my secret. Anyway, I didn't kill him."

"I hope you don't have to tell," said Baruch solemnly.

"I shall ride on, dah-lings," said Tallulah, reining her horse around. "I'm afraid your conversation this morning is locked on a grim topic I would rather forget. I came out to feel the wind in my hair."

Baruch nodded, but she did not see him. She urged her horse into a gallop and rode away in the direction from which she had come.

Mrs. Roosevelt and the others rode on in silence for a minute or two. Then she turned to Baruch with a thoughtful frown. "May we assume that the bomb was planted in or under the bed between the time when Mr. Partridge left the room to come down to dinner and the time when he went back up?"

"Not necessarily," said Baruch. "But suppose we do assume it. What then? What do you have in mind?"

"According to Miss Crawford, he left his room before a quarter till seven," she said. "She says he went across the hall to meet with Mr. Zanuck, though I gather you haven't checked with Mr. Zanuck about that. And he left his room unlocked, since she was able to enter and take the reel of film."

"Yes. Apparently Partridge meant to go back to his room before he came downstairs."

"And maybe did," said Mrs. Roosevelt.

"Yes. And maybe did."

"Very well," she went on. "While he was across the hall with Mr. Zanuck, Miss Crawford entered the room. Then Miss Crawford returned to her room, hid the film, and came down to the living room. She was with you when I came in. How long had she been there?"

"She had just arrived," said Baruch.

"You and I chatted with her for—what?—ten minutes or so? And then Miss Bingham and Mr. Bogart arrived, together. And after that anotherfive minutes or so passed before Mr. Zanuck arrived with Mr. Partridge."

"Yes."

"How long do you suppose it took to install the bomb?" asked Mrs. Roosevelt.

Baruch glanced at Wilkes. "What would you say?"

Wilkes drew a breath and considered. "Oh, three or four minutes," he said. "If you knew what you were doing. If you had planned it. Five minutes would be more than enough."

Mrs. Roosevelt goaded her horse with a heel and rode out ahead of the two men. "I'm afraid it looks rather bad for Mr. Crown," she said.

"I'd say he's a chief suspect," said Baruch. "But what do you have in mind?"

"Let us suppose," said she, "that Mr. Partridge left his room at a quarter till seven. By a quarter after, everyone but Mr. Crown and Mr. Wilkes was in the living room with us. That means there was half an hour during which someone could have entered the room and had plenty of time to install the bomb."

"Yes. Yes."

"But for one thing," she said with emphasis.

"But for what?"

"People in the hallway," she said. "Mr. Partridge crossed the hall to Mr. Zanuck's room. Then Miss Crawford arrived. She was in the room briefly, then went to her own room. A minute or so later she left her room to come downstairs. At some point, Mr. Bogart came out of his room, and Miss Bingham came out of hers. Finally, Mr. Partridge and Mr. Zanuck left Mr. Zanuck's room. We may presume, may we not, that whoever entered Mr. Partridge's room to plant the bomb hoped to do so without being observed? Five people had rooms on that hallway, and all of them were due downstairs at seven. Any one of them might have come out into the hall at any moment. I can hardly believe that someone knowing those facts would have chosen that period of time to enter Mr. Partridge's room and plant a bomb."

"I see your point," said Baruch. "On the other hand, Partridge was out of his room during the afternoon."

"But the bomb was not installed until after he left his room to come down to dinner," said Mrs. Roosevelt.

"How can you be sure of that? A time bomb—"

"It wasn't a time bomb, Bernie. I feel sure of that."

"How? How can you be sure?"

"What time did the bomb go off?" she asked. "Eleven-fifteen? How could the person who installed it be sure Partridge would be back in his room by that hour? If it had gone off at three A.M., the case would be different. But . . . No. It was set off by some other means, probably when he sat down on the bed. I've thought about it, and—"

"You're right," said Baruch. "Absolutely right."

"And Mr. Crown, who had a key, could have returned to the room while we were at dinner and—"

"Yes," said Baruch grimly. "Of course. On the other hand, it remains possible that Joan Crawford did it. What is more, we haven't eliminated Tallulah. She made quite an entrance at dinner, but that could have been a cover. She could have arrived a quarter of an hour earlier, left her car on the road in the dark a hundred yards from the house, sneaked in, and planted the bomb."

"Fanciful, if you don't mind my saying so," said Mrs. Roosevelt. "Anyway, what about the key? Whoever entered Mr. Partridge's room must have had a key."

"Unless he left it unlocked," said Wilkes. "Joan Crawford said it was unlocked when she went in to get the film."

"George can give us the answer to that," said Baruch. "He opened all the rooms after the explosion, as I told him to do, to let them air."

"Then, the key. . ." She paused and smiled shyly. "I was about to say, 'The key is the key.'"

As they rode toward the house, they saw the sheriff's car parked near the kitchen door. Sheriff Thompson stood at the back of the house, talking with a black workman, looking up at the blown-out windows on the second floor. The sheriff's shiny necktie reached only to the middle of his comfortably bulging belly, failing to cover the open gap in his shirt where a button had been lost. He was sipping from a cup of coffee, and in his other hand he held the ragged butt of a handmade cigarette.

"Good mawnin' to y'all," he said to Baruch and Mrs. Roosevelt and Wilkes as they walked toward him from the stable. "Fine mawnin'."

"It is indeed, Sheriff," said Mrs. Roosevelt. "In fact, if it were not for this distressing business of the death of Mr. Partridge, it would be a perfect morning."

"Mawnin' like this," the sheriff said, "y' have to think about the man that's gone, 'bout how he's missin' it. Y' have to hope he's gone on to a better place."

"Amen," said Mrs. Roosevelt.

The sheriff sighed. "Well, anyhow, I s'pose we don't know nothin' more'n we did?"

"Very little," said Baruch as he led them toward the back door. "Except that Mrs. Roosevelt has come to some conclusions that I imagine are valid."

"And what are those, ma'am?"

"Well, first," said Mrs. Roosevelt, "that the bomb was set off by some device other than a clock. How could the murderer have known that Mr. Partridge would be in in his room and in bed by eleven-fifteen?"

"I reckon that's right," said Sheriff Thompson. "Couldn't have been a time bomb. Wouldn't have known what time to set it for."

"That means," said Mrs. Roosevelt, "that the bomb was detonated some other way. It would seem most likely that the bomb was in or under the bed and that his weight on the bed somehow closed a switch."

"Well," said the sheriff, "I'm still not givin' up the idea that he may have been workin' on the bomb himself, gettin' it ready to use to kill somebody else."

Mrs. Roosevelt nodded. "Let's keep that possibility in mind. But if the bomb was planted by someone else, then it had to be done by a person who had access to the room —and access means time to go in and do the job, without being caught in the act or being observed entering or leaving Mr. Partridge's room, plus a key to unlock the door— assuming, that is, that it *was* locked."

They entered the house. A maid was running a vacuum cleaner, and Baruch told her to go and fetch George.

They entered the library. "I am afraid," said Mrs. Roosevelt, "that my speculations all point in one direction: to Mr. Crown."

"Odd fella," said the sheriff. "He hasn't told us the truth."

They sat down in the library: Baruch, Mrs. Roosevelt, Wilkes, and the sheriff; and after a moment the butler, George, came in.

"We have an important question, George," said Baruch. "If you don't know, that's all right, but don't give me an answer unless you're sure."

"Yes, suh," said George.

"You were the first to arrive at the door of Mr. Partridge's room last night, weren't you? So, tell us, was the door locked, or not?"

"It was locked, Mr. Baruch," said George, nodding solemnly to lend emphasis to his words. "I unlocked it when I went back up to open all the rooms and all the windows, to let the house air, like you told me to."

"Then how did Mr. Bogart know Mr. Partridge was dead inside?"

"The door was busted," said George. "He jus' pushed in a piece of the wood and could see in."

"How about the other doors?" the sheriff asked.

"Everybody'd locked their doors, suh. They got valuables with them, I guess."

Baruch nodded. "Thank you, George. That's very helpful. By the way, where is Mr. Bogart this morning? Where are all the guests, for that matter?"

"Well, suh," said George. "We had a little accident in the house this mawnin'. Miss Bingham, she done burned her hand on her curlin' iron. Kind o' bad, I'm afraid. I took her up some bandages and salve. She's in her room, I b'lieve. Mr. Bogart's still asleep, far's I know. Mr. Zanuck and Miss Crawford, they went fishin'. They had some coffee and went out. Said they was goin' fishin'. Miss Bankhead took a horse and went for a ride."

"And Mr. Crown?"

"I haven't see him, suh."

"Would you please go find Mr. Crown then and tell him we want to see him," said Baruch.

They waited in the library while the butler went to find John Crown. The sixteen-millimeter projector remained on the table, and Mrs. Roosevelt eyed it with a degree of disapproval.

"It is always an honor and a pleasure to visit this house," said Sheriff Thompson.

"It's a pleasure to have you, Virgil," said Baruch. "We'll have to get in some shooting before the season gets much further advanced. Is everything all right in town? I mean, did your cousin treat our matter in confidence?"

The sheriff nodded. "Only other person who knows anything is Judge Cranshaw. Seemed like we had to tell him. He'll keep quiet."

"We may have the matter settled before noon," said Baruch.

"Ah most surely hope so," said the sheriff.

"I suppose we need not worry that any of the guests have absconded," said Wilkes.

"Tallulah's car is here," said Baruch. "So are mine, and I noticed the truck is in the garage. Of course, Zanuck and Miss Crawford could be on their way out of the county in a fishing boat. But I don't think so."

"Have you notified Mr. Partridge's business partner?" asked Mrs. Roosevelt.

"I called him long-distance this mawnin'," said the sheriff. "Rousted him out of bed. I told him there'd been an accident. I can't say he seemed much upset."

"It's distressing to think that a man is dead and no one cares," remarked Mrs. Roosevelt.

"That's how he lived, looks like," said the sheriff. "So's nobody'd care."

John Crown arrived. He was wearing black trousers and a white shirt and had not yet shaved. He looked as if the butler had wakened him.

"Close the door, Mr. Crown," said Baruch. "The sheriff wants to ask you a few more questions."

Crown glanced anxiously around the library, at the four people sitting and looking up intently into his face. He closed the door and for a moment stared at it as if it had trapped him.

"What do they call you, Mr. Crown?" asked the sheriff. "John? Johnny?"

"Johnny, mostly," said Crown hoarsely.

"Well, we gotta look at some facts, Johnny," said the sheriff. "Maybe you got an explanation for them facts, and if so . . . But if you don't, it looks kind of bad for you."

"I knew I'd be suspected."

"Everybody's suspected, just about. But you're the *chief* suspect now. You just got promoted."

"Sure," said Crown bitterly. "Why not? I'm the nobody in the house. It would be very convenient to hang me."

The sheriff shook his head firmly. "Nobody's hangin' nobody," he said. "Even if it would be convenient. Which it wouldn't."

Crown sighed. "What makes me chief suspect?" he asked.

"It's a question of keys, Johnny," said the sheriff. "And locked doors. Whoever planted the bomb got into Partridge's locked room. It was still locked when the butler and Mr. Bogart ran upstairs to see what had happened."

"Keys," said Crown. "That's ridiculous." He allowed himself a nervous little smile, and he shook his head. "Utterly ridiculous. You're on the wrong track if you're counting on locks and keys to make me the killer."

"You went in and out of his room to take care of his stuff, right? You had a key to his room."

"That didn't make any difference," said Crown. "When I got there, the room wasn't locked. Anyway, I didn't have the only key. Everyone had a key."

"What do you mean, everyone had a key?"

Crown reached into his pocket and took out a nickel-plated key. He tossed it on the library table. "That's all the key I have," he said. "All I ever had. It will open any door in the house, I imagine. It opens my room. It opened Partridge's room. There was no second key to his room. Ask your servants, Mr. Baruch. Did Partridge or I ask for another key to his room? My key opened his room. Wait a minute."

He picked up the key from the table and went to the library door. He opened it and inserted the key in the keyhole. He had to jiggle it a bit, but it turned the lock, and the bolt slid in and out.

"Simple mortise locks," he said. "They're meant for privacy, not protection. My father is a house builder. He's installed a thousand mortise locks, and he never carried more than two or three keys, to open all of them. Gather up everyone's keys. Every one of them will open that door."

"Damn," muttered the sheriff.

Crown shrugged. "Am I still chief suspect?" he asked. "Or have I been demoted?"

"You were in Mr. Partridge's room at seven o'clock, I believe," said Mrs. Roosevelt.

Crown sighed. "Whenever Mr. Partridge left a hotel room or a bedroom in someone's home where he was a guest, as here, my orders were to go to that room immediately and tidy it up. If he returned, he expected to find it completely in order. He told me he would be going down at seven to join the other guests for dinner, and I knew he was always very punctual, so I was there at seven. There was a bit of unpacking left to do. I did that and arranged his clothes as he wanted them. And I cleaned up the bathroom."

"How long were you in the room?"

Crown thought for a moment. "Maybe ten minutes," he said. "Maybe not quite that long."

"Alone? No one came in while you were there?"

Crown shook his head. He frowned. "I was alone," he said.

"Mr. Partridge did not return while you were there?"

"He was downstairs, with all of you."

"As a matter of fact, he wasn't," said Mrs. Roosevelt. "He was across the hall, in Mr. Zanuck's room."

Crown winced. "He had told me he was going downstairs at seven."

"So you left the room at, say, seven-ten? Did you lock it when you left?"

Crown nodded. "Yes. I had been surprised to find it unlocked."

Mrs. Roosevelt ran her hand down her cheek and pondered for a moment. "When you came to Mr. Partridge's room, and when you left, did you encounter anyone in the hall? Did you see anyone? Did anyone see you?"

"No. There was no one in the hall when I came and no one when I left."

"Where did you go after you left Mr. Partridge's room?" asked Mrs. Roosevelt.

"Down to dinner. Bob—uh . . . Mr. Wilkes here—was having dinner in the breakfast room, and I joined him. After dinner, we stayed at the table, with the rest of our wine, and played pinochle, for quite a while."

"He was with me until almost eleven," said Wilkes.

"Until how long before the explosion went off?" asked Baruch.

Wilkes shrugged. "I'm not sure. Fifteen minutes, maybe."

Mrs. Roosevelt glanced at the sheriff, then spoke to Baruch. "I can't see that we're getting anywhere," she said glumly.

"You ain' been demoted, Johnny," said the sheriff. "I s'pose I should take you over to Georgetown and lock you up, but then I'd have to run back and forth to town ever'time somebody wanted to ask you a question. Best you stay here, I guess. But you behave y'self, heah? Don't you get no ideas 'bout runnin' off."

Mrs. Roosevelt went upstairs to offer her sympathy to Colleen Bingham and see if the young woman needed any help. She found her tinkering with a camera, which she said she hoped to use to take some pictures of the estate and the people there. Her left hand was bandaged in rounds of gauze that held a cotton pad in place on the back, just behind her index finger.

"It was such a stupid thing," she said to Mrs. Roosevelt. "I use that thing"—nodding to an electric curling iron that lay on the table by her bed—"to put a little curl under my ears. I've always been afraid I'd burn my neck or ear, and here instead I've burned a blister on the back of my hand."

"We can arrange for a doctor to come out," said Mrs. Roosevelt.

Colleen smiled. "Oh, I think it will be all right," she said. "It hurt enough to make me cry when I did it; but, except for throbbing a bit, it's all right now."

"Tell me," said Mrs. Roosevelt, "how does it happen that a young man like Mr. Crown has been working as a household servant? I should have thought he would have had other ambitions."

"It is my understanding," said Colleen with a little frown, "that he owed Ben Partridge a lot of money."

"Do you have any idea why?"

"The story Ben told is that Johnny came to Hollywood the same as everyone else, in the hope of becoming a movie star. He didn't make it and was working as an extra at RKO. He needed money and got mixed up with some criminals. Bookies. He was a messenger, so to speak. He carried their money from cigar stores and the like to their office. Since it was illegal money anyway, he decided to take a little from time to time. After a while, it added up to a lot. Then they found out. They threatened to hurt him. He'd met Ben Partridge somewhere, so he went to Ben, and Ben let him have the money to repay the bookies. He's worked for Ben ever since, paying it off."

"I see," said Mrs. Roosevelt thoughtfully. "What an unhappy story..."

6

Baruch sent the butler to assemble his guests for lunch at 12:30. He made a point especially that John Crown should come, and when Crown walked into the living room, he took him aside and said, "A man with the status of chief suspect need not take his meals with the servants, Mr. Crown. Please join the rest of us from now on."

The sheriff had returned to Georgetown, and Zanuck and Crawford were still out somewhere fishing, so the company at the luncheon table was Baruch and Mrs. Roosevelt, Humphrey Bogart and Colleen Bingham, Tallulah Bankhead, and Robert Wilkes and John Crown. They did not talk about the murder. Colleen described her accident and assured them her burn, though ugly, did not hurt much. Baruch talked of the estate, as he loved to do. Bogart spoke of shooting, and Baruch told the butler to leave his household duties for the afternoon and go out and launch clay pigeons for Mr. Bogart.

It was odd, Mrs. Roosevelt thought, how the death of Benjamin Partridge had brightened the faces of most of these people. In Bogart's case, it appeared that the absence of Partridge simply left him no one to scowl at. He looked relieved, actually. Tallulah, with a tumbler of bourbon by her left hand and a cigarette in her right, looked as though she had forgotten the murder entirely. Colleen, though she favored her bandaged left hand and occasionally winced when she moved it, had overnight become cheerful and animated. She had the look of a woman who had been liberated. Only Crown looked troubled. His eyes remained fixed on the table much of the time, and he participated in the conversation only when it was specifically directed at him.

"Your father was a house builder, you say?" Baruch said to Crown.

"*Is,*" said Crown. "He built more than twenty houses last year. In the Buffalo area."

"And you are the daughter of Jack Bingham, aren't you?" Baruch asked Colleen.

"You've heard of my daddy?" she asked, surprised.

"I've heard of him," said Baruch. "I've never met him. An oilman."

"A wildcatter. He's spent all his life looking for one big field."

"He's had his share of success, I understand," said Baruch.

"And put every dime he's ever made back into the ground," she said. "It's in their blood, those old fellows like my daddy. I mean, oil is in their blood. They'd be worth making a movie about, those wonderful characters. When I was a child, Daddy used to haul us around with him summers, and we lived in boardinghouses and ate at tables with the old oilmen. Their talk was..." She laughed and shook her head. "I'll never forget them."

"God, I wish I *could* forget most of my father's associates," drawled Tallulah. "Politicians!"

"My father was a doctor," said Bogart glumly. "What was yours, Barney?"

"I forget," said Baruch. "At my age, you forget things like that." He chuckled. "But I inherited a wonderful name. Do you know what my name means, Bogie?"

Bogart frowned. "Bernard," he mused. "Saint Bernard. It means a big dog."

Baruch laughed. "No. 'Baruch.' Do you know what a 'baruch' is?"

"A horse-drawn carriage," suggested Bogart.

"No. A blessing. In Hebrew, the word *baruch* means 'blessing.'"

"Was it Dorothy Parker," asked Mrs. Roosevelt in mock innocence, "who suggested you only go to the synagogue to hear your name spoken?"

"No," said Baruch. "She's the one who said there are only two things in this world she cannot understand: the theory of the zipper and the function of Bernard Baruch."

After lunch, Baruch and Mrs. Roosevelt walked along the circular drive behind the house, in the bright sunshine they had gone out to enjoy.

"I wonder if it would not be well to take a boat and go looking for Mr. Zanuck and Miss Crawford," said Mrs. Roosevelt. "After all, someone was murdered here last night."

Baruch nodded. "We will bring along fishing tackle, so our encounter with them—if we have one—will seem perfectly innocent."

Wilkes accompanied them. As they pulled away from the little dock before the house, in a twelve-foot skiff powered by a chugging little outboard motor supervised by Wilkes, they could hear the deep reports of Bogart's shotgun, banging away at the clay pigeons being launched by George. When the wind was right, they could even hear Bogart yelling, "Pull!"

"I can't be confident of our chances of finding them," said Baruch of Zanuck and Crawford. "Hobcaw Barony covers a lot of land and water."

Handsome white birds, disturbed by the clatter of the laboring little engine, rose from the waterfront tangles as their boat turned south, then east, through the narrow channels between islands and mainland and over the choppy waters of Winyah Bay. Baruch, pointing, showed Wilkes the way to go, as they circled some of the islands, looking for the small boat Zanuck had taken early in the morning. There was a stiff wind. The boat wallowed in the waves and would have thrown cold spray if it had moved faster. Mrs. Roosevelt wore a thin raincoat over the riding clothes she had donned that morning. She had brought along a small 35-millimeter camera and peered through its viewfinder at the shore birds, turtles, and alligators that all but ignored the passage of the boat.

"This is not part of the estate," said Baruch as they approached the shore east of Pumpkinseed Island. He stood and scanned the shoreline through his binoculars. "But I think we've found them."

Another boat, not very different from their own, was drawn up on the sand and into the edge of the grass. Wilkes steered where Baruch pointed, and they chugged near. The boat drawn up on the sand was abandoned, but when they were within fifty yards Zanuck trotted down through the tall grass and peered at them, shielding his eyes with his hand.

"Ho!" he yelled.

Wilkes slowed the little outboard and guided the boat up to the shore.

"Fishing?" Zanuck asked as he stepped down and grabbed their bow to pull the boat to a landing.

"Looking for you, frankly," said Baruch. "We became a little concerned."

"Doing a little exploring," said Zanuck. He jerked his thumb over his shoulder. "Joan is coming."

Joan Crawford appeared a few yards back in the tall, thick grass—tossing her head to toss back her hair, stumbling over the root clumps and through the sand as she came down to the water's edge. She was wearing slacks, a sweater, and a corduroy jacket, all covered with sand. Her face was flushed, and her smile was determined and artificial.

"You're off the Barony here," said Baruch. "This isn't my land."

"Oh, hell," said Zanuck. He pointed at the islands to the west, in the bay. "The islands are yours?"

"Yes. But not North Island, which is what this is. Makes no difference, actually. We don't go ashore on

Pumpkinseed there. I try to leave that for the birds that nest on it."

"We've caught nothing today," said Crawford. "Fishing—"

"'We fished all night, Lord, and caught nothing.'" Zanuck laughed.

It was apparent they had been doing something other than fishing in the sheltering tall grass of North Island, and everyone was faintly embarrassed—Zanuck and Crawford to have been found, Baruch and Mrs. Roosevelt to have interrupted. Zanuck struck a match and began a struggle against the wind to light a big cigar.

"You missed lunch," said Baruch. "We brought along a basket. What may be more to the point, we brought along a quart of Scotch."

"I'm grateful for both," said Zanuck, "but especially for the latter."

Mrs. Roosevelt climbed over the gunwale and set foot on North Island. Her riding clothes served her well here, on this sunshiny but blustery afternoon. She tossed her raincoat back in the boat. "I will have just a sip of that, uh, loudmouth, Bernie," she said. "Just a sip."

Baruch had, in fact, brought not a quart but a flask and half a dozen tiny cups. They stood on the sandy shore, all of them, and sipped Scotch.

"Any developments in the big detective case?" Zanuck asked.

"I am afraid not," said Baruch. "The sheriff would like to talk with you a bit."

"I am at his service," said Zanuck.

"The time sequence of last evening is much on my mind," said Mrs. Roosevelt. "Would you mind going over a point or two with me, Mr. Zanuck?"

"Not at all," said Zanuck.

"Could we?" She indicated with a gesture that meant, Could they stand apart from the others and talk. "Would you mind?"

Zanuck turned his back on the rest of the party, and they walked a few yards south along the edge of the water. "Are you doing the detective work?" he asked Mrs. Roosevelt. "If so, I'm glad. Frankly, I'm happy to see someone contributing brains to the investigation. In the absence of that element, God knows which of us might be accused."

"Don't underestimate Sheriff Thompson," said Mrs. Roosevelt. "A great deal of ability and intelligence sometimes hides behind a drawl like that."

Zanuck nodded. He stopped and faced the pitching green waters of the bay, squinting at the purple-gray clouds that lay over it to the south and west. "Take Joanie there," he said, biting down on his cigar and drawing on it to encourage the weak flame he had managed to light with his wind-blown match. "She's shrewd and tough, as she had to be to come up through what she came up through. And when she's under stress, she talks like southern fried chicken."

"Did she tell you what she retrieved from Mr. Partridge's room last evening?" asked Mrs. Roosevelt.

Zanuck nodded. "I've seen it. For her sake, I hope that's the last copy."

"It will be burned," said Mrs. Roosevelt firmly. "Just as soon as this distressing business is concluded."

"In her presence," said Zanuck. "Let her see it burned."

Mrs. Roosevelt nodded. "Yes. I am reasonably certain, Mr. Zanuck, that I know who murdered Benjamin Partridge. I would like to review some facts. I don't mean to exclude Mr. Baruch from the conversation, but frankly I do mean to exclude Miss Crawford. I believe the facts will exculpate her entirely, but you can understand that—"

"I do understand," said Zanuck. "Anyway, several of us had ample motive for murdering Ben Partridge."

"We can go into that later," said Mrs. Roosevelt. "Right now I'd like to ask you when Mr. Partridge came to your room."

Zanuck nodded. The wind whirled his cigar smoke around his face, whipping it away behind him. "I wasn't studying my watch," he said, "but I'd call it about a quarter to seven. I was dressing, planning to go downstairs at seven."

"Were you expecting him to come to your room?"

"No. He knocked. I went to the door. He said he wanted to come in and talk. He was all dressed, ready to go downstairs. I handed him a bottle of bourbon and told him to pour himself a snort while I finished dressing. He did, and he started talking business."

"Maybe we'll have to know what that business was, later," she said.

"I hope not," said Zanuck. "I wouldn't mind telling you, but it would be ruinous if the story got out. Anyway, he said he couldn't stay more than a minute or so. He said he'd asked Joan to come to his room before we went downstairs and wanted to go back to spend a few minutes with her."

"Did he say why he had asked her to come to his room?" asked Mrs. Roosevelt.

"Yes. Definitely. And, I'm sorry, but what he said was anything but delicate. He expected to, uh . . . how shall I say?"

"Abuse her," suggested Mrs. Roosevelt wryly, glancing back at Joan Crawford, who was apparently listening to a gestured Baruchian exposition of the glories of Winyah Bay.

"Well. Yes. Something like that. Because he had that film, he was in a position to, uh, make demands."

"But he remained in your room and did not go back to his own, even though she was supposed to be there for his pleasure."

"We got into a very hard argument," said Zanuck. "He became very upset. So did I. I won't deny it."

Mrs. Roosevelt turned away from Zanuck and walked slowly along the shore, farther from the boats. He followed. "May I ask what is the nature of your own relationship with Miss Crawford?" she said in a low voice.

Zanuck chuckled nervously. "Well, I . . ."

"Your *business* relationship, Mr. Zanuck."

"I have an option for her next film," he said briskly.

"You understand, MGM has her contract; but I have option rights to her services as an actress for one film. I have a very fine property I want to make into a major picture."

Mrs. Roosevelt nodded. "I understand. Anyway, Mr. Partridge was in your room long enough for Miss Crawford to have come to his, searched for the film, found it, and taken it away to her own room?"

"Easily," said Zanuck. "She'd have had plenty of time. We were late coming down for before-dinner drinks. I was embarrassed by how late we were."

"He was in your room almost half an hour."

"Yes."

"During that time did either of you see or hear anyone going into Mr. Partridge's room?"

Zanuck shook his head. "We were talking. Our attention was very much fixed on what we were saying."

"Ah. Now, when you left to come downstairs, did Mr. Partridge return to his room? Did he go back to his room before the two of you came downstairs?"

"He . . . well, he opened his door and looked in, that was all. Then he locked it."

"It was unlocked?" she asked. "You're sure?"

"Yes. He opened it and looked in. Then he took out his key and locked the door."

"I see," she said thoughtfully.

"You think the bomb was planted while we were in my room talking?" Zanuck asked.

"Either then or after you came downstairs," said Mrs. Roosevelt.

"Well, his room was unlocked. Anyone could have walked in. Joanie of course did."

"After we all gathered downstairs," said Mrs. Roosevelt, "none of us could have planted the bomb."

"Not quite so," said Zanuck. "I hope the fact has no significance, but Bogie left us for a few minutes just before we went in to dinner. I supposed he'd gone to the bathroom, and probably that's exactly what he did; but he was gone for a few minutes. Actually, when you think about it, the fact *is* insignificant, because Partridge locked his door before we came downstairs. Bogie couldn't have gotten in without a key."

Mrs. Roosevelt nodded, but she frowned and was troubled. "Of course," she said quietly. "He had no key to Mr. Partridge's room."

Zanuck puffed nervously on his cigar. "The solution to the problem, if you don't mind my telling you so, doesn't lie in who had a key and who didn't, what door was locked when and what door wasn't, and so on. It lies in finding out who brought a bottle of nitroglycerine onto Mr. Baruch's estate, and how. You came here on a boat. The rest of us arrived by car, over very rough roads that lead onto the estate from the highway out of Georgetown. None of us drove ourselves except Tallulah. We were driven in by Mr. Baruch's man—Ed, I think his name is—who wasn't terribly careful about running into holes and ruts and bouncing the car around. I can't believe anybody brought in a bottle of nitro that way. So how'd it get here? That's what I've been thinking about."

Humphrey Bogart had fired a hundred shotgun shells and hit twenty-four of the clay pigeons George had launched for him. Returning to the house, he returned the shotgun to its rack in the gun room. He poured himself a Scotch from one of the decanters that seemed always at hand in the house. Tallulah was in the library, drinking bourbon and glancing through a book of prints. She was in a withdrawn mood and seemed averse to conversation. He went out the front door and strolled into the woods behind the house and down the slope toward the bay.

He carried his Scotch with him, sipping as he walked. He wore a heavy tweed jacket, a gray wool shirt, and breeches with boots. His shoulder was sore from the kick of the shotgun, and he rubbed it.

He walked for about ten minutes, until he was perhaps half a mile from the house. It seemed a remote place, away from any road or trail, where scrub pine grew thick on the bank just above the high-tide line; and yet twice he thought he heard someone thrashing through the pine and brush ahead of him.

He finished his Scotch and put the glass down by a tall pine, meaning to pick it up on his way back.

He couldn't see far, except out across the water; and he walked cautiously, recalling what Baruch had said about snakes in the woods and big snapping turtles that lay hidden among the roots of trees in the edge of the water.

He heard someone. No question about it—either another person or a deer or wild hog was moving in the woods ahead of him. "Haloo!" he called.

Whoever was there did not answer. He pushed forward, into the heaviest growth of the pine, where the ground was softly covered with piny-smelling needles. The carpet of needles was disturbed—dry ones had been turned over and the wet needles underneath turned up, leaving distinct, darker brown scuff marks. He had been right in thinking someone had been in the thicket. He pushed branches aside and made his way into the middle. Narrow-eyed, he looked around. He squatted, so he could see under some of the thick, low-hanging branches.

Lying on the ground under a stunted pine—hidden, but not hidden well enough if you were searching—was a small traveling case: a cheap and well-worn brown and yellow model made chiefly of paper. He pulled it out, flipped the catches, and opened it. Inside were bottles, a bowl, a funnel, a thermometer, a hunk of sponge, a few rubber bands, a pair of tin snips, and some scraps of tin cut from a coffee can.

Bogart pulled his handkerchief from his pocket. He wiped his fingerprints off the catches on the case, closed it, and wrapped the handkerchief around the handle. He carried the case out of the thicket and down to the edge of the water. There he knelt again and opened the case. Holding each bottle with his handkerchief, he poured what was left in them into the lapping saltwater. Then he held each bottle underwater until it filled, so it would be sure to sink; and he tossed each one out over the gray-green water as far as he could throw it. He threw everything else from the case after them. Finally he stomped the empty case into shreds of paper and a few splinters of wood and threw all of that into the bay, with the metal catches and the handle.

He paused to light another cigarette, then shoved his way out of the area of pine thicket and started back toward the house.

He walked a few yards, then stopped and stared upward, trying to recognize the pine under which he had left his glass. He moved on a few more yards, still looking up. He almost walked into Colleen Bingham before he saw her.

"Bogie!"

"What you doin' out here, Colly?"

"Just . . . walking." She shrugged. "What are you doing?"

Bogart nodded. "Walking," he said. "Actually, I'm looking for my glass. I left my Scotch glass around here somewhere, meaning to pick it up on my way back to the house."

"You're on your way back? I'll walk with you."

She seemed cold, to the point of trembling, in spite of her heavy brown corduroy slacks and her cream-white turtleneck sweater—maybe because her head wasn't covered and her hair was whipping in the wind. He was sympathetic and put his arm around her. She was in fact trembling.

"Colly," he said. "We're well rid of Ben. All of us. You understand?"

She nodded. "But why do you mention it?"

"So we understand each other."

She sighed. "He was an evil man," she said.

"I'm not sure everybody realizes that," he said. "Those of us who do may have to stick together."

She nodded solemnly, and on impulse he drew her close

and kissed her. She responded warmly, and for a moment they stood, prolonging their kiss.

"Well . . ."

"Hey, Johnny! Odd coincidence," said Bogart. "You out for a walk, too?"

John Crown showed Bogart a quick, instinctive flash of hostility before he gained control of himself and managed a smile. "Yeah. Uh, I was looking for someone to talk to."

"Strange place to be looking. Anything special, or just conversation?"

"Oh, just conversation. I'm not sure people want to talk to me much, now that I'm chief suspect."

"That's so unfair!" cried Colleen. "Johnny couldn't have—"

"Well, I *could* have," said Crown darkly.

"That's right, you could have," said Bogart. "And so could I. And so could Colly. And so could—Look what's coming."

Tallulah Bankhead strode purposefully along the water's edge, her shoes sinking into the mud and sand where it was wet. She had not bothered to pull on a coat or jacket against the chilly wind, and her arms were bare, her legs bare below her skirt. She puffed on the butt of a cigarette, almost angrily.

"Hey, kiddo!" Bogart yelled. "Where ya goin'?"

Tallulah stopped. She fastened a look of fury on Bogart. "I *was* on my way to take a leak, if you must know."

"House is full of bathrooms," said Bogart.

"Not near the satisfaction you get from adding your bit to the ocean," she said. She climbed toward them. "What are you all doing out here *ménage à trois?*"

"Blocking your progress, I suspect," said Bogart.

"Well, damn you, you did," she said. "I suppose I may as well go back to the house."

"Has our genteel host returned?" asked Crown.

"No. He and Eleanor are still out playing detective. I hope they come back with the supposed crime solved. For myself, I cahn't *wait* to know who did in Ben Partridge. I'm going to give the culprit an engraved plaque."

"Don't have it engraved yet," said Bogart. "It may be a long time before this one is figured out."

7

Bernard Baruch never dined alone, not if he could avoid it; and he went to some trouble to people his table with varied and interesting characters, so that dinner conversation could be an intellectual stimulus as well as amusing. He enjoyed, too, dining with people he could impress: with his hospitality, his wit, and his extensive knowledge of an infinite number of subjects. Dinner was for him an occasion, something he looked forward to during the day; and at Hobcaw the evening after the murder of Benjamin Partridge, he firmly turned the talk away from the murder and the investigation.

He had invited Robert Wilkes and John Crown to join the other guests for cocktails and dinner; and, since neither of them had brought dinner jackets, he suggested that everyone wear what he called "country clothes"—tweeds, sweaters, walking shoes.

"Who will make the Amelia Earhart picture?" Baruch asked as the roast beef was served. (The world-famous flyer's disappearance over the South Pacific on her around-the-world flight had occurred only months before.) "I assume someone will make a picture based on her life."

"I wouldn't want to risk it," said Zanuck. "What if she turns up alive?"

"Do you think there's a chance she will?" asked Mrs. Roosevelt.

"My theory is that her plane was forced down by the Japanese," said Zanuck. "Because she was flying too close to some island they're fortifying in violation of their mandate. I bet she's a prisoner."

"Why don't you make the movie that way, DZ?" asked Bogart.

"Sure," said Zanuck, lifting his glass of wine. "Then, when I've spent a hundred thousand dollars and have the movie ready to go, she turns up and we find out that what she really did was land on a paradise island in the Pacific to spend a few months with her secret lover. No thanks."

"I have never been up in an airplane," said Colleen Bingham. "And I never intend to."

"Do you realize," said Mrs. Roosevelt, "that the British flew an Empire Flying Boat from Ireland to New York this summer, as a test of the feasibility of starting trans-Atlantic passenger service? Imagine that! Imagine being able to travel across the Atlantic Ocean in *one day.*"

"I wouldn't buy any tickets," said Baruch. "Those flying boats have to carry so much gasoline that there is no room for people."

"Mr. Trippe, of Pan American, has told the President that he expects to offer weekly service to London within two years."

"I'm not sure I'd like to travel to London that way," said Baruch. "Imagine also being entrapped in the tiny cabin of an airplane and compelled to remain in a seat—nights perhaps in a bunk—all the way across the Atlantic. I rather look forward to mornings in a deck chair, with hot coffee or consommé, sessions in the steam room, afternoons of bridge in the bar, and dinners at the captain's table, on a good liner. I am not ready for the Spartan life of an airliner."

"I can understand going by air in an emergency," said Bogart. "Otherwise, to hell with it. Whoever is in that big a hurry?"

"Mr. Kennedy perhaps," said Mrs. Roosevelt with a smile. "He is ready for the idea."

"He would be," intoned Baruch.

"On the other hand," said Mrs. Roosevelt, "Mr. Trippe also thinks it will be possible within the next ten years to travel to Manila or Hong Kong in less than a week."

"Good," said Baruch. "I hope he goes there. With Joe Kennedy. And . . . Oh, who should we send? The Supreme Court?"

"If the President has his way," said Bogart, "there will be too many justices to pack on one airplane. We'll have to send them out by tramp steamer."

"For myself," said Joan Crawford, "I can't think of a reason for traveling to Manila *or* Hong Kong. I wish Juan Trippe well in his enterprise, but why on earth would anyone want to go *there?*"

"You must forgive me," said Tallulah, "but you have just expressed my own attitude toward California."

"We—"

The butler interrupted. "Excuse me, suh," he said to Baruch. "This telegram has just been brought over from Georgetown, and the boy is waiting to know if there's any reply."

Baruch opened the envelope. (For some reason he would never know, telegrams in their envelopes always had the odor of cheese about to spoil.) The wire read:

UNDERSTAND BEN PARTRIDGE DEAD OF ACCIDENT YOUR ESTATE STOP AM IN WASHINGTON AND PROPOSE TO MAKE BRIEF VISIT TO FIND OUT HOW COME STOP HAVE ARRANGED TRAVEL SO AS TO ARRIVE BY NOON WEDNESDAY STOP ADVISE IF NOT CONVENIENT STOP
WALTER WINCHELL

"George," said Baruch quietly to the butler. "Ask the telegraph boy if he can take dinner in the kitchen and wait until I decide how to answer this telegram. If he's reluctant, offer him a drink or two."

"Yes, suh."

Baruch tucked the telegram in the pocket of his jacket. "California," he said. "It is my understanding that it is to become a county of the State of Oklahoma, as more Oklahomans arrive there and become its chief inhabitants. That is an excellent idea. Then we shall be relieved, perhaps, of California senators, California newspaper publishers, and —as I would hope—California wine."

"It's a great place to make a living," said Bogart. "I just wouldn't want to have been born there."

After dinner, Baruch invited Mrs. Roosevelt to accompany him upstairs, to his suite. They sat down before a small fire burning in the fireplace of his private sitting room, and he showed her the telegram.

"Is there any way we can discourage him?" she asked.

"Oh, many ways, yes," said Baruch. "I can refuse to admit him to the property. But—"

"But if we do, it will only confirm in his mind a suspicion that has no doubt already had its birth."

Baruch nodded.

"On the other hand, if he comes here, he will immediately discover that Mr. Partridge was murdered," said Mrs. Roosevelt. "And then—"

"Not necessarily," said Baruch. "I was thinking about it over dinner. He might not discover it."

"Oh, how could we keep it from him?" she asked.

"Well," said Baruch, "of the people here, it's in no one's interest to have a story of murder screamed at the world. Not by the likes of Winchell. He's a professional scandalmonger, Eleanor, as we well know; and this is a gold mine for him: a house full of celebrities, one of them mysteriously dead. He'll milk it for weeks."

"The story *must* be published, sooner or later."

Baruch rubbed his hands together beneath his chin. "Must it, necessarily?" he asked.

"A murder . . . a trial . . . an execution perhaps. Bernie! We can't—"

"Think about it a minute," said Baruch. He nodded. "Think about it. Almost twenty-four hours have passed, and we have no idea who killed Partridge. Almost all the suspects are prominent people, public figures. Not one of them wants his or her name associated with a murder. If we can't find out who killed the man, we leave it that he died of an accident."

"Bernie! *Really!* An explosion in the man's bedroom! An accident? Even Walter Winchell isn't fool enough to believe that!"

Baruch picked up a short iron poker, reached into the fireplace, and poked the fire vigorously. Sparks rose in sheets and streamed up the chimney. "Eleanor," he said blandly, "he blew himself up with a can of dry-cleaning fluid. He was trying to take a spot off his suit while smoking a cigar, and—"

"Oh, Bernie, really! And blew a whole room out of the house?"

"A *big* can of dry-cleaning fluid," said Baruch. "Anyway, by the time Winchell arrives, how big the explosion was won't be apparent. Most of the repairs are finished now."

"And what if the evidence develops to prove John Crown murdered him?" asked Mrs. Roosevelt.

"Well, Sheriff Thompson is continuing his investigation," said Baruch. "If he comes up with proof that someone killed Partridge, then he makes his arrest and announces what he's found."

"And the accident story?"

Baruch smiled. "We were wrong. It looked like an accident, but the sheriff, through his dogged investigation, found out it was murder. In the meantime, we tell Winchell it was an accident. No big scoop in that. He goes back to New York with nothing to broadcast."

"It will come out," she protested. "We—"

"Eleanor," said Baruch firmly. "This is not New York or Washington. This is Georgetown County, South Carolina. The sheriff has already said he wants to do us a favor. Let's let him do it."

"I think John Crown murdered the man," said Mrs. Roosevelt glumly.

"All right," said Baruch. "Tomorrow Winchell comes. Thursday he goes away without a story. Thursday the President comes. Sunday you and he return to Washington. All the others leave—except Crown; the sheriff arrests him. Everyone important has scattered—the Hollywood people back to California, you and the President back to Washington—*and then,* but not before, the sheriff announces he has concluded Benjamin Partridge was murdered and he has arrested a suspect. When—and if—the newspaper boys call you at the White House, you say you are astounded and appalled."

"But it's all a horrible lie!" she objected. "How can I—"

"It isn't a lie at all," Baruch interrupted sternly. "We don't *know* Partridge was murdered. Maybe he did die accidentally."

"By setting off an explosion in a can of cleaning fluid," she murmured ruefully.

"Or playing with explosives he was getting ready to use against someone else," said Baruch. "Anyway, Sheriff Thompson is in charge of the investigation. Whatever he says happened, happened. What obligation have we to tell Walter Winchell otherwise?"

Mrs. Roosevelt sighed. "Tallulah will get drunk and say—who knows what?"

"Not if her father tells her to keep quiet," said Baruch. "That's another reason I don't want Winchell scandal-mongering around here: I think we owe something to Speaker Bankhead. When I tell him what's going on, he'll put an effective muzzle on Tallulah."

"Bernie, I have my very grave doubts about this."

"I'm trying to protect your name, too," said Baruch.

"Obviously, the President can't come here now."

"Obviously, the President *must* come here now. We must all go along as if we had no idea there has been anything but an accident."

"We all become accessories," protested Mrs. Roosevelt.

"To what? We don't know there has been a murder. We only suspect it. We are not interfering with the investigation. To the contrary, we've given the sheriff important facts. All we're doing is frustrating a professional snoop in his effort to make a dishonest dollar by embarrassing as many prominent people as he can."

She shook her head. "I suppose I'll take your advice, Bernie," she said. "One President after another has relied on it, for many years, so I suppose I can."

"I will take all responsibility for whatever happens," said Baruch.

They assembled in the living room.

"The telegram I received during dinner," said Baruch to all his guests, "was from Walter Winchell. He has heard that Benjamin Partridge died here last night, in an accident, and he proposes to come here tomorrow to inquire into the matter—presumably so he can write and broadcast on the subject. I can hardly refuse to allow him on the premises, but I can warn you—"

"I shall be a hundred miles from here before he arrives," said Tallulah, "and I suggest the rest of you be farther."

"No," said Baruch. "If anyone leaves, it will only encourage him to suspect the worst."

"Worse than what's happened?" asked Colleen Bingham.

"As of the moment," said Baruch, "we know nothing except that Benjamin Partridge was killed in an explosion in his room. We have talked about our various suspicions, but we know nothing more than that there was an explosion and that he is dead. The sheriff has not called the death a murder. He is continuing his investigation. If all of you say that and no more, it is entirely possible that Mr. Winchell will leave here with no scandalous story that can embarrass and even damage us all."

"Every one of us, unless I'm wrong," said Joan Crawford, "has reason to lie to that slimy bastard."

"No," said Baruch again. "Don't anyone lie to him. If he finds you out, the worst possible consequences could ensue. None of us—except, I suppose, one—knows what happened to Benjamin Partridge. We can all say we don't know what happened, and all of us but one will be telling the truth. We were all downstairs. He went upstairs alone. There was an explosion. The sheriff is investigating. His preliminary conclusion is that Benjamin Partridge died in some sort of accident. Until he finds evidence that proves otherwise, his official position is that Mr. Partridge died an accidental death. If we don't feed Winchell speculation and gossip, he will leave here with no story."

"That won't discourage him in the least," said Zanuck. "He'll make up a story, the way he makes up half of what he writes and broadcasts."

"I will advise him—in a very friendly way, of course— that my lawyers will examine every word he uses about Hobcaw Barony and will sue him, his newspapers, and his broadcast network for any libel he publishes. Politicians may fear him. People in your industry may fear him. But he will find himself playing in the big leagues if he crosses me," said Baruch.

"What would you do if Louella Parsons came here, Barney?" asked Bogart with a grin.

"I would have my garden staff throw her to the alligators."

"I'm not sure alligators will eat bats," said Joan Crawford.

"If one eats that old bat," said Bogart, "it will be an instant alcoholic."

"I am going to wire Mr. Winchell to come as he proposes," said Baruch. "If all of us are circumspect, no harm should come of his visit."

"Let's hope some harm comes to *him,*" said Bogart.

"Restraint and circumspection might well begin now, Mr. Bogart," said Mrs. Roosevelt. "We may need to practice at it a bit before tomorrow."

The sky was clear. A bright moon shone on the waters of the bay, its cool, soft light lending the waters and the far shore, the islands, and the towering trees of the near shore —everything visible from the windows of Baruch's bedroom—a new, peaceful, yet faintly forbidding aspect. Baruch slept, snoring softly. Tallulah stood at the window

nearest the foot of his bed, staring at the night. She had
stood there for some time, naked, smoking one cigarette
after another, resentful of the way the bourbon she had
drunk all evening impeded her thoughts.

She was thirty-four years old, a well-put-together
woman: no classic beauty perhaps but a striking, handsome
woman who would have won attention in spite of her pro-
grammed eccentricities. She was a skilled, respected
actress. Her father was Speaker of the House of Representatives. She smoked too much, drank too much, and played
too hard at being Tallulah; but she was talented and intelligent and courageous and independent.

She ground out her cigarette in the ashtray nearby on
Baruch's bureau. Her peignoir hung across the foot of the
bed. Impulsively, she grabbed it, pulled it on, and slipped
quietly out of his room. She crossed the hall, to the suite
that was Mrs. Baruch's when that infrequent visitor to
Hobcaw was in residence. Mrs. Baruch was not here now
—in fact, the rumor was that her health had failed badly
and that she was in danger of death—and the suite was
officially Tallulah's for the duration of this visit. Anyway,
her clothes were there. She went in and dressed in the
clothes she had worn to go riding that morning—the
ragged black sweater and long gray skirt, with shoes this
time. She walked down the hall and down the stairs and
out of the house, into the night.

Zanuck was not asleep. Nor was Joan Crawford. In his
room, across the hall from Colleen Bingham's room, they
smoked—he, one of his big cigars, she, a cigarette—and
he sipped Scotch, and they talked. Crawford wore silk pajamas. Zanuck, in his undershorts, had been on the floor
doing push-ups and had just risen to his knees and reached
for his glass and cigar.

"There may be other prints, DZ," she said. She sighed.
"Ah don' know. Louie Mayer absolutely blew his cork
when he found out. He had umpteen million invested and
saw it all goin' down the drain. He went out and bought
every print he could find. He put the word around. He
paid . . . never mind what he paid. He withheld every dollar

of it from mah salary. He thought he had them all. Then Ben Partridge showed up with this one. Ah cain't promise anybody it's the last one. Ah'm gonna be blackmailed all mah life—"

"Watch out for the honey-chile accent, Joanie," said Zanuck harshly. "You let your adoring public hear that—"

"Ah'm a piece of property!" she cried. "Thass all Ah am. Make millions out of me—"

"Want to be a human being?" Zanuck snapped. "Go ahead. Any time. There's a hundred thousand girls out there who would trade places with you, and happily be a piece of property, any day."

"And what if Ah go to jail for killin' Ben Partridge?" she asked. "Or what if you do? Only you won't. You'll go to the chair. Me, they'll put me on a South Carolina chain gang for the rest of my life."

"Forget it, Joanie. You're not going to jail. Neither am I. They've already destroyed ninety percent of the evidence—by carting off all the debris from Partridge's room and carpentering and plastering and painting over all the damage. Bernard Baruch's a powerful man, and he doesn't give a damn who killed Ben Partridge, so long as he's not embarrassed by it."

"Mrs. Roosevelt, though," said Joan Crawford. "She's an idealist, and honest as a day is long."

"And naive," said Zanuck. "Be grateful she's here. Her presence brings a powerful motive for covering up, keeping quiet, lying to Walter Winchell, keeping secrets. What's more, they're going to burn the film."

"You've seen the film, haven't you, DZ?" she asked quietly. "I mean . . . everybody who is anybody, has."

Zanuck nodded. "And everybody who is anybody thinks it's a star performance. Hon-ey! Looks like you wore out five guys. In my mind, in Louie Mayer's mind, in the mind of anybody with half an ounce of brains, you come off a more interesting woman than anything you've done for the big cameras. Only thing . . . the moms and dads who pay a dime or a quarter to go to the movies every Saturday night—"

"The suckers we live off of—"

"Exactly. We aren't quite sure what they'd think. And we can't take the risk to find out."

She sighed. "Winchell has to know about the film. If he knows Partridge had a print—"

"We're dead," said Zanuck.

"I'd kill him to stop him," she said coldly.

Zanuck grinned. "I don't doubt it in the least."

Tallulah thrashed in the pine thickets. She had fallen to her knees half a dozen times, and her skirt and legs were smeared with mud. She staggered. She was not drunk, but the bourbon in her head disturbed her balance; and in the dark she had tripped in the tangled brush and scratched her legs and arms.

She stopped and stared up at the moon. "Where is it, you son of a bitch?' she muttered. "Make enough damn light to . . ." She peered all around.

The night was a confusion of noises: the whirring and chirping of a million bugs, slitherings that could be snakes or could be frogs or turtles, the grunts of alligators, the whoosh of wings, bats or owls or both. She was a southern woman, born and reared in Alabama, and not in a city either, and none of this frightened her. She was angry that she could not find the place—or hadn't so far, anyway. And she was growing cold.

Pine. That was it, pine! She pushed through the curtain of pine.

"*Yahh!*"

"So! I figured—My God, *Tallulah!*"

"Who . . . ? *You!* Johnny Crown!"

He had been sitting on the ground, and as she took her scare and then stood, trembling and recovering, he rose and walked toward her.

"You," he said hoarsely. "Tallulah!"

"Yes, it's Tallulah," she said. "Who do I look like? And what, pray tell, are you doing out here in the middle of the night, Johnny?"

"Waiting to see who would come. What did you come here for, Tallulah?"

"I came to see what was here, what was so damn interesting to so many of you this afternoon—out here in the pines and brambles. So what was it? What were you all looking for, you and Bogie and Colly? What made you all so nervous when I came along? And why are you out here now?"

He stepped close to her. Her face was ghostly white in the light of the cold, high moon. His frown was a caricature of suspicion and skepticism; and he tipped his head, as if by staring at her that way he could better see through her. "I could give you precisely the same answer," he said. "When I couldn't find anything, I decided to wait, to see who would come. I've been here a long time. I figured someone would show up, sooner or later. I really didn't expect *you.*"

"I don't think you're telling the truth, Johnny," she said.

He snorted contemptuously. "Nor are you," he said. "When are you going to tell them about what happened in England?"

"'How much do you know about that?'"

"In addition to his other endearing qualities, Ben Partridge was a braggart. And he thought it was something to brag about."

"Well, you can snitch on me if you want to, Johnny. It won't prove I killed him."

"If they knew you were out here now . . ."

She tossed back her head and laughed. "And what if they knew you are here, Mr. Chief Suspect? What are we out here looking for, Johnny?"

"You tell me. Bogart was here—"

"And Colly," Tallulah added. "And you and I. At least one of us had a purpose."

"I've told you the truth," said Crown.

Tallulah drew a deep breath. "Of *course* you have, dahling," she said. "Just as I've told you the truth." She shrugged. "Ah, well. You don't happen to have a cigarette on you, by any chance?"

He shook his head. "I don't smoke."

"I should have known. Lost in the middle of the woods in the middle of the night, and I have to encounter a saint who doesn't smoke and doesn't, I imagine, have a sip of bourbon on his person. Am I right?"

"I don't have a drink for you either," he said.

"Well, how about warmth, then? I'm cold. Put your arms around me, Johnny. Warm me up. I'm not particular about how you do it; just make me warm. One liar for another, Johnny. I'm not afraid of you if you're not afraid of me."

Crown took her into his arms and held her close. "I didn't kill him, Tallulah," he said into her ear.

"No, dear, and neither did I, of course. Though your presence out here—and I suppose mine—would be taken by others as a strong indication one of us did. After all, neither of us found what we were looking for, did we?"

8

The train carrying Walter Winchell arrived at the station in Georgetown about eleven. Baruch had sent a man to meet him. Bouncing out of Baruch's Packard at the rear entrance to the Hobcaw mansion half an hour later, the compact, ruddy-faced, white-haired Winchell was wearing a gray suit, a gray hat, and carrying a topcoat over his arm.

Baruch alone met him at the door.

"Mr. Baruch! Good of you to receive me. This is certainly a nice place you have here."

Winchell had made his flat voice and the peculiar rhythms of his radio delivery known nationwide. Baruch was surprised to hear that the man actually spoke pretty much the same way in person. He was a tense little man, with shifty eyes, obsessively self-conscious—conscious, actually, of his image, of the persona he had created for himself, and anxious to maintain it.

"I understand," said Winchell, "you have a house full of celebrities."

"I do now," said Baruch dryly.

Winchell smiled. "Well, thank you. Thank you. I understand even Mrs. Roosevelt is here and that the President is coming tomorrow."

"That's right."

Winchell stood in the center hall of the house, between the gun room and the library, looking around with undisguised curiosity. "Well," he said, "where *are* all these celebrities?"

"You'll see them all before the day is over, I suspect," said Baruch. "Mrs. Roosevelt is in her suite, resting. The others . . . well, you understand, we come here to enjoy the attractions of the estate. I believe two or three of my guests are off fishing. I know Tallulah is riding this morning. One or two of them sleep late. I asked the sheriff to be here to meet you. He is waiting for you in the library."

"Sheriff . . ." said Winchell. He was not skilled at concealing his reactions, and his voice betrayed his disappointment. "Oh, yes. The sheriff."

Baruch and Winchell entered the library, where Sheriff Thompson was sitting comfortably in a leather chair, a glass of bourbon enclosed in his two hands. He put his glass aside and rose. "Well, suh!" he boomed. "Mistah Winchell, is it? Pleased to meet ya, suh."

"Sheriff Virgil Thompson, Mr. Winchell," said Baruch.

"Happy . . . to meet you," intoned Winchell.

"Y'all from N' Yawk, ain' that right?" said the sheriff. "News reportah, as I understan'."

"On the radio every evening," said Winchell.

"Radio," drawled the sheriff, nodding. "Oh, sure. Myself, I rarely turn the thing on; but my wife, now, she wouldn't miss Ma Perkins, keeps track of all them stories. I kinda favor Amos 'n Andy, turn 'em on once in a while."

"You've never heard my news broadcasts?" Winchell asked.

Sheriff Thompson grinned. "Well, now, I may have, now that y' mention it. Winchell . . . Name does seem familiar, somehow. 'Course, for news, now, I do enjoy listenin' to Gabriel Heatter. I do make a point to heah him now and again."

Baruch had stepped to the window to hide his grin. Virgil Thompson knew the name Winchell as well as he knew the name Baruch, and he rarely failed to listen to Winchell's nightly newscast; but he had warned Baruch before

Winchell arrived that he would not allow himself to be intimidated. Baruch could hardly restrain his laughter— not at the sheriff's performance but at Winchell's failure to see through it.

"I understand, uh, Sheriff, that you are investigating the death of Benjamin Partridge," said Winchell.

"I am, suh. Yes, suh. That happened in my county. I'm lookin' into that."

"Well. What conclusion, Sheriff?"

"Ain't come to no conclusion," said Sheriff Thompson, much exaggerating his drawl—in Baruch's estimate. "The man only died day b'fore yestiddy, y'understand. Way it was, he was here, he went up to his bedroom after dinner, and everybody in the house heard a big explosion. Run upstairs and found the gentleman badly injured, in fact dead. No way to know, exactly, how that happened. Can't be sure just what the gentleman was doin', to set off a big explosion like that."

"It was a *big* explosion?" asked Winchell.

The sheriff nodded innocently. "As I look at it," he said, "an explosion big enough t' kill a man is a big explosion."

Baruch stepped to Winchell's side. "Can I send for a drink for us, Mr. Winchell?" he asked.

"Uh, well . . ."

Baruch touched the button to summon George. "It seems possible—I mean, the best judgment we have is— that Mr. Partridge was smoking a cigar and opened a can of dry-cleaning fluid. In the absence of a better explanation, that is what we think may have happened."

"There is no possibility whatever, you think, that, uh . . ."

"That what?" asked the sheriff. "Oh, you mean that somebody blowed up Mr. Partridge, on purpose?" He shook his head. "Thought of that, of course. Have to take that possibility into consideration. Can't find the first bit of evidence, though, that looks that way."

"Mr. Winchell," said Baruch. "Mr. Partridge went upstairs to retire, about eleven-fifteen as best we recall. All the other guests were in the living room, playing bridge, chatting, drinking. Mr. Partridge had been gone a very short time when we heard the explosion. We ran upstairs and found the most ghastly scene. That is about all we know. The room was thoroughly searched. Whatever exploded . . . it exploded."

"A time bomb, Mr. Baruch?" asked Winchell.

Baruch shrugged. "How could it have been set?" he asked. "Who could have anticipated that Mr. Partridge would choose to retire earlier than any of the other guests and would, as it turned out, be in his room between eleven-fifteen and eleven-thirty?"

"A trap set for him," suggested Winchell.

"Which might have been set off by his valet, who went to his room after he left it to put everything in order, or by one of my household staff, who might have gone in to turn down his bed or check his supply of towels," said Baruch blandly. "We've thought of these things, of course."

"Among your guests," said Winchell, "are people with good reason to have hated Ben Partridge."

"If you've got information along that line," said Sheriff Thompson, "it might be evidence of somethin', and I'd be grateful if you'd tell me all 'bout it."

"I can't reveal anything that's come to me as a professional confidence," said Winchell loftily.

The sheriff smiled. "Well, 'course I cain't place much confidence in what you cain't tell me."

Winchell nodded gravely. "Can I see the room where Partridge died?"

"Hello, Bogie."

"H'lo, Winchell. Have a smash of loudmouth. It's okay; it's past noon."

A buffet luncheon was ready. The only guests in the dining room when Winchell and Baruch and the sheriff arrived were Bogart and Colleen Bingham.

"I'll take a sip," said Winchell. "Is that some rye there?"

The butler poured rye for Winchell, bourbon for the sheriff, and a sherry for Baruch as they filled their plates at the sideboard and carried them to the table. Winchell took the chair beside Colleen.

"Well, you got your story?" Bogart asked Winchell.

"Mr. Baruch has been so kind as to allow me to stay overnight," said Winchell. "As long as I've come so far, I'd like the chance to interview each of you."

"What you want to know?" Bogart asked.

"Tell me about the explosion," said Winchell. "Where were you?"

"Sitting in the living room there," said Bogart. "As a matter of fact, Colly and I were sitting on the couch, talking. All of a sudden—BOOM! From upstairs. Zanuck and I ran up. George there ran up." He shook his head. "Awful sight."

"How big an explosion was it, would you say?"

Bogart shrugged. "How big is big?"

"Well," said Winchell, "as the sheriff puts it, it was big enough to kill him."

"I'd guess he was holding it right in his hands," said Bogart.

"Was holding what?"

"Whatever went off."

"Are you guessing it was a can of dry-cleaning fluid?"

"I don't guess about stuff like that," said Bogart. "It wasn't a penny firecracker, I can tell you for sure. Otherwise . . . Who knows?"

Winchell nodded. "Who knows? Otherwise, Bogie, how are things at home?"

"Fine," said Bogart. "How are things at your house?"

"The story I hear," said Winchell, "is that Mary knows about Mayo. I mean, your wife knows you've made a new friendship."

"You'd know more about that than I do," said Bogart. "Mary's in New York, working on a play."

"The story is that Mayo Methot can drink you under the table."

Bogart turned, planted a hand on the arm of his chair and so raised one shoulder high, then cocked his head.

"Winchell," he said with his best Duke Mantee menacing sneer, "*nobody* can drink me under the table. Even you."

Mrs. Roosevelt did not appear for lunch. She and Baruch had agreed that it would be well to allow Winchell to make his appearance, ask his initial questions, and perhaps become convinced he had not chanced on a major story, before she met him. Winchell thought she was in her suite, resting. In fact, she was riding, accompanied by John Crown, who turned out to be a competent horseman ("My grandfather," he explained, "kept horses"), and Robert Wilkes, riding a little apart and keeping a wary eye on the man identified as chief suspect.

The weather had turned warmer, though the clouds building in the west suggested that it would rain by evening. The warm breeze smelled of rain. Mrs. Roosevelt was pleased to be out, happy to have another chance to ride, and for the first ten minutes she kept her horse at a canter, so it was difficult to make conversation. She slowed to a walk as they rode across the dry trail that crossed what had apparently been a dike in one of the abandoned rice fields.

"I must ask you a question, Mr. Crown," said Mrs. Roosevelt. "You told us yesterday, with some emphasis, that you locked Mr. Partridge's door when you left his room shortly after seven. But Mr. Zanuck told us later that just before he and Mr. Partridge came downstairs—only a few minutes later, of course—Mr. Partridge stepped across the hall and locked his door. Mr. Zanuck is equally emphatic in the matter. Do you have an explanation?"

Crown considered for a moment, then shook his head. "No," he said. "No explanation."

"There are only three possible explanations, as I see it," said Mrs. Roosevelt. "One of you is wrong. One of you is lying. Or—"

"Or someone else used a key and entered the room," said Crown.

"Quite so," she said. "The third possibility is that, during the few minutes between your leaving and Mr. Partridge's coming out of Mr. Zanuck's room, someone came to the room and unlocked the door you had locked. Not very likely, I'm afraid."

"So one of us is wrong or one of us is lying. If it comes to taking my word or Zanuck's, then of course—"

"Don't assume that."

"He had his own reasons," said Crown. "Stronger than mine."

"Reasons to kill Mr. Partridge?"

Crown nodded. "Partridge said something about how there was going to be a big confrontation with Zanuck. At Hobcaw. Both of them came here, you know, hoping to encourage Mr. Baruch to invest money in film projects. You may be reluctant to believe anything I may say about the antagonism between them. But if I am arrested and charged with murdering Benjamin Partridge, I really beg you to have someone check into what was going on between them."

"Can you be more specific?"

"Yes. Within the last two years, both of them left studios where they were well established and struck out on their own—Zanuck from Warners, to merge Fox with Twentieth Century, Partridge from MGM to form Par-Croft. Both of them are short of money. Both of them need stars. Twentieth Century-Fox has just one surefire money-maker: Shirley Temple, and the tyke is going to grow up and leave them without anything to equal her. Otherwise, Twentieth has Sonja Henie—but how many ice-skating pictures will the public stomach? Par-Croft has Colleen Bingham under contract, and Raymond Massey."

"And Merle Oberon," said Mrs. Roosevelt.

"Borrowed for one picture," said Crown. "Which would have cost Partridge a fortune. I think he hoped Mr. Baruch would finance *Ironweed*. He hoped Mr. Baruch would be impressed with the prospect of a picture with Merle Oberon in the role of Sissy."

"And Mr. Zanuck?"

"Same thing. He's hoping Mr. Baruch will finance a

project he has in mind for Humphrey Bogart and Joan Crawford."

"And what is that?"

"It's a C. S. Forester novel published two years ago, called *The African Queen*."

"Oh, yes," said Mrs. Roosevelt. "I've read it. The story of the spinsterish missionary and the Cockney river rat, with their rickety old steamboat in the jungle. It would make a marvelous movie, wouldn't it?"

"Zanuck thinks so," said Crown. "Warner Brothers owns the rights and wants to star Bette Davis in it, with some young English actor they've brought over, called Niven—Nigel Niven, I believe it is—but Miss Davis doesn't seem to think the part is right for her and probably won't make the picture. Zanuck has offered to buy the rights. He wants to put Joan Crawford in the female role and Humphrey Bogart in the role of the Cockney. If he can raise enough money, MGM will sell him Joan Crawford's services for the picture, and Warners will sell him Bogart."

"So that's why Mr. Bogart and Miss Crawford are here."

"Yes. Bogart really wants to do the picture. He'd do anything to get out of the rut he's in at Warners: one gangster after another. He thinks this could make him a top star."

"Now that I've met him, he does seem miscast as a gangster," said Mrs. Roosevelt.

"So far as Joan Crawford is concerned," said Crown, "she's interested, and Zanuck's been romancing her to keep her interested."

Mrs. Roosevelt reined her horse to the right and for a moment turned her back toward John Crown, so he would not see her amused smile.

"You see my point?" asked Crown.

"Your point is that both Mr. Zanuck and Mr. Bogart had motive for killing Mr. Partridge," she said. "Mr. Zanuck, though, had no opportunity. Mr. Partridge was in his room with him from a quarter to seven till a quarter past."

"How do you know he was?"

"He says he was."

Crown nodded. "You have his word for it."

Mrs. Roosevelt guided her horse around a fallen limb. "Where else might Mr. Partridge have been that half-hour?" she asked.

"I don't know," said Crown. "But among the places he could have been was across the hall with Colleen Bingham. I need hardly tell you what relationship he had with her."

Mrs. Roosevelt frowned. "You can't exculpate yourself, Mr. Crown, by trying to shift suspicion to others. You are not very subtle about it."

"All I am saying is that I am not the only one in the house with motive to kill Benjamin Partridge and the opportunity to do it."

"Your point is taken," she said, and she goaded her horse into a canter.

Walter Winchell sat comfortably in Baruch's gun room. At Baruch's suggestion, he had made it a sort of temporary and informal office for himself. He had a drink, was smoking a cigarette, and had a reporter's ominous little notepad on his lap. Colleen Bingham sat uneasily facing him. She was wearing a tailored gray skirt with a narrow black belt, and a white blouse with a loosely knotted short black necktie. And, of course, her bandage—today a smaller one—on her left hand. She looked something like a secretary in a small-town bank or a teacher in a country elementary school.

"It's going to change a lot of things for you, isn't it, Colly?"

She nodded. "I'm sure it is."

"Career. Domestc arrangements. You'll miss him."

"I suppose I will."

Winchell nodded. "What do you know about this business, Colly?" he asked. "What really happened here?"

"I don't really know. I'm the last person who'd know."

"You slept with him. How come you weren't in his room when the big bang went off?"

"He went up early," she said. "I was talking with Bogie,

and I just . . . sat there and went on talking. I would have gone up later."

"Lucky," said Winchell. "If you had gone up . . . Tell me, though, Colly, did Ben have a big can of dry-cleaning fluid in his room?"

"I didn't see it. Ask Johnny; he's the one who took care of Ben's things."

"Why did you come here in the first place, Colly?"

"Ben wanted me to come."

"Why?"

She heaved a loud, angry sigh. "Don't play games with me, Mr. Winchell," she said in a hoarse whisper. "You know how it was between Ben and me. If the public knew, I'd never appear in another movie. I know that, and I know you can publish the story any time you choose. So what do you want from me?"

"I want to know if Ben Partridge's death was really an accident," said Winchell, lifting his glass and taking a sip.

She shrugged. "I've told you what I know."

"Uhmm. Well . . . Oh, by the way, Colly, how's everything in Wewoka?"

"Where?" she gasped.

"Wewoka, Oklahoma. How's everybody there?"

"My mother and father live there," she said quickly, her voice thin. "My dad's retired now, almost entirely; and he wanted to live where he'd be near the old oil fields and some of his old oilmen friends."

"How's the baby?"

"What baby?" she whispered.

Winchell grinned. "Your baby. The one they're keeping for you."

Colleen Bingham covered her face with her hands and shook her head.

"I'm not Parsons or Hopper, Colly," said Winchell gently. "I'm just a working newspaper stiff and a good friend of yours. I've known about the baby for six months. I haven't published the story. I don't see any reason to, and I don't plan to. On the other hand, I hope you'll be as good a friend of mine as I am of yours."

She wiped her face with her hands, smearing tears with the tips of her fingers, streaking them down across her cheeks, and rubbing them off. Slowly her face stiffened, and she sniffed and confronted Winchell erect and alert.

"Is the little girl Ben's baby, incidentally?" he asked.

"No! She's not his."

"Then whose?"

She shook her head firmly. "That I won't tell you."

Winchell scribbled a note on his pad. "You know, I haven't thought about this much. I really haven't. But, let's see . . . you took a leave of absence from Warners. When was that, about a year ago? No, a year and a half ago, wasn't it? Went to Oklahoma to be with your daddy, 'cause he was sick, as I recall. That's when you had the baby. Right? Right, Colly?"

She nodded.

"Warners didn't like it that you took leave right then, as I remember. They sold your contract to Par-Croft. You went to work for Partridge and immediately started sleeping with him. How come, Colly?"

"What's so unusual about that?" she asked bitterly. "Crawford is sleeping with Zanuck, here, in this house."

"Well, Ben was no attractive guy. What was it, Colly? Did he know about the baby?"

Collen sobbed. "What are you going to do?" she asked.

Winchell rose, stepped to her, and put his hand on hers. "Colly," he said quietly. "I'm not interested in destroying Colleen Bingham. I want news stories, not the heads of Hollywood stars, shrunk and lined up on my mantel. Help me find out what's going on here. That's all I want. I'll protect you." He closed his hand around hers. "Honestly . . ."

"What if they find out—*you* find out—I was in his room, that maybe I was the last person in his room before he was killed there?"

Winchell shrugged. "So? What were you doing in his room?"

"He knew about my baby," she said weakly. "He had a

picture. And he had a letter my mother wrote, saying the baby was fine and healthy and—"

"Then it *was* his baby," interjected Winchell. "Your mother wrote—"

"*No.* It wasn't his letter. He got his hands on it. She wrote . . . I've never been sure how he got it. Out of the Warners' mailroom, I guess. Anyway—"

"He blackmailed you with it," said Winchell.

"That was his whole life!" she whispered in shrill anger. "He got things on people. He got what he wanted out of them by threatening to tell the whole world what he'd found out. He sneaked around and . . . Mr. Winchell, he had that letter and the picture of my illegitimate child! When he showed them at Warners, they sold him my contract. Cheap. He said the story would come out sooner or later, and that would be the end of me, but maybe he could make a film or two with me before it happened."

"Victim of Ben Partridge," said Winchell. "Victim of the Hays Office. Victim of the Legion of Decency."

"He promised me the role of Sissy in *Ironweed*," she said. "Then on the train, on the way here from California, he told me he'd given the part to Merle Oberon. We had a nasty argument about it. He was furious with me, and he pulled out the letter and the picture of my baby and waved them in my face. He threatened me again. I mean, threatened to publicize the fact that I have an illegitimate child."

"What a wonderful guy," said Winchell.

"That's how I knew he had the letter and picture with him. I thought maybe that gave me a chance to get them. I went to his room Monday night. I knew Johnny Crown would be there, tidying up, putting Ben's clothes in order. I stayed in the room after Johnny left. Johnny didn't mind, didn't worry. After all, I was a member of the household, so to speak. Anyway, I had a few minutes alone. I looked for my letter and picture."

"Did you find them?"

"No. I couldn't find them. I didn't have much time to look. Then . . . Then, after dinner, he went upstairs, and there was an explosion, and he was killed. It scared me half to death. I'd been in his room! You see? If anyone saw me—"

"I see."

"They'd think I somehow caused the explosion. I mean, if it wasn't dry-cleaning fluid—"

"It wasn't dry-cleaning fluid, Colly. Was it? It was some kind of bomb. Wasn't it?"

Colleen Bingham closed her eyes and shook her head. "I honestly don't know, Mr. Winchell. I don't know. . ."

9

"Winchell, *dah*-ling!" shrieked Tallulah; and she swept across the living room and threw her arms around the dapper, dinner-jacketed reporter. She kissed him hard on the lips, leaving his mouth grotesquely smeared with red lipstick. "'Good evening, Mr. and Mrs. America and all the ships at sea!' If there were but one news snake in all the world that I could embrace and call friend, it would be you, Walter, dah-ling. However are you? May I hope cancerous?"

"No, sorry to disappoint you," said Winchell. "And how are you? May I hope syphilitic?"

"Well, I trust not yet—though I just kissed *you*," she shrilled.

"Not where I should like to have you kiss me, Tallulah."

The laughter around the room ranged from the uproarious by Bogart, to the nervous by Zanuck, to the tolerant by Baruch. Mrs. Roosevelt showed what she hoped was a half-amused, not condescending smile.

Winchell had just come down from his room on the second floor, the one directly across the hall from the room where Partridge had died two nights before. That he had brought a tuxedo made it apparent that he had expected to be invited to stay.

105

"Mrs. Roosevelt!" Winchell exclaimed. He broke away from Tallulah, bowed, and strode across the living room. "Please forgive the badinage. It is a great pleasure to see you."

"Mr. Winchell," said Mrs. Roosevelt. "It is my pleasure."

Winchell took her hand, kissed it, and came up beaming. "Not at all, dear lady," he said. "The honor and pleasure are mine." Immediately he lowered his voice. "Please be assured that, whatever news story is breaking here, I will keep your name entirely out of it."

"What story is that, Mr. Winchell?" she asked innocently.

He glanced around and lowered his voice still more. "Well, Ben Partridge *did* die in rather mysterious circumstances."

She nodded. "Inexplicable," she said, frowning. *"Whatever* could he have been doing?"

Winchell smiled. "Let us put the subject aside," he said. "We can talk about it later—if, that is, it is necessary for you and me to talk about it at all."

Baruch hurried to her side. "The sheriff will be at your disposal all morning, Mr. Winchell," he said.

Winchell nodded at Baruch. "The President will arrive . . .?"

"In mid-afternoon, I believe," said Baruch. "I expect a confirming wire. Rye?"

"Ah, thank you," said Winchell. He glanced at the butler, who had overheard and was on his way to the bar to pour the rye. "I hope it won't be inconvenient for me to stay long enough to say hello to the President."

"It would be inconvenient if you should wish to stay beyond Sunday," said Baruch, "because I myself will be leaving for New York on Sunday or Monday and the house will be closed. Otherwise, be my guest as long as you wish."

"Will you leave before the investigation into the death of Ben Partridge is completed?" asked Winchell. "In fact, what of all the others? I mean, the Hollywood people?"

"We are all at the disposal of Sheriff Thompson," said Baruch. "But I am sure he will have completed his investigation before Sunday."

Wilkes and Crown again wore dark suits, but Baruch did not allow their want of dinner jackets to discourage his guests from dressing for dinner. Except for them, all were dressed as they had been Monday night, the men in tuxedos, the women in floor-length dresses. Mrs. Roosevelt wore a light green linen skirt, with a cream-white silk jacket. Joan Crawford's thin black satin dress ran down over her figure like water poured over her shoulders. Colleen Bingham wore autumn orange and yellow and brown. Tallulah's white satin skirt was slit on the side, halfway to her hip, and her black linen jacket was open almost to her waist, in a narrow V that concealed her breasts and stomach almost modestly but wickedly suggested they might be exposed at any moment.

"How much does he know?" Crawford asked Bogart—referring to Winchell, on whom she bestowed a murderous across-the-room glare as he stood chatting with Baruch and Mrs. Roosevelt.

"What are you afraid he might know?" asked Bogart.

She shrugged. "Is he buying the story of the dry-cleaning fluid?"

Bogart sneered and chuckled. "He's not that dumb. The presence of Mrs. Roosevelt is restraining him."

"Then when the President arrives, he'll be restrained more," suggested Crawford.

"We can hope so."

Winchell, as soon as he had opportunity, took John Crown aside. "Tell me about the dry-cleaning fluid, Johnny," he said. "Do you buy the story that Ben may have blown himself up with a can of dry-cleaning fluid?"

"It's possible, I suppose," said Crown. "What else could it have been?"

"A bomb, Johnny," said Winchell. "Maybe someone blew him up with a bomb."

"A lot of people had reason," said Crown. "But what

kind of bomb? How could anyone have brought a bomb here?"

"Half a stick of dynamite," said Winchell. "Maybe only a quarter of a stick. Blasting cap. Some kind of electrical device to set it off. You could carry all that in a suitcase. Easily."

"That assumes a lot, as it seems to me," said Crown.

"Okay, let's hear your theory," said Winchell.

"I don't have a theory, Mr. Winchell," said Crown soberly. "But it seems to me you're talking about a lot of difficult problems. Dynamite and a blasting cap and an electric hookup of some kind to set it off . . . Would *you* know how to put it together and make it go off when you wanted it to? And would you know just how much dynamite to use to kill a man and not blow up the whole house? You're talking about some kind of expert, it seems to me."

"And you don't see one in this room," said Winchell.

"Do you?" asked Crown. "Which one. Bogart? The son of a Park Avenue physician and a fashion illustrator. Fancy education. Andover. Yale—"

"Where he failed," interjected Winchell.

"Zanuck," Crown went on. "His father was a hotel desk clerk. Zanuck's been in Hollywood all his adult life. Where's your blasting engineer?"

"Yourself, Johnny. What's your background?"

"My dad builds houses. I've been in Hollywood since I was old enough to buy a drink. You can check it out."

"The gals . . ." said Winchell, speculatively glancing over Joan Crawford, Colleen Bingham, and Tallulah Bankhead. "If someone built a bomb for one of them . . . and sent it here with her in her luggage . . ."

"A plot to kill Mr. Partridge," said Crown. "If so, why here? Why put a bomb under him in Mr. Baruch's house? It could have been much easier somewhere else. In his car—"

"Okay, Johnny," said Winchell. "Anyway, did Ben have a big can of dry-cleaning fluid in his luggage?"

"Yes, he did," said Crown. "He was a fanatic about keeping his clothes spotless. The only thing unusual would have been for him to be cleaning his clothes himself. That was my job."

"Well, DZ," Winchell said a few minutes later to Darryl Zanuck, "how goes the big Forester project?"

"I'm sorry...?" Zanuck responded, frowning.

"Oh, the African thing," said Winchell. "What do they call it? About the old steam tub that goes down the river. I understand you've bought Joan Crawford's contract—that is, for the one picture. Do you really think she'll make a believable Sister Rose—and Bogart a believable Allnut?"

"Potentially," said Zanuck, "I think it can be one of the finest motion pictures of all time."

"Well, I must say, you're committed to it," said Winchell.

"What do you mean by that?"

Winchell smiled, while at the same time ducking his head aside to avoid a thick puff of the smoke from Zanuck's cigar. "I know what you paid MGM to have Crawford for this picture," he said. "I'm probably the only one here—Crawford herself excepted, of course—who knows what you paid for her."

"Worth it," said Zanuck.

"Important to Twentieth Century-Fox," said Winchell. "What you've got invested in this one already could mean the difference between make and break. Right?"

"I want to make a great picture," said Zanuck.

"Money being, of course, inconsequential."

Zanuck nodded. "Exactly," he said. "Inconsequential."

"Well, I'm interested in something, then," said Winchell. "I've heard a rumor to the effect that Ben Partridge has been putting together a film based on the Edward VIII–Wallis Simpson affair and wanted to star Joan Crawford as Wallis and Les Howard as the King. Were you two competing for Crawford?"

"Ask Crawford," said Zanuck.

Over dinner, he did, in a quiet conversation to the side, which he supposed was not overheard by any of the other guests. "Which is it going to be, Joan? Sister Rose or Wallis Warfield Simpson?"

"What makes you think it's going to be either?" she asked coldly.

"Well, Zanuck admits he'd like to have you for Sister Rose in *The African Queen*, with Bogart as Allnut. But there's a rumor around to the effect that Par-Croft has two writers working on a hurry-up screenplay for a potboiler about the abdication of Edward VIII; and the rumor goes on to say that Ben Partridge put in a bid with Louie Mayer to buy your services for the part of Wally."

"Mr. Winchell," said Joan Crawford, "Ah wouldn't have made a picture for Ben Partridge if he'd been the last producer in America."

"If Louie Mayer had lent you to him, what choice would you have had?"

Her chin snapped up. "I don't have to worry about that now, do I?"

"No, you sure don't."

"Take it easy on the kid, Pops," said Bogart, who sat on Winchell's other side.

Winchell turned abruptly away from both of them and spoke across the table, to Mrs. Roosevelt. "Have you seen Mr. Gallup's latest poll?" he asked.

"Which poll is that, Mr. Winchell?"

"There's a new poll out, on Justice Hugo Black," said Winchell. "You remember, the original poll found that most people thought he should resign from the Supreme Court, now that it's known he was once a member of the Ku Klux Klan. The new one says the contrary—a majority think he should not resign."

"His radio talk must have turned the tide," said Mrs. Roosevelt.

"Well, that and the President's efforts on his behalf," said Winchell. "What kind of Justice do you think he'll make?"

"We have an expert on that, right here at our table," said Baruch, nodding toward Tallulah.

She smiled. "True. The Bankheads have known Senator

Black as man and boy. Hardscrabble kind of man. He'll make a fine judge."

"What about the Klan business?" asked Bogart.

"Bogie," she said. "If you want to get elected out of Boston, you had better be a member of the Friendly Sons of Saint Patrick; and if you want to get elected out of hill-country Alabama, you had better be a member of the Klan. You've got nothing to be proud of in either case—but maybe nothing to be ashamed of, either. Depends on whether you're a believer, and I can tell you from personal knowledge that Hugo Black's no Klan believer."

"He has voted a very liberal line in the Senate," said Mrs. Roosevelt.

"Radical, some say," remarked Baruch.

"The President put his popularity on the line when he made that appointment," said Winchell.

Mrs. Roosevelt smiled broadly. "That is what popularity is for," she said. "It's a currency to spend, to achieve worthwhile objects."

As she had done her first two evenings at Hobcaw, Mrs. Roosevelt retired to her suite while the other guests were still in the living room, still drinking, still playing cards.

When she said her good-nights, Zanuck had organized a poker game; and he, Winchell, Bogart, and Tallulah were intent on their cards and stacks of red, white, and blue chips. The smoke was heavy over their table. Joan Crawford and Colleen Bingham stood behind them, frowning over the cards and shaking their heads at the bets. Baruch stood before the fireplace, adding his observations. Crown sat apart on the couch, drinking.

Wilkes had preceded her to her suite, and as she entered he came out. He had examined the rooms thoroughly before she came in to go to bed.

Mrs. Roosevelt undressed and put on her nightgown and robe. She stacked the pillows and settled down to read in bed: a novel, *Gone With the Wind*. There was talk the book would be made into a movie, and she'd heard speculation that Joan Crawford would play the role of Scarlett O'Hara.

She had read for half an hour when she heard a discreet knock on her bedroom door. She rose, asked who was there, and unlocked the door to admit George, Baruch's butler, bringing her a pot of tea.

"Evenin', Mrs. Roosevelt," he said. "Mr. Baruch thought you might like tea."

"It's a kind thought," she said.

He put the tray down on the table beside her bed. "I wonder," he said, "if you'd mind havin' a word with me. If it ain' too much bother."

"It's no bother at all, George," she said.

"Well, ma'am," he said hesitantly, "I do have somethin' I guess I ought to say. I don't know who else to say it *to*."

"Well. Pull up a chair, George, and sit down," she said. She sat on the bed. "What do you want to say?"

George remained standing. He was a big man, tall and muscular, and his chocolate-brown face was solemn. "It has to do with the death of Mr. Partridge," he said. He clasped one hand nervously in the other. "You understand, I . . . Well, I cain't talk to just anybody. Even Mr. Baruch. Mr. Baruch's a fine man, but I'm not sure he'd want me meddlin' in. He might say it's none o' my business, you know."

"A mysterious death in the house is everyone's business," she said.

"Well . . . It might have to do with somebody takin' a colored man's word against a white man's word," said George cautiously. "Please. Please, ma'am, don't tell nobody what I'm gonna tell you. I cain't no way afford to get crosswise o' white folks. I hear you and Mr. President, you will listen to colored folks."

"Of course, we will. And I understand," said Mrs. Roosevelt quietly. "I'm afraid I understand all too well. I will keep your confidence."

George nodded. "I ain't supposed to hear all that I hear. You know, some folks talk in front of us like we's supposed to be deaf. But I heard a lot of what's been said about the way Mr. Partridge died."

"Yes. I understand."

"The talk is he was blowed up with nitroglycereen. That is, 'cept the talk to Mr. Winchell, who's supposed to think he blowed up a can of spot remover."

"Yes. You've heard that, too," she said. "We—"

"I'll keep the secret, of course," said George. "But anyway, I don't think he was blowed up with nitroglycereen. I think he was blowed up with a stick of dynamite."

"What makes you think so, George?"

George sighed, and he looked around as if he half-suspected someone was hidden in the room, listening. "Up toward the bridge," he said, "they used to be a place where the road run through a low place and was always full of water and mud. Cars and trucks used to get stuck there all the time. Mr. Baruch, he ordered the manager to have that road moved up on higher ground. Man, he come over from Georgetown to do that. Well, on that higher ground they was some stumps and some big rocks. Man, he brought over a case o' dynamite, with all you need to make it go off. Some that was left over was kept. In a shed. Figured Mr. Baruch might want some more work done. So they kept what was left over. My brother Rafe, that's part of his job—I mean, to look after the tools and stuff and make sure nothin's stole. Well... A stick of that dynamite is gone."

"Gone since...?"

"When I see there was an awful explosion, it come to mind right off that maybe... Yestiddy I found Rafe and asked him to check. A stick of that dynamite is gone. They was six sticks left. Now they's five."

"And you don't think you should tell the sheriff?" she asked gently.

"I wouldn't dare," said George, shaking his head. "'Cause I know who took it."

"Can you tell me?"

He nodded. "But if it comes to my word 'gainst his... Also the lady. Their word, against a colored girl's. That's who saw. A colored girl."

"Tell me all about it, George," she said. "I'll keep your secret."

George leaned toward her, so she could hear his low voice. "Guests all come Monday," he said. "In the mawnin', all but you and Miss Bankhead, 'cause the train that comes from Chicago and down through Chattanooga and Atlanta and over here to Georgetown, that train comes in 'bout ten o'clock mawnin's. So we get 'em all in the house and in their rooms 'fore noon."

"All right. Then what?"

"We serve some lunch. Most of 'em is tired, wants to take naps, they say. 'Cept Mr. Zanuck and Miss Crawford. They want to go fishin'. Well. They didn't bring back no fish. 'Cause they didn't go fishin'. Nevah dropped a hook in the water."

"How do you know?"

George nodded. "I know. They asked for a boat. Tom, who takes care of the boats, fixed 'em up with a boat and fishin' tackle. Mr. Zanuck, he steers out into the bay, an' they go chuggin' up toward the bridge. They gits up along the shore some way, they puts the boat again' the bank and stops. They gits out and goes up in a stand o' pine." He stopped and smiled shyly. "You know what they done there," he said with a subdued smile.

Mrs. Roosevelt smiled, too. "I can imagine," she said.

"Okay. Well, after a while they goes on up the shore. By 'm by they come along where the shed is, where the tools and the dynamite and other stuff is. They stop. They go in the shed. They sneak, act like it's a secret, like they don' want nobody know they's there. After a while, they come out. And a stick o' dynamite is missin'."

Mrs. Roosevelt frowned deeply. "Who saw this, George?"

George nodded. "Bunch o' witnesses. Not just one. Tom fixed up the boat an' fishin' stuff for 'em. They stop in the stand o' pine, did what I said. Well, a man named Dave was on his way along, lookin' for driftwood for his stove, an' he seen 'em. Go on up the shore, come to the shed, a niece of mine, she seen 'em agin. Niece name Sarah. She was fishin', only *really* fishin'—caught somethin' for supper that night. But Sarah, she seen 'em go in the toolshed. She didn't know who they was, 'cept they was guests in the big house. She seen 'em go in the shed, and after while they come out. Go back to the boat. Then they go down the bay agin, toward the house.''

Mrs. Roosevelt shook her head and frowned. "Sit down, George," she said. "Don't be afraid. Sit down."

George pulled over the chair that stood before the vanity. He sat down, stiffly erect.

"You say Sarah didn't know this couple who went in the shed was Mr. Zanuck and Miss Crawford. How do you identify them now?"

"Sarah does laundry for the big house. She come. I showed her. She figgered out which was which."

"All right. Let's think a minute, George," said Mrs. Roosevelt. "How could Mr. Zanuck and Miss Crawford have known there was dynamite in a shed on the estate?"

"Couldn't have," said George.

"So they couldn't have gone there to get dynamite to use to kill Mr. Partridge."

"No. But mebbe found it an' then took the chance it give 'em."

Mrs. Roosevelt nodded thoughtfully. "Yes. Yes, that could have happened." She sighed. "Still, how could they have known there was dynamite in that shed?"

"Sign on it," said George. "When they put the dynamite in there, Rafe, he put a sign on the shed. Say, DANGER. DYNAMITE. KEEP AWAY."

"And everyone has kept away but Mr. Zanuck and Miss Crawford."

George nodded. "Well, mos' everbody. Nobody wants to take a chance gettin' near that stuff. But Mr. Zanuck and Miss Crawford, they walk right in. An' when they come back, Mr. Zanuck, he call for aspirin, say he has an awful headache. What everybody say, nitroglycereen makes bad headache; and what they say, dynamite is jus' nitroglycereen mixed up with sawdust and packed in sticks."

"Yes, so I understand," she said.

"They ain't no stick dynamite in they rooms," said George. "We looked. It's gone. Blowed up, I gotta figger."

"The sheriff—"

"Cain't talk to the sheriff," said George firmly. "Sheriff Thompson, he's a good 'nough man; but he wouldn't listen to no nigger on no subject. Put aside that Mr. Zanuck, Miss Crawford gonna say no. Even without that, the sheriff, he gonna smile and say, 'Fine, boy, thass fine, an' thanks.' An' he gonna forget anything I tell him, right off."

"I understand," said Mrs. Roosevelt. "I'm terribly sorry, George."

"Anyway, I got somethin' else to tell," said George somberly. "Don't go exactly with what I tol' just now. Different."

"And what is that?"

George drew a deep breath and sat even more erect. "You b'lieve in conjure? I mean, at all?"

"George . . ."

"My mama, she's a conjure woman," said George in a low voice, hardly above a whisper. "I took . . ." He stopped and looked around, as if once more he felt the need to be sure no one was hiding in the room and listening. "I took a piece of blanket soaked with Mr. Partridge's blood. I took it to my mama. Ain' nobody gonna pay no 'tention, but Mama got her idea who killed Mr. Partridge. It's different from what I tol' you."

"And your mother thinks?"

"Mama took that piece of blanket with the blood on it," said George quietly, soberly, "and mixed it up with some ashes from a fire burnt with nothin' but white oak. Then she put some other stuff on top of it, what she won't tell nobody what it is. Then she prayed over it for a while. Then she came up with an answer."

"Yes. And what is the answer, George?" asked Mrs. Roosevelt.

"Folks laugh," said George gravely. "Even colored folks laugh. But Mama, she found the body of a drownded man, when nobody else could find it. Anythin' you lose, she can find it. She learned from her mother—"

"George. Who does she identify as the murderer?"

George sighed loudly. "Blonde woman," said George. "Not Miss Crawford. Somebody else."

"That makes it—"

"Miss Bingham," said George gravely. "I showed my mama her picture in a magazine, and she says Miss Bingham done killed Mr. Partridge."

Mrs. Roosevelt tried to subdue her smile. "Well," she said. "I suppose the evidence against her is as strong as that against anyone else."

George shook his head. "But she ain' the one stole the stick of dynamite. Mama says nevah mind. Mama says the blonde woman done killed Mr. Partridge. No dynamite. No matta what."

Mrs. Roosevelt poured tea from her pot, into the cup on the tray. "George," she said. "I will keep your confidence. And I will ask you to bring me any other information you get. Anything. Just come to me and tell me."

George smiled for the first time. "Baker Street Irregulars," he said.

"I beg your pardon?"

"Mr. Sherlock Holmes," said George. "In them stories about bein' a detective in London. The boys that helped him. He called them his 'Baker Street Irregulars.' Me an' the other colored folks, we be that for you, Mrs. Roosevelt. We be your irregulars."

"Oh, *very* good!" she said. "And keep an eye out."

George nodded. "Somethin' very funny goin' on. Ain' none of them folks tellin' the truth. An' tomorrow, the President hisself comin'! Cain't let nothin' bad happen while the President at Hobcaw. Take no chance on that."

"Let me know anything you learn, George," said Mrs. Roosevelt. "I will always listen to you."

10

The train the railroads designated POTUS—President of the United States—would arrive at Andrews, South Carolina, about one o'clock. Two cars, the President's armored Pullman and another for the Secret Service and for communications equipment, would be detached from the train there and hauled down the track to Georgetown by a switching locomotive. The President would give a little talk to anyone from Georgetown who might want to come out to the railroad and see him; and, as it was expected, by two-thirty he would be on his way in Bernard Baruch's big blue Packard, to the bridge and then down through the woods to Hobcaw House.

A Secret Service detail was at the house by eight in the morning. They had driven down from Washington in three cars. By the time Mrs. Roosevelt left her suite and went to the dining room to join Baruch for breakfast, they were all around the house, poking into everything, looking at anything that might offer even the remotest hazard to the President.

"I suppose we must tell them about the Monday night explosion," said Mrs. Roosevelt to Baruch.

"I've already done that," said Baruch.

The Secret Service men had brought radio telephones.

These would scramble and transmit speech to the communications car that would be on the siding over in Georgetown. The equipment on the car would relay to the navy facilities at Charleston, where the radio transmissions would be unscrambled and fed into the telephone wires to Washington. The President would have instant communication.

Even though the President would be sleeping on the first floor, they installed a canvas chute on one of his bedroom windows. In the event of fire, they would heave him onto the chute, and he would slide down to the lawn.

They were concerned about the possible existence of explosives in the house and wanted to search every guest's room. Baruch had consented, but the Secret Service men were circumspect about it and would find opportunities when the guests were downstairs.

Zanuck was at the table for breakfast. He and Baruch were to meet immediately after, for their discussion of ways to finance the filming of *The African Queen* or some other picture. Sheriff Virgil Thompson arrived and sat down for a cup of coffee. Robert Wilkes, who had spent some time with the other Secret Service agents, explaining to them what measures he had taken to protect Mrs. Roosevelt, came to the dining room and sat down over a plate of eggs and sausage.

"I can have Winchell wakened," Baruch said when he had finished his breakfast. "Mr. Zanuck and I are going to close ourselves in the library for a little while, for a talk. Winchell does want to see you, Virgil."

"Unless the sheriff is in a hurry," said Mrs. Roosevelt, "I would like to chat with him a bit."

"Ah'm in no hurry at all, ma'am."

"Then . . . And Mr. Wilkes, please stay, if you can."

The First Lady poured herself another cup of coffee, then poured one for the sheriff. She looked out for a moment at the gentle rain. It had begun in the night and seemed likely to continue all day, falling from a sky that hung low over Winyah Bay. She hoped it would stop by tomorrow, so the President could enjoy the sun and get in his fishing.

"The two of you," she said to the sheriff and Wilkes, "examined the body of Mr. Partridge and the room; and, as I understand it, you concluded he had been killed by the explosion of a bottle of nitroglycerine. Isn't that right?"

"An unscientific conclusion," said Wilkes. "But, yes, that's what we suspect."

"Could it have been dynamite?" she asked.

The sheriff smiled faintly. "Could have been cleaning fluid," he said. He glanced around, as if to be sure Winchell was not downstairs and about to enter the dining room. "Dynamite would've made more sense. Nitroglycerine is very dangerous to handle. I can't figger why a body'd want to use it."

"It was the bottle fragment that suggested nitro," said Wilkes. "That plus the odor."

"I got to tell you about that there bottle," said the sheriff. "There was more pieces of it in the corpse. Two more hunks of that same greenish glass."

"Speaking of the corpse," said Mrs. Roosevelt reluctantly. "What's been done with it?"

"We notified that feller Bancroft, in California," said the sheriff. "He sent a wire, sayin' he don't want it, just bury it. Douglas is buryin' it, this mawnin', in the cemetery. Didn't know what church the man was of, if any, so the Methodist preacher's gonna say a few words. Didn't figger anybody here'd be interested in comin' to see the burial."

Wilkes frowned. "The body could, of course, be exhumed if—"

"If necessary," said the sheriff. "It's in a fifty-dollar casket. We sent Bancroft a bill for that."

"What a pity," said Mrs. Roosevelt. "I mean, that no one cares enough about the man even to . . ." She shook her head. "Anyway, what chance is there that he was killed by dynamite rather than nitroglycerine?"

"Could be," said the sheriff. "Who could tell?"

"Well, a scientific investigation—" Wilkes ventured.

"Sherlock Holmes kind of stuff," said the sheriff. "Ellery Queen kind of stuff. Smart guesses. We cain't tell, ma'am, whether it was nitro that went off, or dynamite."

"Or cleaning fluid," said she.

"That's right. Or cleaning fluid."

"But dynamite," said Wilkes, "would have been the most practical explosive."

"How big an explosion does one stick make?" asked Mrs. Roosevelt.

"I don't know," said Wilkes. "But I'd judge a bigger explosion than went off upstairs. From what I've heard and read, a whole stick would have blown the walls out."

"That's my impression, too," said Sheriff Thompson.

"Ah, then . . ."

"But you can cut a stick in pieces," said Wilkes. "If you know how. It's commonly done. They set off half sticks, quarter sticks. People who know how to work with it, cut sticks to whatever amount they want."

"As I understand it," said the sheriff gravely, "it's the blasting cap that's dangerous. You can handle a stick of dynamite pretty safely, long's you don't whack it with a hammer or set off a blasting cap in it."

"I've heard," said Wilkes, "that you can toss a stick in a fire and it will just burn, won't go off. It takes a shock to set it off—which is the function of the blasting cap."

Mrs. Roosevelt smiled. "I am fortunate to have the benefit of your experience," she said.

George, the butler, stepped near. "Mr. Winchell comin'," he said quietly.

Winchell breezed through the door and took a place at the table. He was followed by Bogart, who entered somewhat more slowly and seemed to be nursing a hangover.

"We could have wished for better weather for the President," said Winchell as George poured coffee for him.

"It will change," said Bogart as he drew back a chair and lowered himself gingerly. "He'll bring 'Roosevelt weather.'"

"Ah," said Winchell. "Does it never rain on the President, Mrs. Roosevelt?"

She smiled. "He doesn't even *own* an umbrella," she said ingenuously.

"It rains on the just and the unjust," said Bogart, "but never on FDR. So I've heard."

"No. And the tide won't come in, either," said Mrs. Roosevelt. "Not while he's here."

"I think Tallulah's counting on it," said Winchell, pointing toward the window.

Outside, in the rain, Tallulah rode toward the stable. She was drenched, her blouse and skirt clinging, her hair streaming over her face. She glanced toward the house as she rode by but did not see the people inside the dining-room window. Her face was grim, and she ran both hands over her head to push back the water.

"Eccentric," said the sheriff.

"That's charitable, Sheriff," said Winchell. "Actually, she's a little off in the upper story, if you ask me."

"I think not," said Mrs. Roosevelt firmly. "I believe the sheriff used the correct word—'eccentric.'"

"I'm surprised she's not setting off fireworks," said Winchell.

"Meaning what, Winchell?" asked Bogart.

Winchell glanced around the table. He raised his cup and sipped coffee. "She has reason to be glad of the death of Ben Partridge," he said.

"Do we need to know why?" asked Mrs. Roosevelt.

"Not necessarily," said Winchell. "Except that Partridge died in the midst of a crowd of people, almost every one of whom has reason to be happy he's dead."

"When you're a despicable bastard," said Bogart, "nobody is likely to mourn your passing."

"Ah'd be interested in hearin' what you have in mind, Mr. Winchell," said the sheriff. "You suggestin'—"

"They knew each other in England," said Winchell. "Tallulah and Partridge. She was a successful actress over there. She had a naughty reputation for doing her best work while less than completely clothed, and the reviews of her plays sometimes gave as many words to her underwear as they did to her acting; but she was well thought of in London."

"I can confirm that," said Mrs. Roosevelt. "I have English friends who find it quite amusing that the daughter of the Speaker of our House of Representatives was an actress in a succession of somewhat risqué plays."

"Ben Partridge was in London at the same time," Winchell went on. "He came over from Germany with a reputation as a successful director and sometime producer, and he'd decided to try his hand at the same kind of work in London and maybe then in the States. He bought into a play that Tallulah had signed to do, called *Lady in Earnest;* and shortly—so my London friends tell me—he developed what we might call a strong affection for her."

"But the very sight of him made her sick," said Bogart. "I don't know that. I just guess."

"She was in love with someone else," said Winchell. "A young actor named Charles Spector. She was quite devoted to him, my friends over there tell me. She tried to promote his career. She asked producers to give him parts in her plays. She wanted Partridge to give him the male lead in *Lady in Earnest*. Well, of course, Partridge didn't want Spector around and wouldn't give him a part. Tallulah threatened to walk out of the production. There was quite a brouhaha, they tell me."

"And a misfortune befell Charlie Spector, I bet," said Bogart. "I haven't heard this story before. I'm just guessing."

"Partridge gave him a job as a clerk and bookkeeper," said Winchell. "Very reluctantly. Very, very reluctantly— to keep the peace. He wouldn't let him near the rehearsals for *Lady in Earnest* and had him handling the money from another play, called *Blue Dogs*. Well, *Blue Dogs* closed, and shortly Partridge accused Spector of having embezzled money from the box-office receipts. Spector was tried, Partridge testified against him, and Spector went to prison. He committed suicide in Brixton Prison, the day after he arrived there."

"Leaving a clear field for Gentleman Ben to move into Tallulah's love life," Bogart sneered. "How very lucky for him."

"That's what Tallulah thought, too," said Winchell.

"She accused Partridge of having framed Spector and of having perjured himself in his testimony against him. She was telling everybody what a rat Partridge was. He sued her for libel. The case was not tried, though. After only a couple of weeks, she settled the suit. Her solicitors saw the evidence and advised her that Spector had in fact stolen money from Partridge. She had to apologize and pay Partridge five hundred pounds."

"Did she do his play?" Bogart asked.

"Yes, she had to do that, too," said Winchell. "Either that or pay his production company what it would have lost if she'd backed out. And *Lady in Earnest* was a success. It made money. It was good for her reputation, too. But she hated Ben Partridge. She blamed him for the death of Charlie Spector, and I mean she *hated* him."

"I believe that completes the circle," said Mrs. Roosevelt. "Everyone hated him. Everyone."

"Which is why I express some skepticism about his having died by accident," said Winchell.

Sheriff Virgil Thompson nodded and sucked his teeth. "Ah'm *entirely* in agreement with you, Mr. Winchell," he said. *"Ah* am skeptical, too. But we cain't seem to find no evidence that somebody killed the man. Motives. Motives. There's a lot of talk about motives. But what Ah'd like to see is some evidence that somebody killed the man. Y'understand, we cain't speculate. I mean, you can, but Ah cain't. *Who* killed him, y' suppose? An' *how?* Ah cain't call his death a murder, or accuse nobody of it, until Ah see some evidence."

"But cleaning fluid . . ." Winchell protested. "Is it really possible?"

"Seems most probable," said the sheriff. "Until somebody comes up with a better explanation. I mean, I just cain't see how anybody'd manage to sneak a bomb into the house, an' plant it, an' get it to go off at just the right time."

"But you are continuing to investigate?"

"Oh, *sure,*" said the sheriff. "Mah mind is open on the matter, Mr. Winchell. Entirely open."

* * *

"Tell me something, Sheriff," Mrs. Roosevelt said quietly when they were again alone except for Wilkes. "Have you questioned the Negroes that work around the place?"

"Yes, ma'am. Every one of 'em."

"Did you find out anything?"

"No, ma'am. They don't have much to say. Just . . . just say they didn't see nothin', didn't hear nothin'."

She nodded. "Very well. I just wondered if they might not be a source of information."

"I wish they wuz," said the sheriff. "I'm not like some, that wouldn't listen to anything they said. I'd take what they say into account."

"I am becoming more deeply worried," she continued. "Whatever we may tell Mr. Winchell, you and I know, Sheriff, that someone murdered Mr. Partridge."

"Or that he blowed himself up while gettin' ready to murder someone else. I wouldn't forget that possibility."

"Very well. And the President is coming this afternoon, and we don't know who killed Benjamin Partridge. We are introducing the President into a house where, very likely, there is a killer."

"All their rooms are being searched," said Wilkes.

"Yes," said Mrs. Roosevelt. "Please ask the man in charge of the detail to come in."

"That's Leonard Salisbury," said Wilkes. "I'll go get him."

Sheriff Virgil Thompson watched Wilkes leave the room. "I'm glad to have them fellas here," he said. "I wouldn't want the responsibility . . . Well. Y'understand."

"That's their job," said Mrs. Roosevelt. "To protect the President. It is not their job, though, to solve our mystery. Don't count on their help with that."

"I'm not," said the sheriff. "Ah'm beginnin' to think, though, to be altogether honest, that we ain't gonna find out who killed Partridge. Maybe never."

She shook her head. "Sometimes I feel they all know but you and me. None of them cares. They are all glad he's dead. And I feel quite sure, Sheriff, that more than one of them knows who did it. I keep looking at them, wondering . . ."

"The man was not a very nice fella, from what I gather," said the sheriff.

Leonard Salisbury, chief of the Secret Service detail that now overran the house, arranging everything for the visit of the President of the United States, entered the dining room a few minutes later. He carried in his hand a wooden object, which he laid on the table.

"What's that?" the sheriff asked.

"I'll explain in a minute," said Salisbury.

Leonard Salisbury was perhaps fifty years old: a tall, slender, gray man, with a sharp beak for a nose and a pointed chin, cold blue eyes—he was, in short, Hawkshaw the Detective, in the flesh.

"We are concerned," said Mrs. Roosevelt, "about the President's safety in a house where murder may have been committed Monday evening."

"We would never have consented to his coming here if we had known," said Salisbury.

"There are reasons why he had to come," said Mrs. Roosevelt.

Salisbury nodded: a concession. "Yes, ma'am. We will take extraordinary measures to protect the President."

"I am confident of that, Mr. Salisbury, as I am always."

"Thank you, ma'am."

"You have searched the rooms?" she asked.

He nodded. "And found that," he said, pointing to the wooden object on the dining table.

It had the figure of an oversized pair of pliers: a pair of hinged handles that closed a set of jaws. There was no metal in this tool; even the pin at the hinge was of wood. It was a tool of some kind, smeared with mud that had been wiped off, giving it the discolored look of age—and yet its sharp, clean edges suggested newness, as if it had been but rarely used.

"What is it, and where did you find it?" asked Mrs. Roosevelt.

Salisbury picked it up. "I didn't recognize the thing myself, at first," he said. "One of the boys saw what it was." He turned it over in his hands. "Want to know what this is, Mrs. Roosevelt? This is a *crimper*. I mean, a crimper that's used to crimp a blasting cap."

"Oh, sure!" said the sheriff. "That's what it is!"

"I'm afraid I require explanation," said Mrs. Roosevelt.

"All right," said Salisbury. "A blasting cap—so called —is a sort of thin copper cylinder, a little smaller around than a pencil and about four inches long. It's got an explosive in it: fulminate of mercury, usually. Now, dynamite won't explode just because the fire from a fuse reaches it. It takes a blasting cap—something that will go off when fire touches it. Blasting fuse has powder in it, and it makes a hot fire as it burns. You stick the end of the fuse in the cap, and you crimp it with a pair of crimpers like this. When the fuse burns down to the cap end, the fire from the fuse sets off the explosive in the cap, and that in turn sets off the dynamite or TNT or whatever."

"And you crimp the cap with wooden pliers because otherwise you risk creating a spark that would set off the cap," said Mrs. Roosevelt.

"Exactly," said Salisbury.

"I've seen them," said the sheriff, pointing at the wooden crimping tool. "Every blasting engineer has 'em."

"Right," said Salisbury. "And why would anybody else have one?"

"So where did you find it, Mr. Salisbury?" asked Mrs. Roosevelt.

"In Miss Joan Crawford's room," he said. "In one of her suitcases, under some of her underclothes."

"I don't see how I got much choice but to take you in and hold you in the county jail," said the sheriff to Joan Crawford. She had explained how she came to have the crimper, but he did not accept her explanation.

She stood open-mouthed, her face flushed, facing the

sheriff and Salisbury and Mrs. Roosevelt in the dining room.

"Oh, please," said Mrs. Roosevelt. "After all, Sheriff, only Tuesday we had a chief suspect we were convinced had killed Mr. Partridge, and you allowed him to stay here in the house. I—"

"You got a point," said the sheriff.

"I didn't know what that thing was!" Crawford protested. "I picked it up for a . . . for a sort of souvenir. I swear!"

"Sure you did," said the sheriff grimly. "All right. It looks like we're findin' evidence at long last. You an' Crown, Miss Crawford. Because Mrs. Roosevelt thinks I should, I'll let you stay in the house. But there's gotta be some restrictions."

"Ones that don't come to the attention of Mr. Winchell," said Mrs. Roosevelt. "Otherwise . . ."

"Right," said Sheriff Thompson. "Otherwise, that sleazy rat will—"

"I'd like to understand what's going on," interrupted Salisbury.

"It is not entirely a matter that's any of your business, Mr. Salisbury," said Mrs. Roosevelt. "You will have your explanation, but let me make it to you in private, later."

"Yes, ma'am."

"A'right," said the sheriff. "I got two suspects in the house. Same rules for Crown as for you, Miss Crawford; and I'll tell him as soon as I see him. No more boat rides, okay? You don't leave the house. When you go to your room tonight, I want it somehow fixed so you cain't get out. I'm puttin' a deputy or two on duty in the house, Miss Crawford. You break my rules, you can sit in the county jail till we get this worked out. You understand me?"

She had turned pale. "I understand," she whispered.

"I'm sorry, Miss Crawford," said Mrs. Roosevelt. "I think—"

"Just don't let Winchell find out," she whispered tearfully. "I swear to you I didn't kill Ben Partridge; but Winchell could ruin even me with the word that I'm suspected."

"Nobody wants to ruin you, Miss Crawford," said the sheriff. "Maybe there's an explanation. We'll be lookin' for it. But right now, it's no game no more—not for you and not for Crown. You understand me?"

Crawford nodded again. Her eyes settled on the crimping tool. "I didn't know what that thing was," she said hoarsely. "I—I swear I didn't kill Ben Partridge. Before Almighty God, I swear it! Please don't—"

"Railroad you," said the sheriff. "We won't do that. You can count on it. But you're suspected of murder now, on strong evidence, so if you want to stay outside my jail, you stay put in this house."

11

The train called POTUS pulled into Georgetown on time. Whatever train included the armored presidential Pullman was called POTUS; and this afternoon it consisted of a tiny, chugging, straining 0-4-0 switching locomotive with tender, a single mail car, and the two cars that made it POTUS: the big green Pullman and the Secret Service car that carried the agents and the presidential communications equipment.

It was raining. Hard. Even so, several hundred citizens of Georgetown and the vicinity assembled around the track, many of them carrying black umbrellas, many just standing in the rain and taking a soaking—businessmen in rumpled, tropical-weight suits, wives in flowered frocks, farmers in worn bib overalls with steel-cased watches secured by shoelaces draped across their chests and knotted in vague semblance of watch chains, men and women alike in hats of all sorts, ranging from black wool to tattered straws, from cloches to pillboxes with veils. On the edge of the crowd, cautiously apart, the representatives of the Negro community stood bareheaded, holding their hats in their hands. All had come for one purpose: to see Franklin D. Roosevelt, President of the United States. They expected this to be a day they would remember all their lives.

He knew it. Not for anything would he have disappointed them. Flanked by two Secret Service men, he stepped out from the rear door of the Pullman, onto the railed platform—taking the two or three steps without help. He was under a roof, but the wind blew the rain in, into his face. He grinned, nodded, waved with his cigarette holder, then swept off his old gray hat and took a small bow. They cheered.

The microphones before him were live. "My friends," he said. "There is a silly legend that rain never falls on Franklin Roosevelt. Well, you can go home and tell your children tonight: if it rains and Roosevelt steps out in it, it falls on his head the same as on anybody else's."

While they laughed he jammed his hat back on his head.

"I've returned gladly to South Carolina, this time just for a visit with my good friend, your neighbor Bernard Baruch. I've asked Bernie to shoo some fish in toward the shore, and I'm looking forward to some fishing, if the sun comes out."

He paused to smile and nod, and the crowd responded with a murmur of laughter.

"I can't tell you, really, how much I appreciate all of you coming here to greet me this afternoon. It is very kind of you. And I'll return a little of that kindness now by saying no more and letting everybody get in out of the rain. Thank you all. Thank you so much."

Mrs. Roosevelt and Bernard Baruch had entered the car through one of the front doors and were waiting in the parlor when the President stepped back inside. He handed his canes to his valet, Arthur Prettyman, and sat down. Mrs. Roosevelt bent over him, and he kissed her affectionately on the cheek. Then he extended a hand to Baruch, and shook hands with him.

"Bernie, you know Pa Watson, don't you?"

Baruch turned and shook hands with Colonel Edwin Watson, the President's military aide, a burly, red-faced man.

"Whatever you do, Bernie, don't let Pa near a shotgun.

He'll shoot turkeys, house cats, goldfish, lampshades . . . anything that moves or doesn't move."

"And catch three fish for every one the President catches," said Pa Watson.

The President chuckled as he lit a fresh cigarette.

"We have something to tell you before we leave for the house," said Mrs. Roosevelt. "Something you have to know."

"Nothing ominous, I hope," said the President.

"Something I hope you can ignore," said Baruch. "You're here to relax, and that's what we intend you should do."

"However . . ." said Mrs. Roosevelt, inclining her head a little to one side. "We have to tell you that a man was murdered in Hobcaw House Monday night. What is more, we still don't know who did it. It was almost certainly one of the guests, but we don't know which one."

"You're asking the President to stay in a house with—" Pa Watson began.

"Worse than that," said Baruch. "Walter Winchell is here, snooping, trying to find a story. We've told him the death was an accident—which in fact does remain a possibility—but of course, since all the guests are celebrities—"

"Winchell is in full cry," said the President, frowning. "Why didn't you let me know? I should have postponed the visit."

"We had hoped the matter would be resolved before today," said Baruch glumly.

"If you had not come, Franklin," said Mrs. Roosevelt, "Mr. Winchell would have been certain he was on the track of a big story. As it is, he seems inclined to accept our suggestion that the death was probably an accident."

"Which maybe it was," said Baruch emphatically. "Anyway, Sheriff Thompson is being entirely cooperative. He's promised not to make an arrest or issue any public statement about the case until after you and Eleanor have returned to Washington."

The President shook his head. "I seem to have little choice," he said. "I can hardly go back to Washington."

"But the President's safety!" Pa Watson protested. "Staying in a house with a murderer loose!"

"It's not as bad as it sounds," said Mrs. Roosevelt. "It would appear that the person who did it had ample motive. Indeed, the victim seems to have been so evil a man that we almost have to wonder if his death wasn't justified." She stopped, sighed. "Anyway, the Secret Service detail has been told, and they've searched the house, including all the guests' rooms. We'll tell you all the details on the way to the house."

"Is anyone especially suspected?" the President asked.

"As of this morning," said Mrs. Roosevelt, "I am afraid the principal suspect is Joan Crawford. She certainly had ample motive, and . . . Well, the man was killed with explosives; and this morning, in the search of her room, Miss Crawford was found to have a crimping tool, a device that is used to attach fuse to blasting caps. It was hidden in her luggage."

"Are you playing detective, Babs?" the President asked sternly.

"Certainly *not*," said Mrs. Roosevelt. "I've asked a few questions, suggested one or two lines of inquiry—"

"Playing detective," said the President, turning down the corners of his mouth and nodding.

"I do feel so sorry for Joan Crawford," said Mrs. Roosevelt.

"You felt sorry for Adriana van der Meer, Babs—and remember what that got you into. I thought you'd had your fill of crime solving."

"We've been trying," said Baruch, "to solve the mystery quickly, so it could be cleared up and—if I may suggest it—disposed of quietly. Eleanor has been very helpful."

"It never rains but it pours," said the President. "And I wanted to go fishing."

"I insist you do," said Mrs. Roosevelt. "As soon as the sun comes out. I've been riding, as I had hoped to do, and—"

"Enjoying the holiday!" The President laughed. "After all, why should a little thing like a murder interfere with a carefree holiday? Babs . . . Bernie . . . You really are extraordinary people!"

"I'm afraid I have one more item of news," said Baruch.

"Whoops!" exclaimed the President. "Additionally, you have found the Holy Grail, accidentally overlooked in your wine cellar."

"Holy what . . .? No. It's Governor Byrnes. I'm afraid he won't be able to make it this weekend. I received a telegram from him. The governor is suffering from a severe head cold."

"Jimmy? Not coming? Ah, well."

"And Bill Knudsen," said Baruch. "I telephoned him, as you suggested. His secretary expected him back on the *Queen Mary*, which docked in New York yesterday; but it seems he missed the *Queen* and is coming home on the *Ile de France*, which won't dock until Tuesday."

"Then who is going fishing?" the President asked.

"You and I and General Watson," said Baruch.

"So," said the President. "A true holiday. A gentlemanly crew. And less competition for the fish."

"And not so many people," said Mrs. Roosevelt, "who would have to hear an explanation of the Benjamin Partridge matter."

Seated in his wood-and-steel wheelchair, the President unintentionally amused the guests by giving George a quick and detailed course on the proper mixing of a martini. All of them were together in the living room, at seven. The Secret Service detail had efficiently, almost unobtrusively, searched each guest at the door—the women only with their eyes, the men by a rapid patdown effected while shaking hands. Now the agents stationed themselves in the corners of the room, trying to be inconspicuous but in no way succeeding.

"This is an education, Mr. President," said Walter Winchell. "May I have your permission to teach Sherman Billingsley to mix martinis the Roosevelt way? And serve them at the Stork Club?"

The President laughed happily. "So long as he doesn't call them FDR Martinis or some such," he said. "Five to one, Walter. That's the secret, first-class dry white vermouth and first-class dry gin, five to one."

"I hear," said Bogart, "there's a bar on the East Side that mixes them seven to one."

"Whew!" exclaimed the President. "I'd be afraid to smoke while drinking one of those."

Across the room, Mrs. Roosevelt spoke quietly with the despondent Joan Crawford.

"I *stole* them," said Crawford. "That's what I'm guilty of: theft."

"Oh, my dear."

"I stole that pair of wooden pliers. I found them in that little shed I told the sheriff about. I thought they were some kind of hand-carved antique tool. They were lying on the ground inside the shed. It looked as if nobody would miss them. On an impulse, I did something terribly stupid—I picked them up and shoved them in my bag."

"Tell me about this shed. Where was it? Why did you go there?"

"I can only tell you at the expense of some embarrassment," said Crawford. "But I suppose—"

"Embarrassment is hardly the issue at this point."

"No, I suppose it isn't. I suppose you understand that Darryl Zanuck and I . . . Well, we've had a physical relationship since we've been here. I'm sorry. I don't mean to embarrass you, Mrs. Roosevelt; but that's how it is. We didn't know each other very well before, but we have developed a strong attraction for each other. And, of course, there is a business relationship, at least potentially. When we said we were out fishing, the truth is, we were looking for places to be alone, where . . . I guess I don't have to be more specific."

"No," said Mrs. Roosevelt gently. "You need not."

Crawford lowered her head, and when she looked up there were tears in her eyes. "I am so . . . *humiliated*," she whispered. "Do you know what they are doing to me tonight?"

"What?"

"I've been moved into the servants' wing. I will be locked in my room tonight, as will Johnny Crown. *Locked in,* Mrs. Roosevelt! I—"

"Moved into the servants' wing? Surely that is not necessary!"

"I asked to be. Otherwise, Winchell, across the hall, might find out I'm locked in. A deputy will spend the night in the hall, to see that I don't try to get out. If he were in the main hall—"

"Mr. Winchell would see him."

"I had an option. I could be handcuffed to my bed."

"Oh, my *dear!*"

"The sheriff thinks I'm the chief suspect now. I'm the one most likely to have blown up Ben Partridge. It's a concession, he reminded me, that I'm not behind bars right now."

"This shed you mentioned," said Mrs. Roosevelt. "What was in there, besides the crimping tool you picked up?"

Joan Crawford shrugged. "Shovels . . . tools." She sighed. "Oh, yes—the sign on the outside said there were explosives inside, but I never saw any. Explo—*My God!*"

Mrs. Roosevelt nodded. "Precisely," she said.

"Ah swear! Ah—"

"Swearing is rather pointless right now, I'm afraid."

"Dynamite!"

"Yes."

Tallulah raised a glass. "The world-famous presidential martini. Oh, *God,* Mr. President! It is full of *vermouth!*"

The President laughed. "Of course, Tallulah. What did you suppose?"

"*Gin,* my dear sir! Nobody but the buggery English could drink the stuff at best . . . but to mix woppish battery-acid *vermouth* in it! Frank! For the sake of Jesus Christ!

Every true-blooded American drinks American sippin' whiskey—which means goddamn *bourbon!*"

"In the goddamn backward, subliterate *South* maybe," said Bogart. "Mississippi, Alabama, Loo-seeanah . . . I suppose the stuff kills the bugs in the water. Ninety-proof Listerine."

"Bogart, you—"

"De gustibus non est disputandum," said Pa Watson, tossing back his presidential martini.

"De big drinky is not disputandum either," said Tallulah. She took another sip from the martini the President had given her. "Actually, I suppose the thing *is* palatable, if you like this sort of thing."

"Well, as Lincoln said"—the President laughed—"'If you like this sort of thing, this is the sort of thing you will like.'"

"You aren't Lincoln yet, my darling," said Tallulah, and she bent down and kissed the President fervently on the mouth. "Oh, God, excuse me, Eleanor. I do get carried away."

"I enjoyed the evening, Bernie. I really did," the President said as he and Baruch and Mrs. Roosevelt sat alone much later, in the first-floor suite. "Whatever looms behind the conviviality, everyone managed to keep it behind, and I am grateful. This peculiar job I've taken on affords one few opportunities for relaxation."

"We intend you should be able to relax this weekend," said Baruch.

"It's odd," said the President, "to see people so able to enjoy an evening when all of them are suspects in a murder."

"I know one who was not enjoying herself," said Mrs. Roosevelt. "Poor Joan Crawford is locked in a room in the servants' wing right now. I'm afraid the sheriff has pretty much settled on her as the principal suspect."

"Because of the crimping tool?" the President asked.

"That does look bad for her, doesn't it?" said Baruch. "The very instrument that—"

"Bernie!" the President interrupted, chuckling. "Use your head!"

"I'm sorry," said Baruch, unable to conceal a degree of indignation.

"How about you, Babs?" the President asked. "Do you place a lot of importance on that pair of wooden pliers?"

"Well, I suppose so," said Mrs. Roosevelt. "After all—"

"Did you ever see a piece of dynamite fuse burning, Babs? Did you, Bernie?"

Both of them shook their heads.

"Well, I have. It sputters and spews flame and smoke. If Benjamin Partridge had looked around and seen a fuse burning in his room, he'd have jumped out the window. What's more, someone would have had to light it. It's pretty obvious the bomb wasn't set off by a fuse."

"Actually, we had supposed there was some sort of electrical connection," said Mrs. Roosevelt.

"It was almost certainly detonated by electricity. And there goes your crimping tool. That's used to crimp the end of a blasting cap down on the end of a fuse. An electric detonator cap is an entirely different thing. You don't use a wooden crimper to fasten your wires to an electric cap."

"I never cease to be astounded by the breadth of your knowledge, Franklin," said Mrs. Roosevelt.

"I thank God for that," said the President. "How good it is that you are not astounded by the narrowness of it."

"Then Joan Crawford . . ." Baruch ventured.

"I don't think you have a suspect there," said the President. "That is, you don't have one more likely than any other."

"I'm going to go tell her," said Mrs. Roosevelt abruptly. "I think that poor young woman should know."

"Babs—"

"No," said Mrs. Roosevelt firmly. "I'm going to go tell her."

* * *

Mrs. Roosevelt, still dressed in the tea-colored gown she had worn to dinner, strode purposefully from the suite and to the stairway—followed at a discreet distance by a Secret Service agent. The house was quiet, and most of the lights had been turned off. On the second floor, she hurried along the main hall and then entered the servants' wing, where she had never been before. A deputy sat dozing as best he could, on a straight wooden chair.

"Young man. Young man," she said.

The deputy looked up, his eyes wide. "Mrs. Roosevelt!"

"I want to talk with Miss Crawford. Please let me into her room."

"Oh . . . Oh, well, Ah guess it's all rat."

The blond, apple-cheeked young man pushed himself erect on the chair, then stood. He fumbled in his pocket for a key.

Mrs. Roosevelt turned to the Secret Service man and told him not to wait for her; everything was obviously all right. Then she knocked lightly on the door, just before the deputy unlocked it.

"Miss Crawford."

Joan Crawford lay in bed, in the hard, shadowy light of a little gooseneck lamp. She had been reading and had lowered her book at the sound of the knock on her door. She was wearing black silk pajamas, and as the door opened she was grabbing at her sheet and pulling it up to cover herself.

"Mrs. Roosevelt. I—"

"I am intruding," said Mrs. Roosevelt. She turned her eyes away while the actress arranged the sheet and blanket. "I came to see you because I think I have some rather good news for you."

"Like that I can go back to my comfortable room? Here I can't even offer you a chair."

Mrs. Roosevelt glanced around the little bedroom. It was modestly furnished with the iron bed, a small, square table with lamp, and a simple wooden dresser. Since there was no adjoining bathroom and the young woman was locked in for the night, there was a chamber pot under the bed.

"I'm afraid we need the sheriff's word for that," said Mrs. Roosevelt, "but I am sure you can sleep there again tomorrow night."

"Why the change?" she asked dully.

"Something the President pointed out," said Mrs. Roosevelt. "The bomb that killed Mr. Partridge was almost certainly set off by an electrical device, but your crimping tool is suitable only for attaching fuse to a blasting cap. The evidence against you is not nearly so strong as we thought."

"The President . . . ?"

"Yes. My husband is a wonderful man, Miss Crawford. He knows at least a little about an amazing number of things, and he pointed out that your crimping tool could not have been used to prepare the bomb that went off in this house Monday night."

Crawford managed to smile. "Thank him for me, Mrs. Roosevelt," she said. "And thank you."

"Now tell me about the dynamite," said Mrs. Roosevelt firmly.

"Ah swear to you Ah never saw it! The sign said it was there, but I didn't see it. What's it kept in, a box? We didn't open any box. The shed was dirty inside, and we were only in there a minute or so. I saw the crimping tool on the ground and bent down to get it. Then—"

"Could Mr. Zanuck have picked up a stick of dynamite and carried it away without your knowing it?"

"No. I don't see how. Inside his coat . . . No, I don't think he could possibly have taken—"

"Someone did," said Mrs. Roosevelt.

Joan Crawford shook her head. "Not Zanuck. No. He couldn't have taken it."

"Unless he went back and got it later," said Mrs. Roosevelt.

"It could have been someone else, too. The sign was plain enough. Anyone who came by would have seen it."

"Could Mr. Zanuck have gone back?"

"I don't see how. He was with me . . . Well, I suppose he *could* have. I took a long bath later. And rested on my bed. But it *couldn't* have been DZ, Mrs. Roosevelt! It just couldn't have been."

"I suppose," said Mrs. Roosevelt quietly, "it would be old-fashioned and naive of me to imagine that—since you've told me you and Mr. Zanuck have what you've called a physical relationship—you are in love with him."

Crawford smiled, her face flushed, and she shook her head. "I'm sorry," she said. "I'm afraid that's not the nature of the relationship."

"I understand. Well, then, I shall be going. I feel sure the sheriff will consent to your returning to your own room tomorrow."

"It was so kind of you to come."

"I could hardly have done less," said Mrs. Roosevelt with a warm smile.

She stood and opened the door. The young deputy came immediately, and as Mrs. Roosevelt left the room he locked it again, smiling at her and murmuring good-night as he turned the key, then tried the knob.

She opened the door into the main second-floor hallway. Only one low-wattage bulb burned in a ceiling fixture half-way along the hall, but as she stepped through and reached back to close the door behind her, a patch of bright light suddenly shone on the floor and on the wall. Someone had opened a bedroom door, and the light from the room poured in a door-wide beam into the hallway. She stopped, startled slightly but not alarmed. To a degree, she was obscured, remaining as she was in the faint yellowish light from the weak little bulb down the hall. Her first instinct was to speak to whomever was coming out of the room, but her second instinct was to wait a moment.

It was Zanuck. He was dressed in pajama pants, nothing more. The room was Colleen Bingham's. For a brief moment she stood in the doorway, grinning at Zanuck as he crossed the hall and opened the door to his own room. She was nude.

Zanuck closed his door. Colleen closed hers. Mrs. Roosevelt walked quietly down the hall and descended the stairs.

12

Friday morning dawned fine, sunny, with a light breeze blowing in off the Atlantic. President Roosevelt was up not long after dawn; and still very early, long before any of the other guests came in to breakfast, he sat down over ham and eggs with Baruch and Pa Watson, and they talked about their day's fishing. Baruch suggested that the good weather offered them the choice of fishing the bay or heading south and around the tip of North Island, out into the open Atlantic, where the big fish might be striking. The President chose the deep water; and before seven o'clock he was helped aboard a fishing boat Baruch had hired for the week. Followed by a launch carrying a special detail of Secret Service men, they churned south through water that turned out to be surprisingly choppy. A Coast Guard boat, alerted that the President of the United States might be fishing off the entrance to Winyah Bay, and notified by radio that morning that he was in fact coming out, met the fishing boat and launch not far south of Pumpkinseed Island and fell in behind and two hundred yards back.

The Atlantic, disturbed by the overnight change of weather, was rougher than Baruch had guessed. The boats rose and fell on six-foot waves, each one out of sight of the others and out of sight of land whenever it was in a trough.

The President, ever the good sailor, was exhilarated. A few minutes outside the entrance to the bay, he had a line out and contentedly, expectantly, watched for a strike.

Mrs. Roosevelt, who had stood at her window and watched the boats pull away, came out to the dining room a little after eight. Wilkes sat down to breakfast with her, and shortly they were joined by Sheriff Thompson.

"I should like to suggest, Sheriff," said Mrs. Roosevelt when he was seated, "that we need to reconsider our conclusions about Joan Crawford."

The sheriff grinned. He was in the process of rolling a handmade cigarette, pouring tobacco from a little cloth bag into a tiny slip of paper he had folded with one hand. "You figger that out, too?" he asked.

"Well, the President did, actually."

"President? Well! Man knows somethin' 'bout explosives, huh?"

"He knows that a wooden crimping tool is used to crimp a blasting cap into which you have inserted the end of a length of fuse," she said. "And he is very doubtful that any fuse was involved."

The sheriff nodded. "Tell you somethin' more," he said. "I checked in with Bill Hathaway last evenin'. Bill's the one that done the blastin' on Mr. Baruch's road, you remember. He had dynamite in that shed, which he left 'cause he expected to come back and do some more work for Mr. Baruch; and he lost his crimper all right, like we might have figured. But he sets off all his blasts with fuse, none with electricity. There was never any electric caps in that shed. In fact, he took all the fuse caps with him, figurin' they're too dangerous to leave around. Whoever blew up Partridge didn't get his cap from that shed."

"And the dynamite?" she asked.

"There's a stick missin'."

"So where does that leave us?" she asked. "Miss Crawford admits taking the crimping tool. She says she and Mr. Zanuck entered the shed, and she stole the tool—as a souvenir, so to speak. She denies she or Mr. Zanuck took the dynamite. On the other hand, she could be lying."

"Why'd they go in that shed?" asked the sheriff.

"Her explanation is strong evidence that she is lying," said Mrs. Roosevelt. "She says that she and Mr. Zanuck went in the shed for privacy—that is, so they could . . . do what men and women do, if you follow me. But that is foolish. They had two comfortable and private rooms here in the house. They had no need to go in a toolshed for the purpose."

"Ramshackle, dirty place," said the sheriff. "Couple'd have to be hard up to—"

"Yes. So she's lying about that. So why did they go in there?"

"Take a stick of dynamite, I suppose," said the sheriff. "Doesn't seem right, though. They couldn't have got no blastin' caps from there. Even if Bill Hathaway's wrong about takin' all his caps with him, they was fuse type. Where'd they get what they had to have to set off that stick of dynamite?"

Mrs. Roosevelt shook her head. "Anyway, I don't think you need to lock Miss Crawford in a room any longer."

"I sent up orders to let her out, soon's I got here. Other hand, maybe what I ought to do is take her over to the county jail and see if layin' in there a day and night makes her interested in tellin' the truth about why she and Zanuck went in that toolshed."

"And how would we explain that to Mr. Winchell?"

"Hmmp. We couldn't," said the sheriff ruefully. "If he wasn't here, I could maybe settle this business a whole lot easier. Somebody in this house is lyin', and maybe it's time for a little of what we might call persuasion."

"Apply it to Mr. Zanuck," said Mrs. Roosevelt.

Zanuck came in a few minutes later, with Joan Crawford. Both of them took coffee, and Zanuck let George pile his plate high with scrambled eggs and sausage. Crawford took only a slice of toast, with butter and no jam.

Zanuck was feeling expansive, apparently. Dressed in a tweed jacket with a maroon silk scarf knotted around the collar of a yellow shirt, he ate hungrily and talked about an idea that had come to him overnight: to cast Walter Winchell in a picture.

"You realize, I am sure," said Mrs. Roosevelt, "that Mr. Winchell was once a vaudevillian—a dancer, I believe."

"He's a ham," said Joan Crawford.

"I'm going to make the proposition to him today," said Zanuck. "What it'll do for his ego may just turn his mind away from playing detective around here."

"If you can do that, we'll all be grateful," said Sheriff Thompson.

From that subject Zanuck went on to talk about Charles Laughton and Maurice Chevalier, then about Frederic March and Clark Gable. He told stories about each one—making Mrs. Roosevelt suspect he felt some nervous compulsion to be amusing this morning. He *was* amusing, but she wondered why the sudden effort.

Finally, when he had nearly finished his breakfast, Zanuck rubbed his hands together and said, "Well, Joanie. Shall we do a little fishing this morning?"

Crawford glanced at the sheriff. "No," she said quietly. "I'm not feeling altogether well this morning. I think I'll spend the day in the house."

"Getting out in the air would be good for you," Zanuck persisted.

"I'd like you to postpone gettin' out in the air, Mr. Zanuck," the sheriff said. "Haven't had a real chance to talk with you yet. And I'd like a chance."

Zanuck drew a breath. "Well, I'm at your service, Sheriff."

"Fine. In the library. Wouldn't want Mr. Winchell walkin' in and interruptin' us."

"Uh . . . Mrs. Roosevelt?" Zanuck asked.

"If you don't mind, Sheriff," she said.

"Not at all. And Mr. Wilkes, too. You'll excuse us, Miss Crawford?"

They sat down in Baruch's library. Zanuck took a cigar from his pocket but thought better and replaced it without lighting it. "I hope I haven't been elevated to the status of chief suspect," he said with an uneasy smile.

"Well, that depends," said the sheriff. "Let's see how you answer a question or two."

"Okay."

"Monday afternoon you and Miss Crawford went inside a toolshed just off the main road coming down to the house," said the sheriff. "We'd be interested in knowin' why you went in there and what you did."

Zanuck grinned and shook his head. "Oh, well, I . . . I'm afraid it would be ungentlemanly of me to talk about that."

"Are we to understand, then, that you went to the toolshed with Miss Crawford to indulge in a brief interlude of physical intimacy?" asked Mrs. Roosevelt—the outward innocence of her expression in contrast with the firm, sharp tone of her voice.

"You place me in an awkward situation, Mrs. Roosevelt."

"Not nearly so awkward as the one in which you will place yourself if you do not give us a frank and open answer to the question," she said.

Zanuck glanced at the sheriff, then at Wilkes. "Very well, then," he said. "We went there to . . . to do what you just mentioned."

"And you did?" she asked.

He nodded. "Then we left."

"You're lyin', Zanuck," muttered the sheriff darkly.

"I beg your pardon?"

"Don't beg my nothin'. Just tell the truth."

"Am I hearing an accusation?" asked Zanuck.

"Mr. Zanuck," said Mrs. Roosevelt. "It strikes us as odd that two people with comfortable private rooms in this house say they entered a tiny, dark, dirt-floor toolshed for the purpose we are talking about."

Zanuck grinned. "You never know about things like that. When the impulse strikes—"

"There are things missin' from that shed," the sheriff interjected.

"Oh," said Zanuck. "Are we talking about theft, then?"

"Yes," said Mrs. Roosevelt. "Of dynamite."

Zanuck's face hardened, and so did his voice. "There were explosives in the shed," he conceded. "Or so the sign said. I didn't see any. Or take any—if that's what you have in mind."

"Did either of you take anything from the shed?" asked Mrs. Roosevelt.

"Like what? What was in there that Joan Crawford or I could want? Worn-out, muddy tools?" Zanuck shook his head. "That's crazy."

"Missing from the shed after your visit," said Mrs. Roosevelt, "were a stick of dynamite and a crimping tool —the tool that's used to attach a fuse to a blasting cap."

"And you think Joan and I took them?" asked Zanuck incredulously. "And maybe brought them back here and used the dynamite to blow up Ben Partridge?"

"We are suggesting it's possible."

"And when Joan went in Partridge's room, she planted a bomb we had made?"

"It is possible."

"With enough imagination, all things are possible," said Zanuck wryly.

"You told us, Mr. Zanuck," said Mrs. Roosevelt, "that you and Mr. Partridge were together in your room for half an hour, drinking bourbon and having a business talk. When I asked you what the subject of that talk was, you declined to answer. Would you like to answer now?"

Zanuck shrugged, sighed. "I suppose I have to," he said. "This thing is beginning to breathe down my neck."

"You said something to the effect that revealing what you were talking about could be ruinous," said Mrs. Roosevelt.

"Yes," said Zanuck. "Though not to me. To two other people I think none of us would want to hurt."

"We're good ol' boys, Mr. Zanuck," said the sheriff. "'Cept Mrs. Roosevelt, and she's a fine lady. We know how to keep a secret. We're doing okay with Winchell so far, ain't we?"

"Yes. May our luck hold on that. Well. You have to understand that Ben Partridge was a man without morals, ethics, principles. He was a confidence man, a manipulator, a—"

"There seems to be no question of that," said Mrs. Roosevelt.

"He wanted to make a film to be called *Ironweed*. You heard us talking about that."

"The picture for which he'd promised the female lead to Miss Bingham—and then arranged to give it to Merle Oberon," said Mrs. Roosevelt.

"To be truthful," said Zanuck, "poor Colly should have been smart enough to know it was just another one of his tricks, that he'd never have given her an important dramatic role—any more than I would. Colly's cute. She's beautiful. Producers like to show her off, but—"

"But she's no actress."

"Precisely," said Zanuck.

"Anyway..."

"Do you understand how all this works, Mrs. Roosevelt? The studios have the stars under long-term contracts. A star can't make a picture except for the studio that owns his or her contract. The studios trade around some. In other words, if I want to make a picture with Joan Crawford, who belongs to MGM, I might work out a deal to let MGM make a picture with Tyrone Power, who belongs to Twentieth Century-Fox. It would be a trade, you see. Or, I might pay cash to MGM for the right to make one picture with Joan Crawford. She'd still be under contract to MGM but working temporarily for me."

"A form of slavery, so to speak," said Mrs. Roosevelt.

"Well, some of them call it that," said Zanuck. "But to go on, Ben Partridge had made a deal for Merle Oberon. Actually, he couldn't afford her. I mean, he didn't have the money her studio demanded for her. He was trying to raise it and hoped to raise it here, from Mr. Baruch. In the meantime he was short of cash. But he had an ace in the hole. Joan Crawford."

"How was that to work out?"

"Well... you know about her stag film. It has been understood for years that if the guardians of public morals ever found out about that, she would be finished as a star. She could never make another picture. Her contract would be worthless. Ben Partridge had what we think is the last print. No one knew he had it, but he did; he'd bought it somewhere, probably for a lot of money. He went to Louis B. Mayer and told him he had it. He took a print from one of the frames to prove he did have it. Mayer offered him ten thousand dollars for it. Partridge asked for Joan Crawford—that is, for her contract. They hadn't settled the matter, but it looked as if MGM was going to sell her to him, cheap."

"Despicable," said Mrs. Roosevelt.

Zanuck nodded. "Please believe me when I tell you I was not willing to deal with Partridge along the lines I'm about to describe to you. I found his offer worse than despicable."

"And his offer was . . . ?"

"I want Joan Crawford for a picture I'm trying to put together."

"The African Queen."

"Yes. Partridge knew it. I've already bought an option from MGM, which entitled me to have her star in *The African Queen*. I paid a lot of money just for the option, and I'll have to pay a lot more if the picture is actually made. Partridge knew that. He told me Crawford's contract would shortly belong to him and that he didn't feel bound by my option. He wanted to rewrite the whole deal—sell me Crawford on his terms, to make himself enough to pay for Merle Oberon. If I didn't take his terms, I couldn't have Crawford; and if I tried to force him to honor my option, he'd release her stag film and put an end to her as a star property. Alternatively, he could make Joan take the role of Sissy in *Ironweed*. Anyway, because he had the film, she'd have to do whatever he ordered."

"Blackmail on a very large scale," remarked Wilkes.

"And a typical Ben Partridge deal," said Zanuck. "He had brought the film here to show me. And to show Joan, too. He carried in his trunk a little machine that lets you look at a film by putting your eye to the eyepiece and turning the crank."

"He was going to ask *her* to look at it?" asked Mrs. Roosevelt.

Zanuck sighed and nodded. "To be perfectly frank with you, I was strongly tempted to slug him. I actually thought about knocking him down, going across the hall to his room, and taking the film."

"Did Miss Crawford know what was going on?"

"Oh, sure. Mostly. She knew he had the film. Louis Mayer had told her that. I don't suppose she knew what he was going to propose to me. I told her later."

"You and Miss Crawford seem to be very good friends," said Mrs. Roosevelt.

"We are indeed," he said.

"And you seem to be a very good friend of Miss Bingham's," said Mrs. Roosevelt.

"Well, I . . . Yes, I suppose I am," said Zanuck, alerted and cautious.

"An intimate friend."

"Uh . . . I'm sorry. What does that mean?"

"Inadvertently," said Mrs. Roosevelt, "quite inadvertently, let me assure you, I observed your departure from Miss Bingham's room last night."

Zanuck's expression changed, through a sequence: from grim, half-angry surprise, to embarrassed, smiling acceptance, to frowning concern. "Hollywood is a different world, Mrs. Roosevelt," he said.

"I need hardly be reminded of that," she said. She smiled. "It is a matter of indifference to me, Mr. Zanuck. I really don't care much about how other people conduct their private lives."

"Colly worked for me, Mrs. Roosevelt," said Zanuck. "She was with Warner Brothers when I was executive producer there."

"And all the girls who work for you—" Wilkes began.

"Not all," Zanuck interrupted. He shook his head. "Not all. And . . . is it necessary to embarrass Mrs. Roosevelt?"

"You might be surprised, Mr. Zanuck, to discover how little, actually, I am embarrassed," said she. "However—"

"Perhaps," he interrupted again, "I should tell you the rest of the story. There *is* more. I said it could be ruinous. Joan Crawford is not the only one it could ruin."

"Miss Bingham . . .?"

"Yes. Something personal. It is, in fact, why I was in her room last night."

"I think we better know what you're talkin' about," said the sheriff.

Zanuck sighed loudly. "Colleen Bingham worked for Warner Brothers," he said. "What happened to her is not altogether unlike what happened to Joan Crawford. She is the mother of an illegitimate child. Partridge found out. He threatened to make her indiscretion public, so Warners sold her contract to him—"

"Cheap," said Wilkes.

"Cheap," agreed Zanuck. "He kept her as a piece of property, treated her like a—"

"Slave," said Mrs. Roosevelt.

Zanuck nodded. "Like a slave."

"She hated him, I reckon," said the sheriff.

"I'm sure she did," said Zanuck. "Anyway, when he came to my room Monday night, he also offered to sell me Colly's contract. More than that, really. He offered to sell me Colly."

"Blackmail again?" asked Wilkes.

"He had evidence," said Zanuck. "He had a letter written by her mother, who is keeping the child for her. There was a picture enclosed—prettiest little toddler girl you could ever want to see: Colly's daughter. And, the way we've got this industry organized, if word of that baby got out, Colly'd be crucified. She could never make another picture. That's what the professional guardians of public morals have done to people like her—if you don't mind my saying so."

"So . . .?"

"I took his damn letter and picture," said Zanuck. "I

told him I'd buy her contract for Twentieth. I agreed to pay twenty thousand dollars for it."

"Which you don't have to pay, since he happened to die Monday night," said the sheriff.

"Right," said Zanuck. "That's exactly right. I don't have to pay it. But I didn't have to pay it anyway—and I never intended to. I got his blackmail material away from him, and—"

"Where is it now?" the sheriff asked.

"Her letter and picture? Well . . ." He turned to Mrs. Roosevelt and smiled. "In her room last night, we burned them."

"Mr. Zanuck," said Mrs. Roosevelt. "Are you the father of Miss Bingham's child?"

"I swear I'm not."

"Then who is?" the sheriff asked.

"The letter didn't say," said Zanuck.

"When did you tell Miss Bingham you had her letter and picture?" asked Mrs. Roosevelt.

"The morning after the explosion," said Zanuck. "Tuesday."

"Which means," said Mrs. Roosevelt thoughtfully, "that, if his blackmail constituted a motive for *her* to kill him, that motive continued through the hour of his death."

"Colly?" Zanuck asked. He smiled. "She's a kitten, Mrs. Roosevelt. I'd rather you'd accuse me."

"We are accusing no one as yet, Mr. Zanuck," she said. "A pattern has clearly developed, however. It is a pattern of—shall we say?—disingenuousness. Information is being withheld. I am afraid it is going to be increasingly difficult for the sheriff to extend his complete cooperation —which he certainly has given us so far—if this pattern continues. I suggest you rethink some of what you've told us. I suggest several of you do so."

13

Just after lunch, George came to the first-floor suite, where Mrs. Roosevelt was resting for a few minutes before going out to ride. She had already changed, was wearing her riding clothes, and was waiting for word that her horse was ready. Once again, he refused to sit down, but he said he had something to tell her, something he felt had to be reported even before Baruch returned from fishing with the President.

"Mr. Winchell, he jus' had to go into town this mornin'," he told her. "He come down to breakfast while you and the sheriff was in the library with Mr. Zanuck, and right off he told me he wanted to go into Georgetown. Well, I didn't know what to do. Didn't think Mr. Baruch would want him to go. I was feared Mr. Winchell'd call N'Yawk or send off one of them stories of his, sayin' who knows what. But couldn't hardly tell him he couldn't go. I decided to drive him in myself. That way I could see where he went and what he did."

"Oh, dear," said Mrs. Roosevelt. "What did he do?"

"Well, he didn't call nobody or send off no telegram or nothin' like that. He jus' had me take him to Collier's Hardware. He was in there 'bout five minutes, come out with a big brown sack, said bring him back to Hobcaw.

154

When we get out of the car, Mr. Winchell don't come in the house. He starts off to the woods with his brown sack. I figure I'd better see what he was up to, so I followed him —kind of sneaky-like, so's he didn' see me."

Mrs. Roosevelt was smiling broadly. "Very good," she said. "A Baker Street Irregular."

George grinned and nodded. "Yes, ma'am. He goes in the woods, kind of a long ways from the house, and puts down his sack. What he'd bought was a big can of dry-cleanin' fluid."

"Ah-hah!"

George chuckled and kept grinning. "Well, he takes out this can and a big ball of what we call tomato twine—you know, soft string like you use to tie tomato plants to the stakes. He cuts off a piece of that string 'bout as long as your arm, and he opens the can, and he starts pokin' string down in there. After a while he pulls her out, string all soaked in cleanin' fluid. Then he pours about half that dry-cleanin' fluid out on the ground. He puts one end of the string in the can and stretches the rest out on the ground."

"Then he lit it!" guessed Mrs. Roosevelt excitedly.

George nodded. "And stood *way back*. When that fire in that string gets to that can . . ." George paused to shake his head and laugh. "Well! BANG! She blowed up. Big ball of fire. Blowed that can all to pieces. An' you know what Mr. Winchell say? Out loud, he say, 'Well, I'll be damned!' That's what he say—'Well, I'll be damned!' "

Mrs. Roosevelt joined in his laughter. "Marvelous, George!" she said. "Marvelous."

George nodded. His smile slowly faded then. "Got somethin' else to tell you, though." He reached into the pocket of his black jacket and pulled out a tool. "See that there? One of the boys found that on the lawn behind the house, out there across the driveway. Went to mowin'. Don't mow much this time of year, but grass seemed to need one more go-over, I guess. Stopped on this."

"What is it, George?" she asked, taking the tool from his hand. "I think I know, but—"

"Wire cutters," said George. "Little wire cutters. Somebody could've used *them* in hookin' up a charge of dynamite."

Mrs. Roosevelt frowned over the sharp-nosed little tools. "Rusty," she said. "But not *much* rust."

"One night's rain," said George.

"And they were found . . . ?"

"Could've been throwed out a window," said George.

"Whose?"

"Well, anybody's, almost. Anybody with a room on the back side of the house. That means Miss Crawford, Miss Bingham, Miss Bankhead. And . . . Well, could've been tossed from Mr. Partridge's room. We looked under the windows, but these—if they was tossed—was tossed a long ways, out across the driveway."

"Bogart?" she asked. "Zanuck?"

"Wrong side of the house—unless, of course, he tossed them out of Mr. Partridge's window. Well, wait a minute. They could've been tossed from Mr. Crown's room over in our wing of the house."

"George," said Mrs. Roosevelt solemnly. "I think you should turn these over to Sheriff Thompson yourself. Or let the man who found them do it."

"Well, I—"

"Really, George. You should."

George nodded. "All right, Mrs. Roosevelt. If you say so."

Walter Winchell glanced out the window, seeing Mrs. Roosevelt striding across the lawn toward the stable.

"A unique American," he said dryly. "After God made that woman, he broke the mold."

Bogart smiled faintly and nodded.

Tallulah sipped from the glass of bourbon she had held in her hand so long the ice had melted. "After God made each guest in this house, he broke the mold," she said. "You couldn't find a stranger group of eccentrics. We're all marvelous zanies—including yourself, Winchell."

"I take that as a compliment, Tallulah."

"You would," she muttered into her glass.

Bogart and Tallulah had remained at the lunch table after everyone else left, to smoke and talk. Winchell had gone out with Colleen Bingham but had shortly returned.

Winchell smiled. He stepped to the sideboard to pour himself a splash of rye. As he stood there, he glanced through the door into the living room, where Joan Crawford sat morosely knitting and talking with John Crown.

Winchell sat down with his drink. "Tell me something, Bogie. Just among friends here and strictly not for publication, wasn't there something at one time between you and Colleen Bingham?"

"Gentlemen don't ask questions like that, Winchell," said Tallulah.

"He knows that," sneered Bogart over his Scotch.

Winchell was not fazed. "Colly has quite a history, hasn't she?" he went on. "No one took any particular note when she moved in with Ben Partridge. He wasn't the first producer she'd—"

"Why don't you lay off it, Winchell?" snarled Bogart. "If you want to know something about Colly, ask her."

"Will you answer one question?" asked Winchell.

"No, I will not. To hell with you."

Bogart pushed back his chair, stood, and stalked out of the room.

Winchell remained unperturbed. "I'm trying to figure out the matches here," he said calmly to Tallulah. "It's Zanuck and Crawford, obviously. And then . . . Is Colly sleeping with Bogie, now that Ben's out of the way? Do you know? I mean, not for publication. Just out of curiosity. Bogie and Colly, you think?"

"Really, Winchell!" Tallulah growled.

"He's protective of her. And he's edgy about it, too. I've watched it. And they exchanged meaningful glances. Haven't you noticed? There's some kind of relationship. The story *was* around, some time ago, that they were a pair, in Hollywood. And the word on Colly is that she never sleeps alone. I bet you a dollar she moved from Partridge's bed to Bogie's."

"No, dah-ling," Tallulah murmured in her smokiest

voice. "I myself am sleeping with Bogie. He's a *marvelous* lover."

"Is that true?" asked Winchell.

She shrugged. "What's the difference?"

Mrs. Roosevelt was pleased to be given the same horse she had ridden before, pleased too that the horse seemed to recognize her and turned to nuzzle her shoulder.

"Hello, Mrs. Roosevelt."

She turned and, surprised, saw Colleen Bingham coming from the stable, leading a small gray mare.

"Do you ride?" asked Mrs. Roosevelt. "How very nice. Perhaps you'd like to ride with me."

"It's not a coincidence, I'm afraid," said Colleen. "I heard you say you were going riding, and I asked for a horse, thinking we could ride together. I'd like to talk to you."

"Certainly. I'd be pleased to have company."

The young woman did not have riding clothes—she was wearing a pair of dark blue bell-bottom slacks more suggestive of boating than riding, with a white sweater and a brown jacket—but she swung confidently into the saddle and seized the reins with authority.

"I'm more used to quarter horses," she said, brushing a wisp of wind-blown blonde hair back from her forehead. "I'm a westerner, you know."

"Yes. I do know."

"My father drilled for oil on farms and ranches all over the country. He wouldn't mount a horse if it was the last thing that ever happened; he'd wrestle some old truck or Model T across any kind of countryside: mud, rocks, woods, anything. But the farmers and ranchers thought it was cute to let the little girl ride a horse to carry his mail or lunch out to him; and they put me up on every kind of horse, from the time I was four years old. By the time I was twelve or thirteen, they'd send me ten miles across open country, over every kind of country in every kind of weather. I carried a rifle on my saddle. I was a regular cowboy and never was afraid of any horse. I could ride a zebra, Mrs. Roosevelt."

They rode north from the house, then east, away from the main road out of the estate, onto one of the trails that crossed the abandoned rice fields and woods, toward the inlets and the ocean. It had been Mrs. Roosevelt's thought that she might, perhaps, be able to find a rise from where she could peer out to sea, maybe to spot the President's fishing boat. It was unlikely, but she meant to enjoy the ride anyway.

"We camped out," Colleen told her as they rode. "I think it's so funny that girls and boys today suppose that camping out is wonderful. I've slept in leaky tents weeks at a time, with mosquitoes buzzing around your head all night and slithering sounds on the ground, which might be rattlers or might be gila monsters. I've eaten beans and beef and corn bread, cooked in cast-iron skillets over wood fires, week after week. I've gone two months without a bath—without seeing more hot water than it takes to make a pot of coffee with salt and egg shells in it."

"There is a degree of the romantic in it, you must concede," said Mrs. Roosevelt.

"Romance?" the young woman said. She shook her head firmly. "I've seen my father and his workers walk away hang-dog from too many dry holes—"

"And seen their elation when they hit oil, I should imagine," suggested Mrs. Roosevelt.

"More often dry holes. For every well that produces, somebody puts their life into drilling ten dry holes. People who think the oil business is glamorous don't know about that."

Mrs. Roosevelt glanced with a degree of skepticism at the softly feminine, blue-eyed girl. She was supposed to be a pretty little ornament, without the strength of mind or force of character to be an actress.

"I suspect that people misjudge the motion-picture business in much the same way," said Mrs. Roosevelt.

Colleen glanced at her and for an instant showed her a

bitterly cynical smile. "Yes," she said quietly. "They most certainly do."

"Every life has disappointments," said Mrs. Roosevelt.

"Of course."

Following a track that could not be called a road, they passed across some of the abandoned rice fields, now shallow swampland filled with a variety of lush green water plants. Frogs, turtles, and snakes retreated at the approach of their horses, leaving faint wakes on the surface of the water. Birds rose, wheeled, and settled again. A duckling, seized from beneath, probably by a turtle, disappeared suddenly and without a cry. Mrs. Roosevelt grimaced. She wished she hadn't seen it.

"Mrs. Roosevelt, I noticed that Joan Crawford was not in her room last night. I know where she was. She and Johnny Crown were locked in rooms over in the servants' wing. I—"

"How did you know that?"

"Johnny told me. He and I are quite good friends, you know. He worked for Ben Partridge, and I . . . Well, you know what the relationship was."

"I do, and I believe I know why you entered into it."

"You know?" Colleen asked, frowning deeply. "How could you know?" She paused, then nodded. "Oh. Zanuck told you."

"I was in the hall last night as Mr. Zanuck came out of your room," said Mrs. Roosevelt. "Quite by chance. I had no intention of spying on you. But I saw—"

"Oh! You saw. Then, you saw me . . . ?" Instinctively, the young woman hunched forward and pressed one arm to her bosom. "You must have."

"Yes."

"Oh, Mrs. Roosevelt!"

"You needn't be embarrassed."

Colleen straightened and sat stiffly erect, her face pink. "What I wanted to ask," she said crisply, "is how much evidence there is that Joan Crawford killed Ben Partridge."

"Well, I am not the investigating officer," said Mrs. Roosevelt. "I have looked into the matter and—"

"You know more about the case than anyone."

"Perhaps. Perhaps not. Obviously, I know less than the person who killed Mr. Partridge."

"But was it Joan Crawford? Do you really think it was Joan Crawford? Or Johnny Crown?"

"It could have been anyone in the house," said Mrs. Roosevelt. "Some of the evidence suggests it was Miss Crawford. Some suggests it was Mr. Crown."

"Would they be under arrest if Winchell were not here?"

"Possibly."

"But the evidence is not enough to—"

"I don't know, Miss Bingham. Personally, *I* don't think it's enough to sustain a charge of murder, but the decision is not for me to make."

"Well, I must tell you something."

Mrs. Roosevelt glanced at her. "I cannot promise not to tell the sheriff anything you tell me," she said.

"All right. Use your discretion. You know about the letter Ben used to blackmail me. He had it with him. He waved it in my face on the train on the way down here. I don't know why he was carrying it with him. Or, rather, I didn't know until Darryl Zanuck told me Ben had given it to *him*. Anyway, I saw a chance maybe to get it. I wanted to search his room. I waited until after seven o'clock Monday night, supposing he would have gone down for cocktails. He was a stickler about being on time, so I supposed he went down at seven."

She tugged on her reins to settle her horse, which was shying over something moving in the weeds nearby, then went on. "I expected Johnny would be in Ben's room. Johnny always had to go in after Ben had dressed and gone somewhere—to clean up and arrange everything in the order Ben required. Johnny was there. He was almost finished with what he had to do, and I kissed him and smeared my lipstick so as to have an excuse to stay in the room and repair my makeup in the bathroom. Johnny left. I repaired my lipstick fast, then took a few minutes to search for my letter and picture. I couldn't find them."

"Because Mr. Partridge had taken them with him to show to Mr. Zanuck."

"Yes. But the point is this, Mrs. Roosevelt: that I was in Ben's room after Joan Crawford went downstairs, and she stayed downstairs, as we all saw, until after the bomb went off. If she had planted it, or if Johnny had planted it, then it had to be there while I was searching. And I didn't see it."

"Did you look under the bed?"

Colleen Bingham frowned. "No. I remember thinking I didn't want to get down on my knees in the dress I was wearing. But I ran my foot along under the bed, on both sides, thinking I might find his briefcase under there."

"When you left the room, did you lock the door?"

"No, and I was bothered about that. I couldn't lock it. I didn't have a key. But I knew Johnny Crown would be in trouble with Ben when Ben came back and found his room unlocked. That was something else he could be very unpleasant about."

Mrs. Roosevelt nodded thoughtfully and kept silent. Her thought was that all these people contradicted each other—which, she supposed, could not happen if they were telling the truth. Johnny Crown—she remembered vividly now—had insisted that no one had entered Partridge's room while he was there doing his valet duties. That was curious.

"Is there any possibility at all that Ben really did die from the explosion of a can of dry-cleaning fluid?" asked Colleen Bingham.

"I understand," said Mrs. Roosevelt, "that a can of dry-cleaning fluid really will explode violently if exposed to flame. I have never experienced anything of the kind, but I have been warned all my life not to take chances with the stuff."

"It could have happened, then."

"If he had a large can of dry-cleaning fluid," said Mrs. Roosevelt. "Did he carry anything of the kind?"

"He was a fanatic about spots on his clothes," said Colleen Bingham. "He always had dry-cleaning fluid in his trunk. He had a half-gallon can, I think. At least a quart."

The President couldn't have been happier. He had caught a handsome snapper his first hour out, then had hooked two sea bass. Pa Watson had caught only one mackerel, not three fish for the President's one as he had promised; and Baruch had caught the largest fish so far: a big bass. Satisfied with these catches, the President had consented to the captain's proposal that they put down deep lines and try for shark, something that would fight hard. So far no one had felt a bite from the ocean floor.

They drank beer, ate sandwiches, smoked, and talked —and laughed at two of the Secret Service men who turned green in the rising and falling boat. Baruch was the perfect host. He had a stock of stories—gossip, political tales, risqué jokes, comments. Pa Watson laughed uproariously at everything; and the President clapped his hands and rolled his head back and laughed, too; effortlessly finding joy in a day he had been grimly determined to enjoy—and enjoying it all the more for the ease with which it was fun.

In mid-afternoon, the President sat in the middle fishing chair, heavy pole with oversized reel gripped firmly, trailing a heavy line. He wore a floppy white hat and two sweaters—and a broad, contented smile.

"Bernie," he said to Baruch. "You know, the Missus loves to stick her nose into things like the investigation of this murder, but we can't let her get too deeply involved. I'm not so much afraid of that fellow Winchell, but there are Republican newspapers that'd love to have a story that makes her look foolish."

"I've tried to keep everything circumspect," said Baruch.

"How's it going to turn out?" the President asked.

Baruch pondered for a moment. "You're going back to Washington on Sunday. I'm going back to New York. The Hollywood group is scattering. Virgil Thompson will finish his investigation, and . . . well, I wouldn't be surprised the finding is 'Dead of cause or causes unknown.' "

"When that gets out, there'll be a fuss. Since Babs was here, and I was here, and all those celebrities, the newspapers are going to want to know what happened. Every detail."

"One thing about it is absolutely clear," said Baruch. "Eleanor had absolutely nothing to do with it. It's as if a murder happened in a hotel where she was a guest."

"Who's your money on, Bernie? Who do you think did it?"

Baruch shook his head. "I have to believe it was more likely Zanuck and Crawford than anyone else. But I'm not at all sure we'll ever turn up the evidence to prove it."

"The cleaning fluid story—"

"No chance. The second floor was filled with the stench of a dynamite or nitroglycerine explosion. I'm not an expert, but those who've smelled the fumes off the explosion of nitroglycerine tell me it's an odor you'll never forget or mistake. The sheriff says it smelled like nitro. Wilkes says it smelled like nitro. And what's more important, my butler, George, who watched them do some of the blasting on the road last summer, says it smelled like what he smelled after dynamite went off. And, there's a stick of dynamite missing."

"Yes, I know," said the President. "From the shed where Zanuck and Crawford went." He shook his head. "But that doesn't make a bit of sense, Bernie. If they came here planning to kill Partridge, why on earth would they do it with a stick of dynamite they just *happened* to find in a toolshed on the estate. If they found the dynamite and saw an opportunity in it, still they had no detonator cap. I don't suppose you believe they just happened to be carrying detonator caps and wire in their luggage?"

"No."

"Incidentally, Bernie, where does a person buy explosives and caps and fuse and all that? If you and I wanted to make a bomb this evening, where would we get the fixin's?"

"I can answer that," said Pa Watson. "You buy that kind of stuff in an industrial-supply store. In most any town, you can find a store or warehouse that keeps a case of dynamite and the rest of the necessaries on hand. Dynamite is used for a lot of things, by a lot of different people—road builders to break rock, farmers to blast stumps out of fields . . . It's also used for some illegal fishing, incidentally. You know what I mean? They set off a charge in a stream or pond. The shock stuns or kills all the fish within a hundred yards, and they float up, and the fishermen net them."

"Don't you have to have a license or permit of some kind to buy explosives?" the President asked.

"You do in some states, I suppose," said Pa Watson. "I'll bet in South Carolina you can walk into any store and buy what you want, if you've got the cash."

"And carry it here in your luggage," said the President, shaking his head again. "That's hard to believe, Pa."

"There's another possibility," said Pa Watson. "If you know how to do it, you can mix nitroglycerine yourself—from ingredients you can pick up in a drugstore. It's extremely dangerous, but if you know what you're doing . . ."

"There's the key to everything," said the President. "Whoever killed Partridge had to know a good deal about explosives. Suppose I send a discreet inquiry up to John Edgar Hoover, tell him to get me a quick rundown on the backgrounds of each of these people. Maybe Zanuck worked on a road-building crew one summer when he was a boy. Or maybe Bogart did. That'd suggest something, wouldn't it?"

14

Beaming, exuberant, the President sat in a chair brought from the house to the lawn and posed with his shark for Baruch's camera. Just as their boat had turned into the entrance to Winyah Bay, when he had been about to begin reeling in his line, he had felt the shock of a tremendous strike on his bait. Half an hour later, weary in arms and shoulders, he had fought the eight-foot white tip to exhaustion and hauled it close enough to the boat to be gaffed by the captain and Pa Watson. It hung now on a pole between the shoulders of the captain and Baruch's gardener. The President, with his tackle in hand, cigarette holder atilt in one side of his broad, toothy grin, hammed for the camera.

Walter Winchell had come out, too, with a camera of his own; and he stood down the lawn, joining in the laughter, and taking pictures.

From a window in Bogart's bedroom, Bogart and Colleen Bingham watched the scene below.

Bogart took the cigarette from between his lips. "Thinking about that man retiring in 1941 just scares the hell out of me," he said.

"Well, I suppose there'll be someone else. After all, no man's irreplaceable."

"No, no," said Bogart. "What scares me is that he might

166

decide to go into pictures. He'd be the biggest star in Hollywood. What an actor!"

Colleen stood beside Bogart. His arm was around her waist. She chuckled at his little joke, then turned serious. "Understand, I'd like to have him for President of the United States for another term," she said. "It's hard to think of another man in his chair."

"Well . . ." He shrugged. "We can't have him after January 20, 1941. The Constitution doesn't say he can't, but no President ever ran for a third term. Anyway, he wants to retire, wants to go home. He's fifty-five years old, after all."

She turned away from the window, walked to Bogart's bed, and sat down. "Oh, God, Bogie." She sighed.

"Hey!" He moved to her, put his hands on her shoulders, squeezed. "Take it easy, kid. Nothing bad's gonna happen."

"How can you think so?" she asked.

"What they haven't figured out yet, they're not gonna figure out," he said.

"We're lucky it happened here," she said. "Big-town cops . . ."

Bogart shook his head firmly. "New York's finest would be doing no better," he said, talking with the stiff, drawnback lips that identified him to every American moviegoer. "Sheriff Thompson knows perfectly well that one of us did Ben in, as the New York cops would know if the case was theirs. What he doesn't know is which one of us planted the bomb—which they wouldn't know either."

"They hang people in South Carolina, I think," she said dully. "Horrible . . . Terrifying."

"Forget that," he said firmly. He bent down over her and kissed her on the mouth.

"There's something I have to tell you," she whispered, looking up into his face.

"Colly, you don't have to tell me anything."

"Yes, I do. You misunderstood something. You've got a wrong idea. Bogie . . . you are not my little girl's father."

"Huh?"

"I never told you that you were. If you think about it, you know I didn't. You jumped to that conclusion. I should have told you right then that you weren't but—unless I judged you awfully bad, honey—you even seemed to be glad. I should have told you right then."

"Colly!"

"I needed help and sympathy and friendship, and . . . I lied to you, Bogie. I didn't tell you a lie outright, but I should have explained as soon as I realized you thought she was yours. It was a lie not to explain to you immediately. I'm sorry. I'm really sorry. But I would have told you two years ago, if . . ."

Bogart turned and walked to the window, where he looked down again on the President being photographed with his shark. "It's okay, kiddo," he said. "I'm not cut out to be a daddy anyway."

"I think you'd make a fine daddy," she said quietly. "I can't tell you I wish you were the daddy, because the daddy is the man I really love, Bogie."

"Who's that?"

"Please don't ask."

He turned from the window and took her gently in his arms. "Look, Colly," he said. "I *am* sorry I'm not the baby's father. I really am. But that I'm not doesn't make any difference. I mean . . . Well, you know what I mean."

"All's well that ends well," she said. "Darryl got the letter and the picture. We burned them, like I told you."

"DZ's a good man," said Bogart. "We can trust him."

"It wasn't easy to burn my baby's picture," she said sadly.

"It was smart," said Bogart. "So far Sheriff Thompson seems to be ignorant of the whole idea of taking finger-prints. But if he had that picture and letter and took prints of them . . . Well. It was smart to burn them."

"Think of the lives that are better because Ben Partridge is dead," she whispered.

"Oh, I have been thinking of that, Colly," said Bogart. "You can bet I've thought about that a lot."

* * *

"I'm grateful to you all," said John Crown. "I'm particularly grateful to you, Mr. President—and conscious of an awful intrusion, coming in here and bothering you with something you shouldn't have to worry about."

"Have a chair, Brother Crown," said the President. "Have a chair and a sip of the nectar of the gods."

They were in the President's big bedroom, in the first-floor suite—the President and Mrs. Roosevelt, Baruch, Pa Watson, and Crown. The President, Baruch, and Pa Watson were still dressed in their fishing clothes, Mrs. Roosevelt in her riding clothes; and the President had called for the gin, vermouth, and ice to be brought to the suite. This evening, he said, he would join the Hollywood crowd for dinner; but at the end of a long and pleasant but tiring day he wanted to relax for a couple of hours before facing any element of the public. Crown did not know this but had some sense of it, which made him even more than usually deferential.

"I wouldn't have asked to come in here," said Crown, "except that I think I've chanced on something that could be vital in the investigation of the death of Mr. Partridge."

"Well, of course we're interested in that," said the President. "But did you see our fish? Tonight's dinner. Fresh-caught fish from the Atlantic. Of course I'm proud of that shark, but I guess there's no way to eat any of it."

"Actually, there is, Frank," said Baruch. "The Japanese eat shark meat, gladly."

"Do they? Well, I don't know, Bernie. I understand they eat snakes, too."

"I've tried their shark meat," said Baruch. "They eat it raw, I might tell you."

"Oh, Bernie, *really!*" exclaimed Mrs. Roosevelt.

"It's quite good, to tell you the truth," said Baruch. "They call it *sushi*. Boneless chunks of the meat of various fish, including shark. It's served with rice and sauces. I'm afraid no one in my kitchen here would know how to do it, or I'd offer you a sample before dinner."

"I think I'll pass that one up, old boy," said the President.

"But Mr. Crown," said Mrs. Roosevelt, "tell us what you've found."

Crown nodded. "Until now," he said, "everything I've said has depended on my word. This doesn't."

"We've never been unwilling to take your word," said Mrs. Roosevelt. "Unfortunately, Mr. Crown, you've told us a thing or two that clearly are not the truth." She shrugged. "On the other hand, so has everyone else, so you're in as good standing as anyone, I suppose."

"Well, this is physical evidence," said Crown. "It depends a little on your remembering something: you and Mr. Baruch."

"Remembering what?" Baruch asked.

"All right," said Crown crisply. "Monday afternoon. There were three of you in the gun room—you, Mrs. Roosevelt; you, Mr. Baruch; and Bogart. Mr. Partridge came down from upstairs, and you talked with him at the bottom of the stairs. I was on the stairs above. Do you remember? It was when Mr. Partridge called me a servant and said I had no right to ask to meet Mrs. Roosevelt. Do you remember?"

"Of course," murmured Mrs. Roosevelt.

"All right. Now try to remember something more," said Crown with solemn intensity. "Bogart took out a cigarette and his lighter. His lighter wouldn't work, and Mr. Partridge lit his cigarette for him. Do you remember that?"

"Well, I . . . Vaguely, I guess I do recall something of the sort," said Mrs. Roosevelt.

"I recall," said Baruch. "And what's the significance?"

"Mr. Partridge lit Bogart's cigarette with a rather handsome gold lighter. It's really a very nice thing and must have been expensive," said Crown. "I hope you can remember that. That lighter. That gold lighter. It's important."

Baruch nodded. "All right. I did notice it. Go on."

"Mr. Partridge was very particular about his things. As his valet, I had to wipe fingerprints and smudges off that lighter. He carried it most of the time. But he did not carry it in his evening clothes, in his tuxedo or tailcoat pockets. It's a little bulky and made a bulge. He didn't carry cigarettes or cigars in the evening, for the same reason. In fact, he smoked very little; but he did carry that lighter in the daytime, more I think to show it off than to use it."

"Go on, go on," said Baruch impatiently.

"As I've told you, I was in his room after seven o'clock Monday evening—doing what he required me to do: tidying up his room, putting everything in its place. The lighter was in the pocket of the suit he'd been wearing during the afternoon, and when I hung up the suit I put the lighter on the dresser. It was there. I swear it was," said Crown vehemently.

"Well, you needn't swear, old man, unless this lighter has some significance," said the President.

Crown nodded. "It has. Watch Bogart this evening. Watch when he lights a cigarette. He has it! He has that lighter!"

"Oh, Mr. Crown, how do you know?" asked Mrs. Roosevelt.

"I stopped by his room a little while ago. I was looking for Miss Bingham. I knocked on her door. She wasn't in her room. I tried Bogart's room then. They are old friends, you know. She was there. They were sitting in his room, talking. As a matter of fact they were watching the picture-taking, of the shark, from his window. They were cordial. Bogart invited me in, offered me a drink. Shortly he lit a cigarette. It was with Mr. Partridge's lighter! He was completely casual about it. Didn't seem to care if I saw it or not. But it is the same lighter. I am absolutely sure of it."

"Is it engraved with Partridge's initials or something?" asked Baruch. "I mean, for you to be so sure—"

"When you see it—as you may do tonight—look at it," said Crown. "No, it has no initials on it. But you'll agree it's most unusual. It would be an amazing coincidence if Bogart just happened to have one like it."

"Well, we can check the room Partridge had," said Baruch. "His things are still there. Except for what was destroyed in the blast, everything's still there, waiting for the investigation to be finished so we can ship it all to his partner in California."

"Now, what you're saying," suggested the President, "is that Bogart was in Partridge's room after you left it and before Partridge returned and was killed."

"The lighter was on the dresser when I left the room," said Crown positively. "Bogart was not in the room after the explosion, was he? What other explanation is there but that he was in the room between the time I left and the time Mr. Partridge went up and died in the explosion?"

"I am very much afraid, Mr. Crown, there is another possibility," said Mrs. Roosevelt. "Why is it not possible that Miss Bingham took the lighter and gave it to Mr. Bogart, who you say is her friend?"

"Colleen . . . ?" asked Crown.

"I said before that you have not been entirely truthful," said Mrs. Roosevelt. "You have insisted that no one came to Mr. Partridge's room while you were tidying up. Miss Bingham herself acknowledged to me this afternoon that she came to the room while you were there and indeed remained there after you left."

Crown stared open-mouthed at Mrs. Roosevelt, then glanced at Baruch and the President. "She . . . she said that?"

Mrs. Roosevelt nodded. "Yes. Yes, indeed. And she told me she was there looking for something. What was that, Mr. Crown? What was she looking for?"

"If you know"—he sighed—"why do you need to hear it from me?"

"Your credibility will be much improved if you tell us the truth," said Mrs. Roosevelt.

"All right. She was looking for a certain letter and a picture. I had searched for them earlier and couldn't find them. She came to look for herself, and when I left the room she was still there, looking."

"What letter?" asked the President. "What picture?"

"It was something Mr. Partridge was using to blackmail her," said Crown. He glanced from the President to Mrs. Roosevelt, then to Baruch and Pa Watson. "I need hardly tell you, his business career might well be said to have been built on blackmail, extortion, and maybe worse. If you don't mind, sir—and with all due deference—I'd rather not say what was in the letter and picture."

"The fewer people who know, the better," said the President.

"Yes. I'm sorry. It's not that I don't trust anyone here, but—"

"You insisted you locked the door when you left the room," said Mrs. Roosevelt.

"Well, of course I didn't really," said Crown. "Colleen didn't know the room keys were interchangeable. She didn't know she could have locked the door with her own key."

"You lied," said Mrs. Roosevelt. "On those two points —in saying no one came to the room while you were there and in saying you locked the door when you left. Why?"

Crown drew breath and stiffened. "I wanted to protect her," he said. "I thought . . . Don't you see? If it had been known he was blackmailing her and known that she was the last person in the room before he died there, everyone would have jumped to the conclusion that she somehow planted a bomb and killed him."

"You almost took it on yourself," said Baruch.

Crown shrugged. "You couldn't have proved I killed him," he said defiantly. "In the end, you would have had to prove how I got explosives into the house and how I set them off." He shook his head. "Until you get some kind of answer to those two questions, you won't be able to convict anybody of killing Benjamin Partridge."

Baruch stood, shook his head angrily, and strode to the window. "Partridge's room in the hour when the bomb might have been planted has taken on the aspect of Grand Central Station at nine in the morning," he complained. "Everyone in the house seems to have been in there: most of them surreptitiously. Crawford, Bingham. Now Bogart."

"That leaves you, Tallulah, and Zanuck," said the President. "I . . . Oh, good. Thank God. Here's George with the necessary. Come in, George. Come in! You've got the ice? The shaker? Oh, good! Couldn't have come at a better time."

George put down his tray and slipped out of the suite.

"I am terribly sorry to have troubled you with this, Mr.

President," said Crown. "It is supposed to be a relaxing weekend for you, and instead you are confronted with murder."

The President's attention was fixed on the measuring of his gin and vermouth. "As a matter of fact," he said without looking away from his work, "the matter presents something of an intellectual puzzle. Rather intriguing, I'd say—except of course for those who are suspects."

Crown sipped cautiously on one of the President's martinis, pronounced it delicious, pronounced himself honored to have been allowed to share the President's cocktail hour; and, being short of conversation on any subject but the crime that had been committed in the house, he grew more and more distressed and took his leave.

"Ah," said Mrs. Roosevelt when the door closed behind Crown. "To return . . ."

Pa Watson opened the closet and retrieved, first, a somewhat shaky tripod easel, then a blackboard. He mounted the blackboard on the easel, and Mrs. Roosevelt brought out two pieces of chalk and an eraser. All this had been supplied by Baruch, who explained that occasionally he plotted stock-market moves on the blackboard.

Mrs. Roosevelt began to set up a diagram on the blackboard, entering names on a line across the top and times down the left side. As they talked, she began to build a chart, writing and erasing as they put the entries in place.

HOUR	CRAWFORD	BOGART	ZANUCK	BINGHAM	CROWN	PARTRIDGE
6:45	?	?	His rm.	?	?	Z's rm.
6:50	P's rm.	?	" "	?	?	" "
6:55	Her rm.	?	" "	?	?	" "
7:00	W/Baruch	?	" "	?	P's rm.	" "
7:05	" "	?	" "	P's rm.	" "	" "
7:10	" "	W/Baruch	" "	W/Baruch	Dinner	" "
7:15	" "	" "	On way dn.	" "	Dinner	On way dn.
7:20	All but Crown in living room. Crown at dinner in breakfast room.					
8:30	?	Bogart gone for five minutes or so.				

"Where was Brother Crown after he finished his dinner?" the President asked as he took a small sip from his second martini. "And where was he when Bogart was absent from the living room? For that matter, where was he when the bomb went off?"

"We can account for him all that time," said Baruch. "He thought he was going to have to eat in the kitchen, like a servant. That's what Partridge had suggested. In fact, my people served dinner to him and to Wilkes, the Secret Service agent assigned to Mrs. Roosevelt, in the small breakfast room at the back of the house. He came down for dinner about 7:15, and he and Wilkes sat together at dinner until 8:30 or so and then played pinochle at the table until not very long before the blast."

"It would simplify your investigation," said the President, "if Crown had been at large in the house from 8:30 until the blast. He could have returned to Partridge's room any time."

"The question," said Pa Watson, "is how long it would take to set a bomb. Don't exaggerate that. Five minutes is plenty of time—if you have your bomb ready and know what you are doing. Look at your chart. Crawford was in the room alone for maybe five minutes. So was Crown. So was Bingham. So was Bogart."

"And Tallulah," said Mrs. Roosevelt. "She could have been in the house before she came in to dinner."

"So which one was capable of it?" asked Pa Watson. "That's the question. Crown said it. It comes back to that, every time."

"Bogart, Zanuck, Crown," said Baruch darkly.

15

The table was set for eleven—the President at the head, Mrs. Roosevelt to his right, Pat Watson to his left, Baruch at the far end, the other guests along the sides: Joan Crawford, Tallulah Bankhead, Colleen Bingham, Humphrey Bogart, Darryl Zanuck, Walter Winchell, and John Crown. One of the Secret Service agents had been able to lend Crown a dinner jacket for the evening, so everyone at the table was dressed for dinner. The room was lighted by candles. Their points of flame gleamed in reflections of the silver and crystal. A basket of autumn flowers made a centerpiece. On the lawn outside, a small orchestra of black musicians played jazz and blues—muted by the closed windows but still audible and a pleasant background to the dinner conversation.

Champagne was poured.

Baruch rose. "Ladies and gentlemen, I give you the President of the United States!"

They drank.

The President raised his glass. "I give you our gracious host, Mr. Bernard Baruch."

They drank again.

Baruch: "And, ladies and gentlemen, the President's most charming lady, Mrs. Eleanor Roosevelt!"

Mrs. Roosevelt stood. "Ladies and gentlemen," she said. "Let us drink to a most pleasant week—that, in spite of a distressing problem we've had. And allow me to express the gratitude I am sure all of us feel toward Mr. Baruch, who has coped brilliantly with a difficult situation and given us all the benefit of his most generous hospitality."

"Hear, hear," said Bogart as he lifted his glass in salute.

"I should like to offer one more toast," said Baruch. "To the fisherman who caught most of our dinner. Let me assure you it is neither mud turtle nor boiled typewriter keys."

The day's catch was presented on platters, to the polite, quiet applause of the table. It was served with chilled Rhine wine, and condensation soon streamed on the glasses. The fish was white and flaky, surrounded on each plate with boiled potatoes and assorted vegetables in butter.

"I've an odd story," Tallulah said to the President as they were eating. "I wonder if you've heard it."

The President leaned toward her, listening past Pa Watson.

"You know," Tallulah said, "that Mussolini made a big speech in September."

The President nodded. "A triumph, by all accounts. To a crowd supposed to be a million people."

"Well, maybe," said Tallulah. "But outdoors, of course. I've heard that a big thunderstorm broke over the field while he was talking, that he never did get to finish his speech, and—get this—he was abandoned by all the Germans, who ran for shelter and left him standing bedraggled in the rain. The story is that he was soaked through and had to find his way to his car, which took him back to his hotel alone but for a couple of Italian lackeys, and thoroughly wet and cold." She laughed. "Guest of honor!"

"Herr Hitler," said the President, "is not known for polished manners."

"He's an oaf," said Bogart, leaning across the table to join the conversation.

Baruch, at the other end of the table, could not hear and

asked Winchell what the President and Tallulah were talking about.

"Hitler," said Winchell.

"That man is a menace to civilization," said Baruch.

When dessert and coffee were brought, the President inserted a cigarette in his holder. "Uh . . . got a light, Bogie?"

Bogart reached past Mrs. Roosevelt to touch flame to the President's cigarette—with a handsome, somewhat bulky gold lighter.

Crown's eyes flared, and his chin snapped up. Mrs. Roosevelt's glance shifted quickly from lighter to him, with a lift of her head meant to suggest that he calm himself. Baruch involuntarily leaned forward, to stare the length of the table at the gold lighter.

Pa Watson was unsubtle. "Beautiful cigarette lighter you've got there," he said, his eyebrows raised high.

Bogart eyed the lighter appreciatively, then snapped another flame out of it to light his own cigarette. "Gift from my first wife," he said. He returned it casually to his jacket pocket.

Tallulah, wholly innocent of the significance of the lighter, shrugged and remarked. "Weinvogel had one something like that. Personally, I never spend money on fancy lighters. I must have lost a hundred of them, here, there, and everywhere."

Conscious of the awkwardness of the moment, Mrs. Roosevelt smiled at Baruch and said, "Bernie, do tell us the story of your encounter with King Edward VII. I doubt that many of this company have heard it."

Baruch nodded, and told the story with pleasure. "Well," he said, "I was in Paris in 1907 or '08—I forget which—and was invited to a private viewing of an exhibit of paintings, at the Salon. I arrived at ten-thirty or eleven in the morning and was shown in by my host. In those days, we were very conscious of correct dress for every occasion, and I was wearing frock coat, high silk hat, et cetera—rather hoping it was the right thing and self-consciously looking at what other gentlemen were wearing to see how I compared.

"Shortly, there was some bustle, a small group entered, and we recognized King Edward. He was wearing a silk hat, black jacket, gray striped trousers, spats—all very much what I was wearing, as I saw it—and, since he was known for his great emphasis on correct dress, I felt confident then that I had chosen correctly. Anyway, he bustled through, looking at the pictures, obviously not much interested in any of them, while my party stood back and, I am afraid, gaped. Just before he left, he looked around and apparently asked who I was; and to my complete amazement, I was summoned to step forward and be presented to the King.

"He was very gracious. He asked a question or two and made small chat for a minute or so. Then, just when I supposed the interview was over, suddenly he gestured to me to step aside; and very quietly, so that no one else would hear, he leaned close and said to me, 'Your being an American probably accounts for it; but, my dear chap, I had imagined *everyone* knew a *short* jacket is always worn with a silk hat at a private view in the morning.'"

Not everyone knew what was funny, but all laughed. Baruch leaned back, content to have amused the company.

"Royalty has deteriorated so badly," said Tallulah. "I—"

The windows rattled from the shock, and the boom of a big explosion filled the room.

"*Oh, my God!*" shrieked Tallulah. "Not again!"

Baruch had turned pale. He pointed silently, hand and arm trembling, toward the window. "*Outside . . .*" he croaked.

Bogart was on his feet. Followed by Zanuck and then by Winchell, he bolted for the door to the butler's pantry; and, passing through, he raced across the kitchen and out the back door. The three of them ran across the lawn and driveway, into the forbidding darkness of the night.

Soon they stumbled. "Where the hell . . ." Bogart mumbled. The night silence had returned—except for the excited murmur of talk, both from the house and from voices in the darkness, maybe in the woods.

"Gen'mens," said a deep voice. A broad black face appeared in the gleam of light from the windows of the house. "Thish yere way."

The black man beckoned and walked away into the darkness. Bogart, Zanuck, and Winchell followed, stumbling in the dark. Behind them, Secret Service agents milled about with flashlights. "Here!" Bogart yelled, but their concern was with protection of the President, and they did not follow.

"Gen'mens," the black man ahead of them muttered again.

They followed him. It was not easy to keep up. He did not run, but he strode rapidly, sometimes trotting, across muddy ground, ground tangled with vines, then rocky ground, making his way—so far as Bogart could tell— eastward.

"Hey!" Winchell protested breathlessly.

They did not stop. They hurried on. The black man plodded his way ahead, Winchell struggled behind, and Bogart and Zanuck stumbled through the darkness, through patches of briars that clung to their clothes, through water that soaked their shoes.

"I got an idea we're out of our minds," muttered Zanuck.

"I was out of my mind to come here," grunted Bogart.

Suddenly they came on the black man. He had stopped and was standing in their path: a big man, dressed in bib overalls and a white shirt, with a tattered straw hat on his head. He was barely visible in the faint light of the moon, but his broad black face was open and solemn.

"Name's Rafe, gen'mens," he said. "Ah don' know what's you lookin' fo', but Ah'm looking' fo' mah missin' stick o' dynamite. You want know what's happen? Somebudy blowed off mah missin' stick, I bet ya."

"From the toolshed," said Zanuck darkly.

Rafe nodded. He pointed ahead and to their left.

They could hear muted voices, some laughing. They could hear splashing.

"Sumbitch," Rafe muttered angrily. He turned and strode forward.

Winchell, who had caught up during this pause, grabbed at Zanuck's sleeve. "What . . .?"

Zanuck jerked loose. "Keep up or drop out," he growled.

Rafe, ahead of them in the dim moonlight, stalked forward, signaling them to follow quietly. Glad of his slowed pace, they followed in single file. He reached the edge of a steep bank, stopped, and raised a hand behind him: the signal to stop. They edged forward nevertheless and came up beside him. He glanced at them and pointed at the water below.

A dozen young men and women were waist-deep and deeper in the water: all black, all naked, as far as could be seen. The surface of the water—it was a narrow inlet off the bay: green water choked with roots and water vegetation—was strewn with dead and dying fish; and these young people were happily gathering them, scooping them up in their hands and throwing them to companions on the bank: other near-naked young men and women, who caught them and stuffed them into gunny sacks. All these youngsters—aged twelve to eighteen, from the look of them—were smeared with mud and water. They giggled and chattered as they gathered fish and filled their long sacks.

"What I do, gen'mens?" Rafe asked in a low, quiet voice. "What Mistah Baruch want me to do?"

"What *can* you do?" asked Winchell.

"Run down. Raise hell. But not much good," said Rafe. "They kilt the fish already. They gone have a big fish fry tomorrow night. Everybody gonna have a *big* fish fry."

"Leave 'em alone," muttered Bogart.

"That explains where the missing stick of dynamite went," said Zanuck. "So long as that's understood, I don't much care what they do."

Rafe shook his head. "Dangersome," he said sadly. "I'm only glad nobody hurt."

Bogart sighed. "There goes the theory that it takes a blasting engineer to set off a big explosion," he said.

"I kin tell you how they set it off," said Rafe. "Set 'er up on a hunk of wood and push her out in the water, then hit her with a twenty-two rifle bullet. One shot, if you kin shoot straight."

"You've done it yourself, hey, Rafe?" asked Zanuck.

He grinned. "Might have. Before they put me in charge of the dynamite an' I didn't no more dare take any." He looked down at the young people in the water. "I put the rest of it where they can't get it."

"Let's forget it," said Zanuck. "We'll tell Baruch what happened. He's been worried about what happened to the missing stick, and he'll be glad to know it's gone."

Rafe nodded. "G'night then, gen'mens," he said, and he turned and walked away into the darkness of the woods.

Bogart, Zanuck, and Winchell started back to the house.

"Fool's errand," Bogart grumbled as he stumbled over a root and nearly fell. "Run out in the middle of the night . . . Damn!"

"You gentlemen have tipped something, you know," said Winchell. "Talk about a missing stick of dynamite. Talk about what it takes to set off an explosion. I thought Ben Partridge was supposed to have died in the explosion of a can of dry-cleaning fluid."

"We don't *know* how he died," said Zanuck sullenly. "But obviously it wasn't from the missing stick of dynamite, 'cause there it went, to kill fish."

"Did you, or the sheriff, or anybody ever think to try blowing up a can of dry-cleaning fluid, to see if it would really explode with enough force to kill a man?" asked Winchell.

"Hell, no," said Bogart.

"Well, I did," said Winchell. "It could do it. It's entirely possible. If he was holding it in his lap. It could kill him. Did you see the body? Was it burned, or—"

"Winchell, for God's sake!" snapped Bogart.

"I've got one big question," said Winchell. "So far as I'm concerned, it's the key to everything. Where's the shattered can? If it was dry-cleaning fluid, you'd have a blown-apart can. Where is it?"

"You'll have to ask the sheriff," said Bogart.

The boom of the explosion had alerted the sheriff, all the way across Winyah Bay. He had driven to Hobcaw to investigate; and, on his arrival at the house, Baruch asked him in for a sip of whiskey. Mrs. Roosevelt suggested they both join her and the President in the first-floor suite.

"Ah git one of those 'bout oncet a year," the sheriff said, referring to the explosion. "Them boys and girls like to have them a big fish fry. It's an illegal way to fish, but since they only do it oncet in a very long time . . . I guess it's up to you, Mr. Baruch."

"I wish we could discourage it," said Baruch. "Aside from the destruction of so many fish, I'm afraid someone's going to get hurt. But . . ." He shrugged. "I wouldn't want you to break up their fish fry."

"The explosion here Monday night was not, then, of the missing stick of dynamite," said Mrs. Roosevelt. "That brings us back to nitroglycerine and what would seem to be the insuperable difficulty of smuggling it into the house."

"I've believed it was nitro all along," said the sheriff. "We found that heavy bottle glass, you remember—a big chunk of it in the room, plus chunks of it in the corpse. There was no fingerprints on any of that glass, incidentally. None that we could find, anyways."

"Nitroglycerine," mused the President. "Where in the world did it come from?"

"There's places in Georgetown County where you can buy dynamite," said the sheriff, "but no place I know of where you could buy nitro." He shook his head. "So how'd somebody get it here? On the train? Don't seem likely."

"I've come to a conclusion about that," said Mrs. Roosevelt. "Fortunately, in Bernie's library there is a set of *Encyclopedia Britannica*. After reading about how it's done, I've come to the conclusion somebody *mixed* the nitroglycerine, right here on the estate. Outside the house, let us hope."

"That just about eliminates all these Hollywood characters, Babs," said the President. "How could any of them—"

"It is not so difficult as you might think," she said. "It requires nitric acid, sulphuric acid, and glycerine—chemicals that are used for many other purposes and can be bought readily. The mixture is . . . well, it's dangerous. But if you know what you're doing: the proportions and so on—"

"It's not difficult," said Pa Watson. "The stuff is not manufactured and shipped. That would be too dangerous. It's mixed near the place where it's going to be used. That means that a lot of people know how to mix it, not just chemists or engineers."

"According to the encyclopedia," said Mrs. Roosevelt, "the mixing can be extremely hazardous, unless you control the temperature. If you watch the temperature carefully, you can mix it with quite acceptable risk."

"If you know the proportions," said Baruch.

"If you had once seen it done," said Mrs. Roosevelt, "or had heard the process described in detail, I suppose you could do it."

"And you could carry everything you needed quite safely in your luggage," said the President.

Mrs. Roosevelt nodded. "This all means, of course, that the crime was not of the moment, not of passion or an impulse, but was planned. The person who did it came here prepared."

"Which absolves Zanuck and Crawford," said Baruch.

"Not necessarily," said Mrs. Roosevelt. "They are absolved of committing the crime with the missing stick of dynamite. We still don't know why they were in the toolshed."

"I've pondered a lot on another element," said Baruch. "Why, if someone wanted to kill Partridge, did he or she elect to do it *here?* I can only guess it was a question of *time*—that Partridge had just done something or was just about to do something that moved the killer to strike on Monday night."

"Having, however, planned it long enough to have accumulated the chemicals and blasting cap and so on," said the President.

Mrs. Roosevelt stood and went to the blackboard. "Let's analyze motives," she said.

In the next few minutes, as they talked, she wrote:

BOGART	P maybe blocking African movie. Career. Maybe love affair w/ Bingham. Maybe father B's child. (P threatening to reveal?)
ZANUCK	Same, as to movie. Big money loss for Z. Maybe love affair w/ Crawford, maybe w/ Bingham—both being blackmailed by P.
CROWN	Treated badly by P. Built-up resentment. Wants movie career, maybe P blocked it. Love affair w/ Bingham? Possibly.
CRAWFORD	Blackmail by P. Career threatened. Humiliation.
BINGHAM	Blackmail by P. Career threatened. Abused. Disappointed over lost movie part.
BANKHEAD	Long-standing resentment. Nothing new. (Note: Irrational.)

"I'm interested in the cigarette lighter," said the President. "Did either of you recognize it?"

"I can't be sure about that," said Baruch. "I did see Partridge light Bogart's cigarette Monday afternoon. I do recall a gold lighter. I can't say the one Bogart showed at dinner tonight is the same one. It is similar."

"He was completely casual about it," said the President. "Why would he show it that casually—and say it was a gift from his first wife—if he had stolen it from the room of a man who was mysteriously murdered in that room the same day?"

"Ah don't b'lieve I know what y'all are talkin' about," said Sheriff Thompson.

"The only thing to do is search Partridge's room," said Baruch. "I'll explain, Sheriff, on the way up."

The President and Pa Watson were initiating a game of double-handed solitaire as Mrs. Roosevelt left the room with Baruch and the sheriff and accompanied them to the second floor.

The lock had been replaced, and to open the room, Baruch had to fumble in his pocket and come up with a new key, a complex, notched key. The new lock could not be opened with every key in the house.

At the door, Mrs. Roosevelt realized this was the first time she had entered this room. For a moment she hesitated, not sure she wanted to see what she might see. Once inside, however, she found the room had been repainted, recarpeted, and all the damage had been repaired. There was not a sign that a powerful explosion had killed a man in this room only four days ago.

Partridge's personal property had been laid out in order by Baruch's household staff: part of it on the new bed, part on the new dresser. His clothes still hung in the closet. She sensed something cold, intrusive about the quick, systematic examination of all these personal, even intimate, things that Baruch and Sheriff Thompson now impatiently began.

"Cuff links, tie pins . . ." Baruch murmured as he looked over what had been put in the top drawer of the dresser. "No lighter. But, look here. A cigar cutter. A cigar cutter and no lighter. No matches."

"Here's some cig'rettes," said the sheriff, pointing at several packages of Wings laid out on the bed. "Just two cigars, though. Anyhow, the man did smoke."

On the way up, Baruch had sent word to his butler that he wanted him in the restored room, and George now appeared in the door.

"Come in, George," Baruch said. "We're looking for

something and can't find it. Mr. Partridge had a gold cigarette lighter. It seems to be missing. You were in charge of
gathering his things together, getting them ready to pack.
Did you see a gold cigarette lighter?"

"No, suh," said George solemnly. "No lighter of no
kind, I don't believe. I don't recollect seein' no cigarette
lighter."

"What all was taken out of the room?" the sheriff asked.

"Only what was . . ." The butler paused and looked at
Mrs. Roosevelt. "Only what was ruined, what was bloody.
Nothin' like a lighter. Nothin' like that."

"How about what was in his clothes?" Baruch asked. "I
mean the clothes he had on."

"I can answer that," the sheriff said. "They took everything off him over at the funeral parlor, and I've got what
he had, in an envelope in my office. Almost nothin'. No
lighter, fer sure."

"Did you go through the pockets of the clothes in the
closet here?" Baruch asked George. "Through his luggage?"

"Yes, suh. He had some cash money in his pants. I
wrote down how much it was and put it in the drawer
there."

Sheriff Thompson picked up a crumpled paper with big
numerals printed in pencil. "Hundred eighteen dollars and
fifty-seven cents," he said. He picked up the stack of bills
and riffled them. "'Pears right."

Mrs. Roosevelt looked into the drawer. There was an
assortment of tie clasps and cuff links, gold and diamond
studs, a thick black fountain pen, an onyx ring, and . . . She
reached in and picked up a small jeweled object.

"What's that?" Baruch asked.

The object was a decorative buckle, with a clip on the
back to hold it in place on a shoe or on the fabric of a dress
or hat. It was not of gold or silver, only some cheap white
cast metal; and the little jewels that decorated it were rhine-
stones.

"Where did you find this, George?" she asked.

"That . . . Oh, I remember that," said George. "It was on

the floor, there by the door. Seemed like they oughta been two of 'em—you know, a set—but we never did find the other one."

Mrs. Roosevelt nodded. She stared at the buckle for a moment. "Will it be all right with you gentlemen if I take this?" she asked. "I'd like to find its mate."

16

"The President has done us a favor," said Mrs. Roosevelt at breakfast. The guests had been wakened by George and told their presence at breakfast was desired. "He invited Mr. Winchell to go fishing with him this morning; and Mr. Winchell, much honored, went off not much after dawn, to troll a line in the pitching waters of the Atlantic. Mr. Baruch went as well. Sheriff Thompson has joined us for breakfast—a bit cool though it is this morning. And, ladies and gentlemen, I propose to solve the difficult problem of the death of Benjamin Partridge, here and now."

She sat at the head of the table, served coffee from a silver pot by George. The week's guests were present at eight o'clock: none of them very comfortable but dutifully in their places. The sheriff sat at the far end of the table.

"I am," said Mrs. Roosevelt, "perhaps unduly optimistic. I've reached a point, however, where I am satisfied in my own mind that I know who killed Benjamin Partridge; and I should like—as would the sheriff—to settle the matter once and for all."

"We might decide," drawled the sheriff, "that the world's better off with the man dead and decide to do nothin' much at all. 'Cept we gotta do somethin' 'bout that fella Winchell."

189

"I've been wrong," said Mrs. Roosevelt, "in my early suspicions. I reached a firm conclusion rather early. For the wrong reasons. Probably the wrong conclusion, actually. I suggest, though, that all of us have a vital interest in solving this mystery, and I solicit your cooperation in doing so."

"Do you expect someone to confess?" asked Zanuck.

"If anyone wants to," said Mrs. Roosevelt, "we might save some time and some embarrassment for those who did not kill Benjamin Partridge."

"Oh, hell," said Tallulah. "I killed the son of a bitch. I've always wanted to."

"Ain't many people drink bourbon for breakfast," the sheriff said. "Might make 'em say they killed Christ."

Mrs. Roosevelt smiled at Tallulah, who had in fact poured a six-ounce glass of straight bourbon to drink with her coffee and had already nearly finished it.

"I'm glad to be able to say, Tallulah," she said, "that, in my judgment, the Speaker's daughter did not murder Benjamin Partridge."

Tallulah snorted. She had come down to breakfast in her silk pajamas, barefoot, and she smoked as she sipped bourbon. "Hell," she said. "Less honor to me."

The sheriff smiled. "Less is right. I'm ready to hang a medal on the man or woman that did in that arrogant bastard."

Mrs. Roosevelt smiled. "I should not go quite that far."

"I would," said Bogart. He had come down to breakfast in gray flannel slacks and a blue blazer, and he looked like the juvenile ("Tennis, anyone?") lead he had once played on Broadway. He held his hand to his mouth and dragged deeply from a cigarette. "I'd hang the Congressional Medal of Honor on the man who rid the world of Ben Partridge."

"Well, that brings us to you as a suspect, Mr. Bogart," said Mrs. Roosevelt. "There are reasons, you know, to believe you set the bomb that killed Mr. Partridge."

Bogart shrugged. "Aside from the honor I might have wanted, what?" he asked.

"Your cigarette lighter, Mr. Bogart?" said Mrs. Roosevelt. "Will you put it on the table, please?"

Bogart flushed, and he reached into the pocket of his blazer and took out the gold lighter. "All right, there it is," he said. "What significance?"

"It was Partridge's," said the sheriff.

Bogart smiled—a lopsided, ironic smile. "You're right," he said. "Temporarily it was his. But it was first mine, and now it's mine again. What's more, I don't propose to give it up."

"That needs a little explanation," said Zanuck. He had pulled a cigar from the pocket of his tweed jacket; and now it lay on the table by his plate, unlighted. He picked it up and rolled it between his fingers and in his lips, moistening the tip. "If that was Ben's—"

"It was mine," said Bogart firmly, almost angrily. "And is mine. He took it from me on a sucker bet."

"Explain, Mr. Bogart," said Mrs. Roosevelt.

Bogart sighed. He pondered for a moment. "Too much loudmouth, one time," he said. "You ever hear of the game you play with the numbers on dollar bills? It has to do with how many times you'll find the same two successive numbers in the serial numbers of bills. Well, Partridge knew the secret—which is that you'll find them a lot more often than once in a hundred, which is what ordinary math would suggest. I don't know the mathematics, but statistically you'll find the same numbers—like 69, 44, 21, 87, or whatever—a lot more often than once in a hundred. I still don't know why, though I've read the explanation. Partridge and I were at a party one night, and he wanted to play this game. I'd had too many smashes, and I went along with him. I won four or five dollar bills from him, and then he offered to bet my lighter against ten dollars. I took it. I won twenty bucks, I think it was; then he won my lighter, which was worth two or three hundred. Mathematically, he was bound to win it, within a few bets—and he knew it. The damned thing was not just worth the money but had a sentimental value to me. I offered him two hundred instead, and he just laughed and pocketed my lighter. After that, every time I saw him, he shoved it under my nose—*my* goddamn lighter, that my first wife had given me, which meant more to me than the two hundred bucks, and he knew it. He enjoyed rubbing my nose in . . . Well, you know what. Winning it in a dishonest game was one thing, but rubbing my nose in it was another. But that was his way. The son of a bitch."

"The question," said Mrs. Roosevelt, "is how and when you got it back."

Bogart glanced around the table. "I went in his room—and picked it up."

"When?"

"Not a hell of a long time before he was blown up," said Bogart. "Believe me, that's occurred to me, too."

"You entered his room Monday night?" asked Mrs. Roosevelt.

"I went up just before we went to dinner," said Bogart. "I suppose everyone thought I'd stepped out to go to the bathroom."

"But actually, you went to Mr. Partridge's room."

"Right."

"To take the lighter?" the sheriff asked.

Bogart nodded.

"No!" shrieked Colleen Bingham. "No, Bogie. You had a better reason. We have to tell."

"Now we do," said Bogart, shaking his head. "You talk too much, Colly."

Colleen shoved her plate away. "Bogie went to his room for me," she said. She looked around the table. "You all know why. You all know about my baby." She sobbed. "To hell with everybody! I've got a lovely little girl, and I don't give a damn who knows it. I'm not married to her father, and that's that! Ben Partridge . . . He wasn't even *human!* He knew about my baby, and he had a letter that proved she was mine."

"Colleen . . ." said John Crown.

"Bogie . . ." she whispered. "He wasn't my baby's father. He could have been, but he wasn't. He's a wonderful man. I'd have been happy to have a baby of his. But Bogie's not . . ."

"Colly—"

"You're not her father, Bogie," Colleen said firmly. She looked around the table again. "Something I said to Bogie Monday made him think maybe he was. I sort of recognized that was what he thought, and I let it stand that way —because I needed his help. He went into Ben's room to see if he could find the letter my mother sent—that Ben had stolen from the Warner Brothers studio mail—that proved I am the mother of an illegitimate child. By the time he went up to look for it, I already knew he couldn't find it, because I had looked for it and couldn't find it. I—"

"Because he'd given it to me," said Zanuck grimly. He picked up the cigar by his plate and shoved it in his mouth. "I'm sorry, Mrs. Roosevelt, but you're going to have to tolerate a little cigar smoke this morning. Ben had given me the letter, as I've already told you, Mrs. Roosevelt. He thought he was selling it to me—"

"Which is why I couldn't find it," said Bogart. "But I did find my damn lighter. I stuck it in my pocket. I made up my mind to take it out and light the first cigar Partridge showed in my presence—and when he raised hell about it, I intended to bust his nose."

"What a waste of effort," said Tallulah. "Couldn't you have 'busted' something more important?"

Sheriff Thompson grinned across his coffee cup. "Somebody busted something important," he chuckled.

"Is somebody going to hang for the murder?" Joan Crawford asked the sheriff. She had brought her knitting with her and was nervously clicking her needles. "Is good riddance good riddance, or not?"

"Depends, I suppose . . ." said the sheriff.

"That brings us to you, Miss Crawford," said Mrs. Roosevelt. "Which of you wants to tell us—you or Mr. Zanuck—why you went in the toolshed where the dynamite was stored?"

Crawford looked hard at Zanuck. Then she spoke.

"He'd told me he had a print of the film. He didn't have to tell me he knew that. I knew he did. Louie Mayer had told me—"

"Happily, I imagine," said Bogart.

"He'd have liked to kill me," said Crawford. She put her knitting aside. "Christ! Pour me a little of that bourbon, Tallulah. No, he wasn't happy. He told me he was selling my contract to Par-Croft. Ben couldn't wait to rub my nose in that. When we got here, he told me he was buying my contract, cheap, from MGM—and why. He had the film with him, he said. He'd let me see it, just to let me see for sure that—"

Zanuck interrupted. "He was going to present Mr. Baruch with a proposition: Joan Crawford in the role of Wallis Warfield Simpson, Duchess of Windsor. He knew I had an option for Joan's next project, and he told me he'd circulate her stag film and destroy her as a star property if I didn't release her and let her do *his* film. He—"

"He summoned me to his room," said Crawford. "For what he called 'a quickie,' just before we went down to dinner—just to show he had me under control."

"She'd told me," said Zanuck. "Joan wants to do my African film; and as soon as we got here, she told me what Ben Partridge had over her. I mean, she told me all about it even before he did."

"Motive enough to kill him," said the sheriff.

"Three times over," Zanuck agreed.

"Which," said Mrs. Roosevelt, "returns us to the subject of why you and Miss Crawford entered the toolshed where explosives were stored—only hours before Mr. Partridge died in an explosion."

"We—" Crawford began.

Zanuck interrupted. He put aside his cigar and blew smoke through his words. "He had the film with him. It was in his room. We decided it was worth the risk to try to break into his room and take the film. We were out in a boat. Actually, we'd decided we'd take the boat all the way across the bay to Georgetown if necessary, to find the tools we might need to break into his room. We spotted the toolshed from the water. We headed the boat into the shore and climbed the bank. And we found what we thought we might need—a big screwdriver, pliers, a pair of wire cutters. We took that stuff."

"But not a stick of dynamite," the sheriff said.

"No," said Crawford. "But I did take the wooden pliers —what you've called crimpers. I saw them lying in the dirt and picked them up. I thought . . . Well, I've said what I thought. Anyway, it was a mistake. We didn't need the tools. Partridge left the room unlocked. I went there for his 'quickie,' found the film, took it, and left."

"And threw the tools out your window," said Mrs. Roosevelt.

She nodded.

"If all this is the truth, then," said Mrs. Roosevelt, "we pass on to Mr. Crown. You had access to the room, Mr. Crown. You had motive. And you have proved very much a liar in answering questions. What do you say now?"

Crown shrugged. "All right," he said. "From the beginning you've thought I killed him." He sighed. "So, all right. Prove it."

"We can't," said Mrs. Roosevelt. "Because you didn't. At least, I think it's very doubtful that you did."

"So who did, then?" demanded Zanuck.

Mrs. Roosevelt reached into her bag, beside her chair, and took out the rhinestone buckle. "Whoever owns the match to this little buckle," she said. "Unless I'm terribly wrong."

She put the buckle on the white linen tablecloth, in the midst of the dishes.

"We can search," said the sheriff. "Actually, I guess I might as well tell you—while we're sittin' here talkin', two of my deputies is goin' through your rooms. Anybody want to tell us where to look?"

Tallulah leaned over the table and looked at the buckle. "I have a pair like that," she said. "Whenever did I lose one of them?"

"Uh . . . So do I," said Colleen Bingham.

Joan Crawford smiled. "Of course, I have some as well."

"Yes, of course," said Mrs. Roosevelt. "And probably the gentlemen have some, too. None of you want us to know who killed Mr. Partridge. I myself am not sure I want to know. But I do know, I think, and I intend to settle the matter."

"You might leave well enough alone, Mrs. R." said Bogart.

"I might," she said with a faint smile. "But that leaves everyone suspected. Do you want to leave it that way?"

Bogart shrugged. "I'm honored," he said.

"Who killed the bastard, Eleanor?" asked Tallulah. She had risen and was pouring more bourbon into her glass. "Who gets the medal I'm going to have struck?"

Mrs. Roosevelt smiled wryly. "It is difficult to believe so many people can talk of such a matter in such a way," she said. "But all right. Let's see."

"You really know?" Bogart asked.

"I think so," said Mrs. Roosevelt. "Let's look at what we know."

"Let's do," said Tallulah, sitting down and taking another sip from her glass.

Mrs. Roosevelt nodded. "Mr. Partridge," she said, "was killed by the explosion of a small quantity of nitroglycerine. I don't know how much. Maybe a pint. You couldn't transport it into Hobcaw Barony—not, anyway, without a high degree of risk, an unacceptable risk. Conclusion: that the nitroglycerine was mixed here, on the estate, probably somewhere in the woods."

The people around the table had turned somber, intent. Of them all, only Tallulah looked unconcerned. She sipped bourbon and seemed likely to lose all contact with reality.

"The nitroglycerine," Mrs. Roosevelt went on, "was planted under the bed, almost certainly. Installing the bomb, so it would be detonated when someone sat down on the bed, took no more than five minutes, we may suppose. During the half-hour, six forty-five to seven-fifteen, Mr. Crown, Miss Crawford, and Miss Bingham were in

Mr. Partridge's room. An hour later, Mr. Bogart was there."

"How do you know Tallulah wasn't there?" Zanuck asked. "We might as well complete the set. Maybe everybody was in his room but me."

"Miss Bankhead could have been there," said Mrs. Roosevelt. "But she wasn't. As you yourself told us, Mr. Zanuck, Mr. Partridge locked his door before he came down to dinner, and Miss Bankhead did not have a key until after dinner. What is more, she did not know that any of the keys to the rooms on the second-floor hall will open any of the rooms."

"No," murmured Tallulah. "God, I wish I'd known!"

"So the nitroglycerine could have been planted by Miss Crawford, when she went in to get the film, or by Mr. Crown when he went in to tidy the room, or by Miss Bingham when she went in to search for her letter and picture."

"Colleen . . .?" whispered Crown.

"She knows I was in the room after you were, Johnny."

"You lied about that, Mr. Crown," said Mrs. Roosevelt. "I suspect your motives will stand examination. But . . . to continue. Whoever installed the bomb under the bed had to get down on his or her hands and knees and—"

"And lost the rhinestone buckle!" exclaimed Zanuck. "Crawling around, she knocked it off."

"Yes," said Mrs. Roosevelt. "Which of course means it was not you, Mr. Zanuck, or you, Mr. Bogart, or you, Mr. Crown."

"Then Colly or me . . ." whispered Crawford.

Mrs. Roosevelt nodded. "And whichever of you lost the rhinestone buckle has long since disposed of its mate," she said. She looked at the sheriff and shrugged. "I am sure your deputies' search will prove fruitless. Whichever one of them lost the buckle is surely intelligent enough to dispose of the other one."

"Which puts us back in the dark," said Zanuck. "Completely in the dark."

"No," said Mrs. Roosevelt. "There is other evidence that, I am afraid, points to just one person here."

"Who?" Crawford asked fearfully. "What evidence?"

Mrs. Roosevelt sighed. "Think about the nitroglycerine," she said. "Whoever mixed the nitroglycerine had to know precisely how to do it. It is a touchy procedure that will kill you if you don't know exactly what you are doing and don't do it exactly right. But it was done. Who would know how to mix nitroglycerine?"

Colleen sighed heavily and closed her eyes. "Someone who grew up in the oil fields," she said.

"Yes," said Mrs. Roosevelt. "They use it to shoot wells. They set off gallons of it in the bottoms of new oil wells, to crack the oil-bearing rock and increase production."

"That's right," said Colleen, her voice trembling. "My daddy mixed it. He used to talk about it all the time, about how dangerous it was and how careful he had to be. From the time I was ten years old, I knew what nitroglycerine was made of and how you made it."

"Yes," said Mrs. Roosevelt. "And even if you do it correctly, and don't blow yourself up, you can still be burned during the mixing. Isn't that right?"

"Burned? How?" asked Zanuck.

"The first step in making nitroglycerine," Mrs. Roosevelt explained, "is to mix the two acids, nitric and sulphuric. Even if you know the right proportions and work very carefully, the acids boil. If you pour them together just a little too fast, the acids will boil violently and—"

"And burn your hand!" cried Colleen. "Nitric acid and sulphuric acid don't like each other and boil when you mix them—and the mixture can boil out and burn your hand. It *hurts*, too, I might tell you." She lowered her head and wept. "It hurts . . ."

Mrs. Roosevelt nodded. "You burned your hand Monday afternoon when you were mixing the nitroglycerine. Monday evening you wore gloves. Tuesday morning you pretended to have burned your hand with a curling iron and asked for bandages. Am I wrong?"

Colleen shook her head. "No..." she murmured. "You're not wrong."

"Colleen!" sobbed Crown. "Oh, God, no! Not you!"

Bogart pushed back his chair, and he stood. "Shut up, Colly," he snapped. "Don't say another word. Not until we have a lawyer for you."

17

Sheriff Virgil Thompson removed his little round gold-rimmed spectacles, breathed on each lens in turn, and began to polish them with a rumpled handkerchief. "Ah don' like the way this is turnin' out," he said.

Colleen Bingham, accompanied by a solicitous Johnny Crown, had just gone upstairs to get her coat.

"I wish . . ." said Mrs. Roosevelt, and she stopped, her voice caught. "I wish you didn't have to take that poor child to jail."

The sheriff shook his head. "Ah don't like it at all," he said.

"Why couldn't we just forget it?" asked Tallulah, tossing back the last of the bourbon in her glass. She got up to pour some more. "Why do we have to let the ghost of Weinvogel reach out from the grave to make another tragedy?"

"Just forgettin' it be hard to do," the sheriff said, frowning. "I don't suppose it's . . . out of the question, though."

"Too many people know," said Bogart.

"Cahn't we trust each other?" Tallulah asked.

"We all have a lot to lose in any *part* of it being made

public," said Joan Crawford. "So far as I'm concerned, the secret is safe with me."

"It's safe with all of us here," said Zanuck. "The problem is . . . Winchell."

"I wonder," the sheriff said speculatively, "if she took good care of what y'd call the physical evidence, meanin' the bottles of acid and all like that."

"You won't find any of that stuff," said Bogart. "If you want to arrest me for destroying evidence, go ahead; but I threw everything in the bay Tuesday afternoon. Of course, I've known since then that Colly was the one who killed Partridge."

"I think you might give us a bit of explanation, Mr. Bogart," said Mrs. Roosevelt, her eyebrows high. "That is really a surprising revelation."

"I went out and shot clay pigeons a while," said Bogart. "I came back in and picked up a drink, and I went out for a walk. I was in the woods, along the shore north of the house, and I thought I heard somebody. I called, but nobody answered. So I walked into a tangle of pines, a little pine grove you might call it, and there I . . . Well, I . . ."

"Go on."

"Well, I saw a little suitcase lying on the ground, sort of hidden but not very well hidden," Bogart went on. "I recognized it. It was Colly's. You see . . . Well, Colly and I use to, uh, spend a night together now and then, in hotels; and she'd bring her things in this little case. I opened it, and there was what you just mentioned, Sheriff—her acids and glycerine and all the stuff she'd used to mix the nitro. I got rid of it all. I poured the chemicals in the bay and sank the bottles. I threw everything else in the water."

"Did she know you did this?" asked Mrs. Roosevelt.

"Yes. I ran into her a few minutes later. She was the one I'd heard. She'd come out there to do what I just did. I didn't have a chance to tell her then, because Crown came along, then you, Tallulah; but I told her later. I told her I'd keep her secret."

"That makes you an accessory to the crime," said Mrs. Roosevelt.

"I suppose it does," said Bogart.

"But at that time you thought you were the father of her child, I believe," said Mrs. Roosevelt.

"Yes. When we first got here, Monday morning, Colly came to my room crying and told me what Partridge had done to her—I mean about the part in *Ironweed*. She was so upset I thought she was capable of suicide. Anyway, during the conversation she told me she'd had a baby two years ago and that Partridge was blackmailing her. I don't know . . . I took it wrong. I thought she was telling me I was the father. It was possible, after all."

"Has she told you who *is* the father?" asked Zanuck.

"No," said Bogart. "But I'm gonna guess it's Johnny Crown."

"Do you suppose he helped her kill Partridge?" the sheriff asked. "Maybe she made the bomb and he planted it."

Bogart shrugged. "You had better ask." He nodded toward the door. "Here comes Crown. Ask him."

Crown walked in, his face long and flushed. "She'll be down in a minute," he said hoarsely. "She's on her bed, crying. She's afraid. Afraid to be locked up in jail."

"We been thinkin' on that," the sheriff said. "Maybe we can find some way she won't have to."

"Can I go back up and tell her that's what you're thinking?"

"Yes, and tell her to come down. We gotta talk more."

Crown hurried out. While he was gone, the company sat around the table, smoking glumly, staring at the dishes. Zanuck pulled on his cigar and made a point of blowing his smoke away from Mrs. Roosevelt. The empty chair where Colleen had sat faced them as if in silent reproach. Bogart poured himself half a tumbler of Scotch.

Crown ran down the stairs. They could hear him coming. "Hey!" he yelled. "She's gone!"

"Christ!" barked Bogart. "She could—"

"She'll kill herself!" Crown screamed. "Help me find her!"

"You bet!" the sheriff cried. "Deputies!" He trotted for the center hall of the house. "Where's mah goddamn deputies?"

"She can't have gotten far, Johnny," Zanuck muttered grimly. "We'll . . . Where do we start?"

"You out the back. Me out the front," said Bogart.

Tallulah had already stalked out, heading on her own quest, bourbon in hand.

Joan Crawford and Mrs. Roosevelt stayed for the moment at the table, stunned and unsure of what they could do. "It is for us, I suppose, to introduce an element of thought into the situation," said Crawford.

Mrs. Roosevelt nodded. *"Where,* do you suppose, she might have gone?"

Bogart had run down the lawn in front of the house, into the woods that fronted Winyah Bay on the lower slopes. He reached the edge of the water just as the big skiff, powered by a roaring outboard, wallowed past in the heaving water.

"Colly!" he yelled. "Colly!"

She glanced at him and shook her head, and abruptly she shoved the outboard engine sharp to the right, turning the bow of the skiff to the left, away from the shore and out into the windblown water. In a moment he was looking only at her wake, as the boat rose over one wave, slid down its face, and plunged into another. She was heading for the south shore, two miles away.

Crown caught up with him.

"She ain't trying to kill herself," Bogart said glumly. "She's trying to escape."

Crown stared helplessly after the boat, as the distance between it and the Hobcaw shore lengthened. He wept. "Oh, God!" he cried. "She—"

"C'mon, kid," Bogart urged, grabbing him by the arm

and leading him back toward the house. "We can't do a bit of good standing here."

"She kin git drownded," said one of the deputies solemnly. They stood under the columns at the front of the house. "Them waters kin git treacherous this time of year."

Mrs. Roosevelt had commandeered the Secret Service radiotelephone equipment, ordering the transmission of a message to the Coast Guard and to the South Carolina state police to send all possible assistance to a young woman who was trying to cross Winyah Bay in a small boat in the face of a freshening wind and growing waves.

All of them felt helpless, frustrated. The sheriff and his deputies, Mrs. Roosevelt and the rest of the guests who had been together at breakfast, all stood staring across the whitecapped waters. The boat was out of sight now, though they knew the outboard motor had not yet powered it to the far shore.

"Git in the car and git over theah," the sheriff said to his two deputies. "If she don't drownd, she come ashore. Whut I'd give for a airplane right now!"

"There is nothing for *us* to do but wait," said Mrs. Roosevelt. "I wish there were . . ."

They went back in the house. Tallulah headed immediately for the bourbon, grabbing it impatiently from the sideboard and pouring. Bogart took more Scotch. Zanuck took Scotch. They sat down in the living room.

Crown, sitting with his head down, his hands clasped between his knees, nodded despondently. "She only killed him because I didn't have the courage. If I'd done it, she wouldn't have had to."

Sheriff Thompson sat not much differently—except that his generous belly overwhelmed his belt and lay almost on his lap. He began to roll a cigarette. "Why don't you tell us why you say that, son?" he said. "We was tryin' to find cause to just *overlook* the death of Benjamin Partridge."

Crown nodded and sighed. "I don't know how much you know, how much you don't know," he said quietly. "I was a bit player at RKO. Colleen was a star at Warner

Brothers. We fell in love. Two years ago." He stopped and looked at Bogart. "She stopped seeing you when she—"

"I get ya," said Bogart.

"Then she got pregnant," said Crown. "At first we thought that was wonderful. Then we remembered that her contract said she wouldn't get married. You know. She was supposed to be the virginal nude, Colleen Bingham." He sighed again. "So she decided to visit her parents and have the baby. After that . . . Well, we weren't sure what we would do. Anyway, she went to Oklahoma and had the baby, and her parents kept it for her."

"Then someone made the mistake of writing a letter," said Mrs. Roosevelt.

"Yes," said Crown. "Her mother wrote Colleen a letter, enclosing a picture of the baby. It was an innocent enough letter, saying the baby is fine and healthy and here is a snapshot you should show to Johnny Crown. But Partridge—"

"The son of a bitch went through the studio mail," Zanuck interrupted. "I was executive producer at Warners. I caught him at it and wanted to fire him, but—"

"She had an illegitimate child," Crown continued. "He faced the Warners with the evidence of it, and they sold him her contract for a pittance. He didn't come to you, Mr. Zanuck. He knew you'd break his nose for a thing like that."

"And we're talkin' 'bout puttin' this little girl in jail for killin' him," said the sheriff, lighting his handmade cigarette.

"This is when I first met him," said Crown. "Colleen was his *property*. He made that clear. He had her contract, and if she didn't do exactly what he told her, he would put an end to her career. That's what he told her. As for me, I was small potatoes compared to her. But I was in the same boat. I was the father of an illegitimate child, which meant that I could never have a career in pictures if it was found out."

"And they call themselves 'Legion of *Decency*,'" sneered Tallulah.

"The 'morals' clause," said Crown. "Every contract has one. Anyway, he told us he'd make us both big stars. But we worked for him. He put me to work as a personal servant, and he made Colleen his mistress. We hated it, but what could we do? It was that way until the night he died."

"He went too far, apparently," said Joan Crawford. "Drove her over the brink."

"Oh, he talked about telling the world our daughter's mother was a tramp," said Crown bitterly. "He asked her how it would sell in Wewoka, Oklahoma, when they found out the little girl in the Bingham household was Colleen's bastard."

"Partridge was the bastard," grunted Bogart.

"Her morals were . . . Well, they were as good as anyone's in this business," said Crown. "I know about you, Mr. Bogart. And, in fact, I know about you, Mr. Zanuck. She even told me what she did when you burned the letter and picture for her. That seems natural to Colleen. She . . . Well . . . Doing *that* just seems to her like a friendly, loving thing to do."

"As good as using it to promote a contract," observed Crawford.

"What were you doing in the woods the other night, Johnny?" Tallulah asked. "When you made me warm?"

"I'd followed Colleen," he said. "I suspected . . . I *had* to suspect. When she went to the woods that afternoon, I had to know if she was going to destroy or hide some kind of evidence." He shrugged. "The woods were full of us, it seemed. You, Miss Bankhead. Mr. Bogart. I went back and searched the area where I knew she had been. I didn't find anything, so I waited."

"And found *me*—inspired by the same curiosity!" Tallulah laughed. "You are a warm person, Johnny!"

"Yes. And you will understand now, Mrs. Roosevelt, why I lied about who had been in Mr. Partridge's room and who had not."

Mrs. Roosevelt nodded. "You make a poor conspirator, Mr. Crown," she said. "Your lies were transparent. Besides that, although you called everyone else 'Mr. So-and-so' and 'Miss So-and-so,' in moments of excitement you referred to Miss Bingham as 'Colleen.' I guessed your relationship was more than casual."

"He was cruel to us both, Mrs. Roosevelt," said Crown soberly. "I wouldn't want to describe the humiliations to which he subjected us. I'm glad he's dead—except for the danger now to Colleen."

"I, for one, am only sorry he died so quickly," said Tallulah. "I should have liked to sit and sip bourbon and watch him flayed alive."

"I am sorry he died here," said Mrs. Roosevelt. "And this week."

"An' so'm I," said the sheriff. "Though maybe—" He shrugged. "Maybe it'll all work out for the best."

"If she doesn't drown," said Mrs. Roosevelt glumly.

She did not drown. The Secret Service radiotelephone —through a roundabout circuit—reported an hour later that her skiff, though filling with water and on the verge of sinking, had reached the entrance to the swampy channel between the bay and the Santee River, where a state police boat had pulled alongside and rescued a frightened young woman. An hour after that—at noon—Colleen Bingham was returned to Hobcaw House, where everyone waited for her.

The deputies—not knowing why they had been ordered to take this young woman into custody but knowing she had run away and that she seemed irrational and capable of running again—had handcuffed her. She was led into the living room, dressed in a damp raincoat, her head covered with a blue and white scarf she had knotted under her chin, her legs and feet smeared with mud, and her eyes red and wet with tears.

Crown leaped up and threw his arms around her. "Colleen! Colleen!"

"It'd been better for you, young lady, if you'd put a little more trust in folks," said the sheriff. "You boys take the handcuffs off her and wait in the car. I'll be along."

The older of the two deputies gravely unlocked the

manacles on Colleen's wrists. Mrs. Roosevelt gave her her hand and led her to the couch, where she guided her to the center place, the closest to the fire in the fireplace. George was ready with a pot of tea, and he poured and handed her the cup.

Colleen was stunned. She sighed and shook her head. But she sipped from the cup of tea.

"Let's see here, now, Miss Bingham," the sheriff said. "We heard some talk earlier 'bout how you knew the right way to mix nitroglycerine. Then there was some talk you burnt your hand mixin' up a batch. That is, Ah recollect somethin' like that; but you gotta understand, Miss Bingham, that Ah'm a little deaf, and sometimes Ah miss important points. Ah don't 'member you're sayin' nothin' 'bout how maybe you put that batch of nitro in Mr. Partridge's bed. I mean . . . Ah don't remember nothin' of the kind, do Ah?"

Colleen's eyes shifted back and forth from John Crown, to Mrs. Roosevelt, to Bogart. She shook her head tentatively.

"No," said the sheriff emphatically. "Didn't think Ah'd heard nothin' like that."

"Odd thing about Weinvogel," said Tallulah. She was on her feet but tottering. "You'd think a man of his years and discretion would know better than to light a cigar while he had an open can of cleaning fluid in his lap, now wouldn't you?"

"Indeed," said Mrs. Roosevelt with a measured smile. "Wouldn't you think so?"

"Yeah," said the sheriff. "Yeah. Ah'd think so. But . . ." He shrugged. "Guess he didn't. So . . . Well. Ah've got impawtint duties waitin' over in town. Been a pleasure to know all you folks. Special pleasure to know people that've got, uh, the good sense to know when to keep their mouths shut."

"We have that," said Crawford firmly. "Whatever faults anyone may find in us, we do have that."

The sheriff nodded. "Figgered," he said. "Oh. By the way. Ah've been invited to a fish fry the colored folks is

havin' tonight. Second big 'splosion this week, y'know—
them fish. Plannin' on bein' there. Plannin' on having a
good time. Maybe some of you will be there. Hope so.
Pleasure. Pleasure. Bye-bye."

"Tea," muttered Bogart as the sheriff left the room.
"Seems to me you'll never warm up on that, Colly. What
you need, honey, is a smash of loudmouth. And so do I."

18

The column of flame rose into the night air, tall and thin and swaying, like a skilled dancer. Other flames, shorter, thicker, flickered under willow frames; and the fish smoked and sputtered and dripped.

George, Baruch's butler, danced in the orange light: without shirt, his smooth dark skin gleaming with sweat. A girl, lithe and beautiful, danced opposite him. Rafe—the man who had led Bogart, Zanuck, and Winchell to the blasted pool of fish—carried an armload of wood forward and dumped it on the main fire. A hundred people—mostly young, with some older people present to lend dignity—tended the fire and the cooking fish, capered, sang, and laughed.

"Damn, Bernie!" said the President. "I'm so glad we came!"

"So am I, Frank," said Baruch. He replaced his pince-nez on his nose, yet stared over it at the dancers and the singers and the fires.

Mrs. Roosevelt sat beside the President, nodding with the rhythm of the guitars and drums that sounded from behind the fire. "Dynamite does produce a lovely fish fry, doesn't it?" she said.

"Let's forget it was dynamite that did it," said Baruch. "In fact, I don't want to think of explosions."

Mrs. Roosevelt nodded. Colleen Bingham danced in the firelight, with Johnny Crown. She was a dancer. That was how she had won her place in Hollywood, originally; and she danced spectacularly, breaking away from Crown, making George momentarily her partner, then returning to Crown, then shifting to a young man whose muscular body took her interest for a moment.

Winchell had been a dancer. He capered into the firelight and offered himself to Colleen. She faced him and danced with him.

"How did she plant the bomb?" Baruch asked Mrs. Roosevelt.

Mrs. Roosevelt sighed. "She mixed a pint of nitroglycerine," she said. "She attached an electric blasting cap to it with electrical tape. The trigger was a sponge, separating two little cards of wood—the whole thing wrapped in tape. To each piece of wood, she had attached a bit of tin cut from a coffee can. They were her electrical contacts. One was bent into a sort of L; the other was flat. She attached the wire from her battery to each. As long as they were apart, the current did not flow. When you applied pressure to the sponge, you compressed it, and the two pieces of tin made contact. All she had to do was insert this device into one of the coils of the bedsprings, and when anyone sat down, the tin contacts would come together and complete the circuit. She had tested it on her own bed springs."

"So when Partridge sat down . . ."

"Boom," said Mrs. Roosevelt. "No more Mr. Partridge."

"But where'd she get the chemicals and the blasting cap?" Baruch asked.

"It seems to be no difficult matter, when you know what kind of store to go to and what to ask for," said Mrs. Roosevelt. "She left the station at Evansville, Indiana, shortly after Mr. Partridge had given her the bad news about her role in *Ironweed*, and bought all she needed—the chemicals and bottles and thermometer, the battery, the sponge, wire—in a couple of pharmacies and a hardware store. I've already suggested to the President the need of some federal legislation about the purchase of the ingredients of explosives."

The President, sitting in his wood-and-steel wheelchair and attended carefully by Pa Watson, looked up. "What are you talking about?" he asked. "I didn't hear a word you said."

"We were discussing the weather," said Mrs. Roosevelt with an easy smile.

"Ah, so I thought," said the President. "You don't need to know, then, what John Edgar Hoover sent us from Washington this afternoon."

"Pictures of the best castles he has made in his sandbox this week, I suppose," said Mrs. Roosevelt.

"A rundown on our fellow guests," said the President. "He warns us that Tallulah may have Red sympathies."

"I am disappointed," she said. "I had hoped he had done something good with his little shovels and buckets. Maybe his playmate did. Mr. Tolson?"

"Babs—"

"Look at Mr. Winchell," she said. "Our last problem. Isn't he enjoying himself?"

The President looked at Walter Winchell. It was true that the man danced well, with the looseness of a professional. Winchell had put aside his jacket and tie and danced in his shirtsleeves, opposite a black girl, then opposite Colleen, then opposite the spare, grinning black girl once again.

Sheriff Virgil Thompson sat on the ground not far from the President's wheelchair. The first to be served a piece of fish, he was eating it with his fingers. Bogart sat not far from him, tugging Scotch out of a pint bottle. Zanuck leaned against a tree, smoking a big cigar and drinking. Joan Crawford, having shed her shoes, ran down toward the fire and joined the dancers.

"Where's Tallulah?" the President inquired.

"I'm afraid to ask," said Mrs. Roosevelt.

George came up from the fire, bearing plates heaped

with sizzling white fillets of fish. He grinned at Baruch as he bowed and put the plates on the ground.

"Thank you, George," said Baruch.

Someone had begun to beat a drum, and the insistent rhythm came to dominate the night. Colleen and Crawford broke away from the other dancers and danced alone in the center of the ring nearest the fire. The orange firelight gleamed on their sweating bodies.

Crown climbed the slope toward the President and Mrs. Roosevelt. Reaching their side, he sat down.

"Mr. Crown."

"I don't know how we'll ever thank you," he said to Mrs. Roosevelt.

"If you try, you're apt to spoil it all," she said. "Just forget it, Mr. Crown. That's what all the rest of us are trying to do."

He nodded. "Thank you, Mrs. Roosevelt. Mr. President. Mr. Baruch."

"Heard for the last time, Mr. Crown," said the President. "Have you had anything to drink?"

"Have you mixed anything, Mr. President?"

"Unhappily, I have not," said the President. "Drink some Scotch, Mr. Crown. A smash of loudmouth. It seems to be the best we can do this evening."

Winchell at last broke away from the dancers. He climbed the short slope and dropped to the ground beside the President. From Mrs. Roosevelt he accepted a huge greasy hunk of fish and began to eat hungrily.

"Vaudeville is not dead everywhere," said the President grinning.

"More's the pity," said Winchell. "Though I couldn't keep up with it anymore."

Winchell's straight, white hair shifted on the night breeze. His face was beet red. He nibbled cautiously on the fish.

"My wife," said the sheriff, "tells me you're a really big man on radio, Mr. Winchell. Sorry I didn't entirely recognize the name."

Winchell reached for a glass of Scotch handed to him by

Mrs. Roosevelt. "Reminds me of something, Sheriff," he said. "Got a minute?"

"Always got a minute," the sheriff said.

"Well, let me show you something then," said Winchell. He rose heavily from the ground, abandoning his fish and his Scotch. "Something I wanted to show you."

Sheriff Virgil Thompson rose too, huffing.

"Right over here," said Winchell, walking a little out of the light of the fire. "Here." He picked up a small canvas bag from its place between the roots of a tree.

"Whut . . .?"

"Just take a look," said Winchell.

The sheriff opened the little bag. Inside was a twisted, torn hunk of metal, which he pulled out and peered at in the dim orange light. "Whut . . .?"

"The can," said Winchell. "Partridge was killed when a can of dry-cleaning fluid blew up. Right? Well, I was taking a walk and came on that blown-up can. Must have been the can that blew up when Partridge tried to light his cigar. Don't you figure? Lucky I found it, huh? You'll need it when you make your report."

"Uh . . . yeah," said the sheriff. "We, uh . . . we'd been lookin' for that. Nice work of you to find it, Mr. Winchell. Nice work. And thanks. We— Oh, my God!"

Tallulah Bankhead stumbled close to the big fire. A wild cheer went up as she seized George by both hands and broke into a staggering, abandoned dance.

"Ho!" shouted the President. "Bravo, Tallulah! Bravo! Bravo!"

Tallulah was wildly drunk. As she flung herself into George's arms, then broke loose and scampered away from him, leaping, twisting, throwing her arms about her, she threw up her skirt, revealing her naked hips. One of her gyrations broke loose the buttons on her blouse, and she tore it off and threw it in the fire. Dancing with her breasts naked, she shrieked and laughed.

"Oh, *Franklin!*"

The President laughed. He shrugged. "Another generation, Babs," he said. He glanced at the gaping, frowning Baruch. "Modern times."

"But," said Mrs. Roosevelt, "think of poor Speaker Bankhead. A daughter who . . . Franklin, she *drinks* too much!"

The President nodded. "So it appears."

POTUS rolled slowly northward in the deepening darkness of Sunday evening. The President relaxed in his favorite chair in the rear car, sipping sparingly from an evening drink, smoking, glancing over the newspapers that had been delivered aboard at one of the stations a few miles behind them. Mrs. Roosevelt knitted. Pa Watson dozed.

"It was good of Bernie, wasn't it?" said Mrs. Roosevelt.

"I had a good time," said the President.

"They are going to marry," she said.

"Who?"

"Johnny Crown and Colleen Bingham, of course."

"Oh, them, of course," said the President. "The marital arrangements of the rest of them are so tangled it would take a League of Nations debate to begin to make sense of it."

"Well . . ."

"Let's pretend we never met any of them and know nothing of their affairs, Babs. Wasn't that, in fact, what was agreed to?"

"In essence," she said, looking down at her knitting. "Though I have second thoughts, I must tell you. Bernie and the sheriff simply . . . Well, they acted like *barons*, as if they have the right to settle things that involve—"

"Babs. Patience."

"But really the law should have been allowed to take its course. Shouldn't a jury have—"

"Let it go, Babs," he said. "It is well settled."

"I suppose so," she said. "It is difficult for me, though, to accept the idea of a little group of powerful men—"

"We had best listen to Winchell," said the President, glancing at his watch. "He made much of making some kind of wire connection between South Carolina and his broadcast network, and God knows what he may say."

They listened to two or three commercial messages before the familiar, mock-excited voice of Walter Winchell came on the air—

"Good evening, Mr. and Mrs. North America and all the ships at sea! *Let's go to press!*

"Flash! The President of the United States . . . and the First Lady . . . spent the past few *days* at Hobcaw *Barony,* the palatial South Carolina estate of Bernard . . . *Baruch!* On Monday night, famed but controversial Hollywood producer Ben Partridge . . . *died* . . . in an explosion in a room at Hobcaw House! *Cause?* No one knew for sure. Had Partridge been . . . *murdered?* No! As it turned out, he died in the explosion of a can of dry-cleaning fluid that exploded when Partridge—stupidly, it must be said—tried to light a *cigar* while spotting his suit! *This reporter* . . . exploring the grounds of the estate, *found* the shattered can that had contained the lethal fluid—*blown* from the window and *lost* a hundred yards away! So . . . ends the wild career of one of Hollywood's most colorful personalities! Benjamin *Partridge!* Dead at fifty-two! Movie and theater personalities Joan Crawford, Humphrey Bogart, Colleen Bingham, Darryl Zanuck, and Tallulah Bankhead, who were in the *house* at the time of Partridge's *death,* joined tearfully in mourning the death of a respected movie producer. *Meanwhile,* in New York . . ."